HARDDRIVE

HARD DRIVE

CYBER FANTASIES COME TO LIFE WHEN MEN HOOK UP ON THE NET

EDITED BY
MIGUEL ANGEL

alyson books
los angeles | new york

MANUFACTURED IN THE UNITED STATES OF AMERICA.

THIS TRADE PAPERBACK ORIGINAL IS PUBLISHED BY
ALYSON PUBLICATIONS,
P.O. BOX 4371, LOS ANGELES, CALIFORNIA 90078-4371.
DISTRIBUTION IN THE UNITED KINGDOM BY
TURNAROUND PUBLISHER SERVICES LTD.,
UNIT 3, OLYMPIA TRADING ESTATE, COBURG ROAD, WOOD GREEN,
LONDON N22 6TZ ENGLAND.

FIRST EDITION: APRIL 2001

01 02 03 04 05 10 9 8 7 6 5 4 3 2 1

ISBN 1-55583-590-2

COVER DESIGN BY MATT SAMS.

Contents

More Than You Bargained For

Better to Have Lusted and Lost...

Boys...and the Men Who Make Them

Lasting Impressions

Home Is Where the Heart Is

More Than You Bargained For

Looking for Sex...Simply Sex

Conrad Max MacDonald

It was this past July that I met Tim. There was no fanfare. I fucked him. I don't know who he was. That's right—I could have been fucking your boyfriend or some woman's husband. But that's what you get when you go looking for a hot fuck on the Internet. No, I know what you're thinking: How could someone be so heartless? Well, I am a gay man. I have a dick, and I get horny. What? Do you think straight men are the only ones who are allowed to say "I need to fuck"? Tim is also responsible for finding me a boyfriend and helping us stay together. Sound remarkable? This is how it happened.

There I was on a hot, crowded subway, screeching through the underground of Toronto's joke of a subway system. I remember this day because it was a day beyond all days. I was as horny as hell. Can you blame me? Hey, it was July, and the city was scorching. There was a frickin' heat wave coming in from the Atlantic that turned Toronto into an oven. I was dying. So there I was, trying to make myself as comfortable as possible on the subway while pressed against some woman's tits and some bike courier's spandex-covered crotch. The only problem was Mr. Bike Courier was starting to get a hard-on and caught me looking at it.

The subway pressed on, going from station to station. People got on and off. It usually ends up that more people get on than off.

I have been pushed, shoved, moved, groped, felt up, and I'm not even on a date. As the train pulled into the next station, I spied a small opening near one of the doors. I moved quickly to it and set my briefcase down. A few seconds later I was joined by the bike courier. He and I were almost so close that we could kiss.

By now you're probably wondering what happened. Well, the cocky bastard started undoing my fly. I looked around to make sure no one else was checking us out. The coast was clear. I couldn't believe what happened next. Buddy boy pretended to drop his bag next to my briefcase and reached down to pick it up. In the process of picking it up he happened to stop at my fly, whip out my cock, and start to give me head right there. Do you know what it is like to be shocked, stunned, and relieved all at the same time? Bingo! That's what I was.

He started gently licking the head with his tongue. Teasing me. I knew he was trying to provoke a reaction out of me. But I wouldn't give. Then he began to give little licks to my cock. He rolled his tongue up and down the shaft, making my cock twitch to attention. I was beginning to ooze precome; I could feel it. That beautiful, dark-haired, brown-eyed man with South Asian features, a goatee, enough piercings to choke a horse, a beautiful lean body, and a huge throbbing cock was lapping up my precome like it was sweet nectar of life.

In only a few more stops or train jolts I was going to come. I couldn't believe I was letting that guy give me head on a crowded subway car. The whole event was like something out of a porn movie. I loved every minute of it. My insides were on fire as he wrapped his full mouth around my cock and began to milk it for more precome. I couldn't take much more. Though I had tried to suppress my desire, I moaned, and he heard it and then stopped. The fucking bastard got me hard and left me on the edge. He reached down, picked up his bag, said this was his stop, did up my fly, and took off. I was hard, horny, hot—overheated—and now had a case of blue balls. Shit, man, this was not going to be my day.

I live about 20 minutes by bus from the subway station, and it was rush hour, so the buses were packed. Again, I was pushed, shoved, moved, and generally felt up all over. I was not in a mood to be touched. I had blue balls and didn't want to jerk off. I knew whacking off to a porn video wasn't going to do it for me. The bus left the station and within 25 minutes, thanks to traffic, I walked through the door of my apartment.

As usual, in the middle of my apartment floor, there was mail. The pile consisted mainly of bills, catalogs, and fliers. I stepped over the pile and headed for the bedroom. I removed my shoes, let my jacket hit the floor along with my now-beyond-sweaty shirt, my good Hermès tie, my dress pants, and my underwear. Then, standing in a pile of sweaty business clothes, there I was, free to do whatever I wanted. Then I caught a whiff of myself. I could smell the bike courier. The scent of his mouth was mixed in with the sweet odor of my crotch and my own body odor. My cock smelled like a mixture of smoker's breath, Pepsi, and the odor of his mouth. Though that encounter did turn me on, I wanted much more than just a blow job. I wanted hot man sex. But what I needed was a good shower, so off I went.

My Friday evenings usually consist of meeting my friends for dinner, a movie, a club, and then a bathhouse. That was not going to do for that night. After I'd dried my body off I called my friends up and canceled our plans. They accused me of having a date, but I set them straight. I don't date; I just fuck. I don't find the guys that I fuck worth getting to know. I called up my favorite Chinese food place, placed my order, walked over to my computer, switched it on, and began to check my E-mail. It wasn't long before I was online and coasting through cyberspace, not really looking for anything specific.

I have never really understood what possessed me to go into Gay.com, but there I ended up. I was in the middle of trying to come up with a description of myself when the door buzzer rang. My order had arrived. I think I was somewhere between chomping down on a water chestnut and munching on udon noodles when I came up with my description and handle: "MuscleGruff, 29, six foot, good-looking, goatee, dark-skinned, fit, football player's build, 8½-inch shaved and cut cock, versatile, always too damned horny, not looking for love so don't ask to stay for breakfast. Private chat is OK." I call myself MuscleGruff because I have a goatee and piercings, and anyone who doesn't like them can bite me. I also have a tattoo on my hip and a few muscles. I've been told I look hot. I don't think I do, but my look gets me laid.

If you haven't ever been inside a chat site, there are many "rooms" you can go into. You can find a chat room for every type of guy you are looking for. It is almost as though you are ordering from a cybermenu of sexual preferences. If you want a muscle boy or a daddy, you can find one. Or if you are really into chubby guys who dress like Divine, you can even find that too. Because I wanted hot sex with a really hot guy, I went into the local chat room for guys from Toronto. I think I was in this room for only five minutes before my curiosity was piqued by the description for a guy named TimWestEnd: "Really cute, 29, 5 foot 9, pierced, tattooed, pure bottom, looking for black guys, very horny. Boyfriend is a jerk and away. Need hot sex, not looking to stay for breakfast. Private me."

Guess what I did.

We discovered that we had actually chatted previously about a year before. I kind of remembered that we wanted to get together, but we never got around to meeting. So we chatted for a few minutes about why his boyfriend was a jerk—he had taken a job where he works night and day. They hadn't had sex in almost a month. He was going to crawl out of his skin, he said, if he didn't get laid soon. Then he asked me what part of the city I lived in. As luck would have it, Tim and I lived five minutes' walking distance from each other. We were practically neighbors.

There were a few more minutes of chitchat, and we decided to fuck...I mean...meet. Because we both lived in the area, we knew the landscape pretty well. A little way down the road from my apartment is a park. I asked him if he wanted to have sex in the park, and he typed back that he needed to get his man pussy poked anywhere. I just laughed and typed back an "LOL" at him. But he was completely serious. So who was I to say no? We decided to rendezvous in 30 minutes. I shut down my computer, finished my dinner, put on something that was easy enough to be taken off, grabbed my bike, and headed off to the park for my meeting with TimWestEnd.

On the way to the park I began to get butterflies. Sure, I've had sex a million times before. I have fucked complete strangers and loved every minute of it. But something in my stomach told me this was going to be different. To be perfectly honest, I really didn't know if Tim was his real name. But I thought, *What the hell! He's only a fuck*. I stopped at our meeting point and chained up my bike.

It was easy to recognize Tim. He was sitting in a pair of high-cut denim shorts, combat boots, a tank top, and a baseball cap. We could have been twins because Tim had piercings and a tattoo in almost the same places that I did. He was cuter than I thought he was going to be. His description didn't say that he had blond hair and the deepest blue eyes. To say I was turned on would be an understatement. I walked over to the park bench where he was sitting and introduced myself. The look of astonishment on his face said it all. We clicked. He wanted me, and I wanted him just as badly. I suggested we go for a walk into the more secluded section of the park to help break the initial tension. You know, I never could understand that part of meeting someone for casual sex—the first 10 or so minutes being uncomfortable, that is. I've always thought that you're just meeting for sex and not to buy a house together, so intentions should be direct and to the point without wasting any time.

Surprisingly, Tim and I were the only ones in that part of the park. The sunlight was almost gone for the day, and I felt comfortable enough to remove my tank top. I could see Tim's eyes bug out at the sight of my hairy chest and my big nipples protruding through the fuzz. It wasn't long before Tim removed his tank top too. There, sticking out from his chest, were the best nipples I had ever seen on a white man, and they were pierced with one ring each. I felt my cock start to grow as he began to play with the rings. Tim was a tease.

We came upon a bench and decided to sit for a minute and talk. To my surprise I found out that we had a lot in common. We liked the same movies, ate similar foods, and thought that outdoor sex was a gift from God. We sat and watched the sun set; darkness came quickly. I told Tim somewhere in the conversation that I was a nudist, and he said he wanted proof.

I didn't have to be encouraged twice. I began to put on a strip show for him right then and there. Unfortunately I didn't have much to take off. In my wisdom while getting dressed, I'd wanted to show off my best assets, so I wore just shorts, a tank top, combat boots, and a baseball cap. I removed my shorts and let my cock hang freely between my legs. Tim told me to stand there and wait for him; he was going to strip for me.

He slowly began to undo his belt and unbutton his shorts. I was salivating over every moment. I felt my throat go dry and my cock swell at the same time. He had the most amazing body. He was completely hairless all over from his neck down to ankles. As Tim began to tease the beast (that is what I call myself when I get extremely horny), I couldn't help but touch my cock. He turned his smooth and shapely ass toward me. It was one of the most beautiful sights I had seen in a long time. Tim's butt was completely hairless, and to prove it he spread his ass cheeks to reveal a clean and hairless rosebud. Then, as if on cue, he turned back to me and kissed me deeply. I don't usually like to kiss guys I'm going to just fuck, but I decided to make an exception.

Tim's body was exquisite. I ran my hands over his chest. His skin was soft and supple, like a beautiful piece of fruit. I leaned in and took his nipple ring into my mouth. I alternated between pulling on the ring and licking his nipple. Tim began to moan. I switched to the other nipple and gave it the same attention. I could feel Tim's cock getting hard against my stomach. I had to have him. I grabbed him and pulled him on top of me on the nearest bench, and we began to kiss even more passionately. It took only five minutes before we were licking each others' body parts. I could feel our cocks grinding against each other in a type of dance. Tim spun himself around so that we were in a sixty-nine and began to suck my cock, and I began to suck his.

I could feel his seven-inch piece of meat throbbing inside my mouth. There was enough precome oozing out of his cock to lubricate a jet engine, but my mouth lapped it all up. I felt Tim's hot mouth slide up and down my brown love shaft. I could hear his greedy mouth hungrily sucking up every drop. He wanted my cock; he lusted after it. I could feel his own cock throbbing as much as mine was. I noticed his tight rosebud staring down from above me.

I've seen a lot of butt holes in my life, but I swear this one did look like a pussy. I wanted to fuck that man.

I began to lap at his hole. I stuck my tongue deep inside his ass and buried it between the quivering lips of his pucker. Tim began to moan louder. I could feel his hips move against the rhythm of my tongue. He was getting off on being eaten out. I loved it. I wanted to tongue-fuck him more and more. I was like the guys you see in straight porn eating a pussy with the woman moaning to beat hell. Then Tim surprised me. He sat up on his knees and then right down on my face. He began to moan louder and louder. I was getting so turned on, I couldn't stand it. He got off my face, pushed my legs into the air, and did the same to me.

Now, I'm one of those guys who loves to get rimmed if it's done right. And Tim knew exactly what he was doing. He pushed his tongue in and out of my ass like a pro. My hole responded right along with him. I couldn't stand it. Tim was eating me out just as well as I had done him. My cock was now running with precome like a leaky tap. His cock was throbbing and coating my face. Tim pushed himself up and stood up near my head. He reached into his pants, which had almost gotten lost in the grass, and pulled out a large package of lubricant. As if I couldn't tell what was going to happen next! Tim wanted his man pussy poked.

Just as it is in some kind of sexual fantasy, Tim opened the package of lubricant, lubed up his hole as he turned around to face me, straddled me, and sat right down on my black pole. I was so shocked, I didn't know what to say. I tried to push him off me but having Tim bare down on my cock was ecstasy. He became amazingly strong, almost animal-like. I asked him about condoms, and he told me he didn't use them, ever. He loved, he said, getting fucked bareback. I could feel his tight, puckering hole wrapping around my cock. Since I didn't know where he had been, I told him to stop. He wouldn't. Tim wanted my creamy chowder up his man pussy, and he wasn't going to take no for an answer. The more I struggled, the more he loved it.

I know about all the risks of bareback sex with guys, and I didn't like it one bit. Suddenly Tim became forceful with me. He told me he wasn't going to let me up until I had come inside of him. Every time Tim pushed down on my cock he caused another sensation of pure sexual bliss to rise in my body. I tried to plant my hands down on his chest to push him off, but he grabbed both of my hands and held them behind my head.

Suddenly it dawned on me that Tim was raping me. A man who is a pure bottom was riding my cock against my will. Quickly, thoughts began to run through my mind about HIV and all the sexually transmitted diseases you can get from unprotected sex. But Tim didn't care. There I was, helpless, lying on a park bench with my hands held, being raped by a bottom while he smiled and grunted with sexual glee.

After about 15 good minutes of riding me, Tim began to *really* pour it on. He used his right arm to balance his weight and began to bounce ferociously up and down on my cock. The sounds of his ass slapping against my hips as the sweat built up on our bodies began to break through the night. The smell of hot man sex was filling the air—along with the smell of Tim's ass, which was now beginning to leak the mild odor of shit. It took only another two minutes, and I was on the edge.

I remember breaking my hands free, grabbing his hips, shoving my cock right up inside him, and releasing the hottest load of come I had ever let go. Tim, quickly afterward, grabbed his cock and jerked off. He came instantly. The sound of Tim coming was almost primal. It was as though he had been in heat and was finally set free from his sexual prison. Finally, he dismounted.

I raised my head up just a little, and there was my hot jizz and Tim's shit all over my cock and crotch. I hate nothing more than a guy who isn't clean and can't hold it.

Tim bent over to kiss me on the lips and then whispered to me that he would clean me up. To my horror, he leaned over and started cleaning my dick with his tongue. The cocksucker cleaned my dick so well that I looked like I had just come out of the shower. Speechless, I pulled on my clothes, and Tim began to put his on as well. He asked for a good-bye kiss, but I just pushed him away in total disgust. He left, waving good-bye.

I walked through the door of my apartment with my bike in hand, still in total disbelief of what had just happened. I knew I needed to call it a night, and so I went to bed.

I was online a few times again after that when TimWestEnd tried to chat in private with me, but I never accepted. I told anyone in the chat room who would listen about my experience with Tim. A few guys couldn't believe what had happened. A couple of insensitive guys told me to stop bitching and just enjoy what I'd gotten. But I still felt raped, taken advantage of, and violated. I wondered if I should press charges against Tim. But how do you prove that some guy with a fabulous body, a great mouth, an ass that felt like a pussy—who I'd met over the Internet and then met in a park at dusk—had raped you? The police are not going to post his picture, and *America's Most Wanted* isn't going to air the story. So I let it go.

I sometimes wonder, though, if there was something I could have done to prevent what happened. I am not HIV-positive, but it kills me that this guy is out there doing this. I never logged on as MuscleGruff again.

A few months later I got the courage to go online again. I came up with a new handle: BoyfriendMaterial. And I altered my profile: "Looking for a guy who can give me a reason to stop cruising Gay.com. Check out my Web site and tell me what you think."

My experience with Tim made me do a lot of soul-searching. I had rethought my original vow not to stay for breakfast with a guy. Maybe staying for toast and cappuccino wouldn't be so bad. If the right guy offered.

As luck would have it, the right guy did come along. He had been to my site. And he had slept with TimWestEnd too. His name is Paulo. Paulo's description of himself was encouraging: "Latin, 32, good-looking, piercings, goatee, six foot, and tired of being used for sex—reformed slut looking for a boyfriend. I make great waffles."

TimWestEnd had handcuffed Paulo to rape him during their encounter. Tim strapped Paulo face up, cuffed both arms, rode him bareback, and cleaned his dick in the same manner that he had done mine. When Tim was done, he robbed Paulo, unhooked one of his hands, left the key, and quickly took off.

Paulo and I made plans to console each other and talk offline. Our first date was at an Italian restaurant. We talked about what Tim had done to us. I got angry for Paulo. His eyes began to fill with tears for me. Neither of us tested HIV-positive or got an STD from our encounters. We were both lucky. We held hands and shared a seemingly endless bowl of fettuccine Alfredo and glasses of wine. We also made plans to get together again. The evening went well and didn't feel like a first date.

A month later, on a sunny September morning, I was awakened by a kiss. It was Saturday. Paulo and I had made love all night. His alarm clock glowed 10 A.M. Paulo had made me breakfast in bed: waffles with maple syrup and sliced fruit. He also had brought in a bottle of Hershey's chocolate syrup just in case I liked chocolate on my waffles. As I began to eat, Paulo asked if he could pour some chocolate on my cock and lick it off. I declined, citing flashbacks to Tim, and we both laughed.

After we finished feeding each other waffles, we made love again. Paulo and I have stayed around for breakfast with each other for three months now. And neither of us has logged on to chat with other guys since we found each other.

Pig

By Phillip Mackenzie Jr.

When I get home from the gym, Alex is in the kitchen, looking like he's just rolled out of bed. It's 10 P.M.

"Hey, man," I say as I drop my bag and head for the refrigerator for water.

He grunts something at me and turns away. I hear him shuffling back down the hall.

Not that I expect anything else. Whatever I say or do is always met with the same slightly quizzical stare.

"As always," I say aloud, "good to see you. Nice chatting with you. But I know you're busy, so don't let me keep you."

Alex has a way of making me feel not just inconsequential but slightly ridiculous. He looks at me as if I'm a laboratory chimpanzee, as if he's amazed that words come out of my mouth despite my being a lesser life-form.

At first I mistook his behavior for poor social skills, until one day when I asked him if he was shy when he was a kid too. With little more than a look, he insinuated that he could talk to me but simply didn't find it worth the effort.

Believe me, I've tried. I talked about my job—until he made it clear that what I did was a drain on society. I talked about music—until he accused me of contributing to the downfall of culture. I tried to talk about books, but that seemed to cause him physical pain.

Sighing heavily, I drop myself onto the kitchen chair and kick my shoes off.

I hate having a roommate. The second bedroom made a great office—and a great place to store all the crap that wouldn't fit anywhere else, like the bike I barely rode anymore, the extra stereo I'd refused in a fit of immature vindictiveness to let my ex take when we split up, and the weight bench that served as a place to put the boxes of books my brother dumped on me when he moved to Montana with his girlfriend two years ago.

But I really needed that membership at Crunch, and the trip to Florence was too good to pass up. And don't get me started on the rigorous demands of appropriate attire and hair as well as the combined introduction of the new Macs and DVDs. Well, all of it put my credit card through a too-vigorous workout. Which was all OK, until the record company folded one morning, and after three weeks I was forced to take a job as a personal assistant to a B-list producer who inevitably took it out on me when no one returned his calls—which no one ever did.

Which explains my roommate, Alex. An assistant professor of anthropology, he is actually poorer than I am, but that doesn't stop him from assuming an air of superiority, which is now primarily manifested through a steadfast refusal to interact with me—or even to engage in rudimentary conversation.

I have a fairly realistic estimation of myself and a very good idea of my place on the food chain, but I also know I'm not stupid, can be fairly witty, and can embark on a superficial discourse on current events, which is pretty much all that is asked of you in L.A.

And when I finally realized I needed a roommate, I imagined something along the lines of *Three's Company:* a set of fun-loving misfortunates, sitting cross-legged on each other's beds, bemoaning our love lives, and cooking up pasta primavera in our little kitchen. Instead I got *Apartment Zero*.

It's amazing how exhausting it is. And frustrating. Is it any wonder then, given the beating my ego takes on a daily basis—combined with the double whammy of the drought in my dating life and spike in my libido—that I've begun spending more time and money than I should in computer chat rooms?

Fuck it, though. The thing is, in there I can be anything I want. I'm not some beaten-down, beaten-up, walking advertisement for early-21st-century ennui. I'm an out-of-control, uninhibited, radical, streetwalking, turn-me-upside-down-and-fuck-me-sideways alley cat of a sex monkey.

I can walk through the door, strip out of my clothes, slide my ass down over the thick, hard shaft of some straight frat boy sitting alone in his room, and let him ride my tight hole until he shoots his sticky load into my guts, and then I can get up and walk away while he's dribbling into his pubes. I love that. Who cares if it's actually some fat, middle-aged, Judy Garland queen tickling his pecker with one hand and the keyboard with the other? Who the hell knows what he's fantasizing about either?

Not that I'm hard on the eyes in the real world. Despite my current financial restraints, I've never given up my gym membership, which has succeeded in not only relieving the stress of my current state of affairs but also resulted in a physique that demands display in a Dolce & Gabanna black silk tank top. My abdominal muscles are visible without flexing even when I stand at the opposite end of the hallway from the full-length mirror on the bathroom door.

Yes, I'm bragging. I've earned the right. At least I'm not like Alex, still waiting for that gamin, starving-artist look to come into vogue.

I feel my dick starting to uncoil inside my jock, and I slip a hand inside my shorts to encourage it before I realize Alex might make another foray into the kitchen and find me sitting here playing with myself, giving him one more thing to feel superior about.

That's another thing about having a roommate. If you can't walk around naked, you sure as hell can't jerk off in the kitchen.

Alex's door is directly across from mine, so I always have to make sure mine is closed firmly if I'm going to get it on with myself. I hear it click when I close it, but I give it an extra nudge just to be sure. Then I walk over and turn on my computer.

As I'm slipping my shirt over my head, I hear that I have mail.

My mother; read later. My ex; discard now. Frank; well, let's see what he has to say.

"I have tix to *Jeff Stryker Does Hard Time.* Tonight, 8 P.M. Wanna go?"

I'm glad I didn't check my E-mail until now. What's with these porn stars doing theater? We want to see your dick or your ass or both. We want to watch you come. In close-up. That's it. Period. We don't want you to do anything else. Ever. And we sure don't want to hear you talk. Got it? Good.

I plop my ass down on the chair and head straight into Man2Man. First I check out the supposedly live guys. One guy is fingering his asshole, but the digitization makes it look like he's breaking his finger. Another guy has just come and is starting to go limp. Damn; missed the show. But looking at his still-oozing slit restarts my cock, so I head for a chat room.

Darkman is there, and so is AssCrazy. They always are.

"Hey, Toybox." (That's me...OK, I know...but I was under pressure when I came up with it.)

"Hey, guys. Anything up?"

"Me," says AssCrazy. "I just got back from that Jeff Stryker show."

"Jesus, she is so tired," says Darkman.

"Maybe, but that pole makes my loins ache," AssCrazy responds.

Hung4U pipes in: "I saw Ryan Idol in *Making Porn,* and I'd take him over Stryker any day."

I am wondering again if AssCrazy is really Frank, when Rdy4Bear logs on and almost immediately heads for a private room with Darkman.

Hung4U and AssCrazy are still debating the finer points of porn-star appendages when someone new logs in. NickName. That's actually kind of funny.

"Hi." The Instant Message pops up on my screen.

"Hi," I shoot back.

"Toybox, huh?"

"Yeah, Nick: Toybox. What of it?" OK, so I'm a little crabby still.

"It isn't any lamer than the other ones," NickName says, seemingly trying to tone things down.

"Thanks."

"Wanna get outta here?" he asks.

"Sure," I say. I like the direct approach. It cuts through the bullshit, acknowledges why we are all there, and saves time. We click to a private room.

"Take off your clothes," he says.

I slip my shorts down to my ankles and slide a finger along the edge of my jock, feeling the sweaty dampness of my curly cock thatch. I'm wondering what this one is into as I massage my crotch. I'm cool with being ordered around in here.

"Tell me," he says.

"My shirt is off. I'm rubbing my hands over my chest. I just worked out, so I'm a little sweaty."

"Smell your pits," he insists.

I turn my head and sniff. It's a little gamey but not bad.

"Tell me."

I'm a little thrown. What am I supposed to say now? "I stink," I type back tentatively.

"You fucking pig."

My terminal almost snarls, and my dick twitches hard. Oh, yeah. Oh, yeah, baby. This is gonna be hot. "I am. I am a pig. I'm a filthy fucking pig," I type back hurriedly.

"Show me your little pig pecker."

I slip my jock down around my thighs, and my dick rises up, pulsing from its nest of brown curls. I slide my hand down under my balls, squeezing them, rolling them around inside the sac.

"DON'T TOUCH IT!" his words scream back at me.

"I'm sorry."

"You don't do anything unless I tell you to."

"OK," I start to type and then erase it and type, "Yes, sir."

"DON'T CALL ME 'SIR,'" he screams back.

Shit. Maybe I should have typed, "Yes, Daddy." Crap. Who is this guy anyway? Peppermint Patty? Fuck it, it's Saturday night, and of course I don't have a date, so if it's going to be a little daddy-boy scene, I can get into that.

It's certainly different. I haven't done that scene yet. I don't really think it's something I'd get into out in the real world, but in here, like I said, you can be anything you want for 20 minutes.

"Get down on your knees," he tells me.

I assume this is figurative, but just in case, I push the chair back and kneel down.

"I'm on my knees," I let him know.

"Do you want my cock?"

"Yes, please," I type, praying it's the right thing to say.

"Beg for it," comes his response.

All right. This is a little much. But, OK, my dick is bouncing happily away down there, so what the hell: "Please show me your cock. I need your cock. I really need it. Please give it to me."

"I don't think so."

What the *fuck* is going on here? I reach down and palm the head of my dick, slicking it with ooze. Screw this guy. I'll touch myself if I want to. I start typing again: "Please. I really want to see your big cock. I want to touch it. I want to suck it."

"Can you suck it good?"

"Yeah. I can make it feel real good," I tell him.

"Can you take it all the way down? Can I fuck your tonsils?"

"Yeah. Oh, yeah, I can take it. Let me show you," I play along.

"Are you gonna make it hard enough to fuck your little toy box?"

"Yeah. It's gonna be so hard. It's gonna rip right into my hot, tight ass."

"OK. You can touch it," he allows me.

Finally! Jesus Christ.

I run my hand down my dick in a long, slow, shuddering stroke and then slip my fingers down under my balls, which are tightened up around the base of my shaft. My middle finger finds the tight knot of my asshole, and I start rubbing in tiny circles.

"I'm taking it out now," I type one-handed. "I'm unzipping your pants and slipping my hand inside. Oh, God, it feels so good."

"TAKE YOUR FUCKING HAND OFF YOUR PITIFUL LITTLE PRICK RIGHT NOW!"

My dick bounces, and I actually gasp as I jerk my hand away. Fucker. What a dick. But I have to admit, this little game has its hot side. I'm harder than I can remember being in a long time. Hmm.

Maybe there is something to this after all.

"I'm sorry," I type back lamely.

"If you want my cock, you give it the attention it deserves. Do you understand me, pig?"

"Yes."

"That means both hands. Now open your mouth."

I actually do this! What am I thinking?

"I'm just gonna give you the head because you didn't listen," he teases.

But his efforts are working. I feel it. The slick rubbery head of a monster shaft rubbing my lips and leaving them slick with precome. I can smell the heated funk and taste the salty tang of cock. The head of my dick is purple with frustration, weeping golden liquid, begging for attention.

"Your mouth is sweet, little pig."

My fingers are no longer on the keyboard. They're buried in wiry curls of hair, full of wrinkled ball flesh, my mouth stretched by cock, my tongue aching sweetly from pressure and friction as he pumps my face.

I reach up to type: "God! God! God! Yeah, fuck my face! Fuck it! Fuck my throat!"

"OH, YEAH!" The words hit my screen—and at the same moment I hear them. I mean really *hear* them. From across the hall.

What the hell? I'm thinking. "Alex?" I type and then erase it.

My heart is pounding in my throat, and my dick rapidly deflates.

"Take that cock. You cock pig," flashes across my screen.

Oh, sure. Snotty, rimless-glasses-wearing, intellectually pretentious Alex as *über*-Daddy? Right.

No way. I settle back down on my knees and start typing again, my cock swelling as I fall back into the mood. I give him what I hope will thrill him more: "Yeah, it feels so good. You taste so good. God, I love your cock!"

"Stand up," he says.

I stand, my cock jutting out and dripping on my keyboard. I swipe the sticky drop with my finger and put it my mouth.

"Bend over," comes his next order.

I lean forward, placing both hands on my desk.

"Ask me to eat your ass."

With one hand I begin typing: "Please. Please eat out my tight hole. Stick your tongue up my asshole. Make it nice and wet."

"Oh, your ass tastes sweet. Nice and sweaty." At least I get a compliment from him.

He has me back in that mode. "Oh, God, yeah," I say. "Tongue my hole. Jesus, you're so good. God!" I am feeling it again, the sandpaper roughness of a man's face between my cheeks, the rasp of a tongue against my puckered crack, the nip of teeth, the blast of hot breath. Fuck, this guy is hot! Goddamn, he's hot!

"You think you can take this big cock up that tight little hole?"

"Yeah. Fuck, yeah," I assure him.

"You want me to plant a big load right up there, don't you?"

Oh, Christ. I almost come. My untouched prong jerks, and my balls spasm, ready to spew their contents all over my screen. I grit my teeth and clamp a hand around the base of my shaft to keep from shooting and then jerk it away guiltily. I get back to the keyboard: "Yes, I want your load. I want to feel your hot come inside me."

I feel hard thighs against the back of my legs, hands pulling my ass cheeks apart, a thick finger sliding into me—and then another. I feel a long, hot, thick pole of flesh against my back and low-hanging, hairy balls against the smooth flesh of my butt.

"I'm ready. Fuck me now, please," I type jerkily.

"I'll fuck you when I'm good and ready, pig," he says, clearly not willing to relinquish his control.

"I'm sorry," I type almost wearily. Jesus H. Christ—this could get old.

"Don't you tell me when to fuck you. I oughtta leave your ass right here for that."

"Please don't. Please don't leave. I just love your cock so much, I got carried away." I work to give him a plea.

"I was gonna be gentle because you were a good little pig, but now I think I'm gonna rip you apart."

"Please. Yes! Fuck your little pig as hard as you want."

"Yeah, your little pig hole feels nice and tight."

I'm past caring. Call me a pig, swear at me, treat me lower than whale spit on the bottom of the ocean. I don't care at this point. Just give me a cock up my ass.

"TAKE THAT COCK!" he screams at me as I feel a huge mass of male muscle breach my chute and slam into my guts like a red-hot poker.

"YEAH!" I scream back.

"FUCK!" he howls.

And again...I *hear* it. From across the hall.

I fly backward from my computer, my dick swinging crazily as I leap at the door. Cracking it open, all I can see is a light coming from under Alex's door. I tiptoe across the hall and press my ear to the door. I hear the clicking of keystrokes; that's all.

As I scurry into my room, I pause, ready to click the door shut. But, heart pounding crazily, I slowly swing it back open. My unhandled rod is jumping and jerking, and sweat trickles down between my pecs.

It is Alex. Alex who fucked my throat and slapped his balls against my chin. Alex's shaggy bush I had buried my nose in. Alex's tongue that had wormed up inside me, setting me on fire and making me beg for the monster cock he crammed into me a few seconds later.

"You love my big dick, don't you, dick pig?" he had typed during my frenzied foray across the hall.

"Oh, yeah, your cock feels so good. God, fuck me harder!" I type back frantically, pulling my desk and chair away from the wall so I can sit in full view of the door.

What if he opens the door? It's Alex. Weird, dark, cynical, mean Alex. Skinny, punky, freaky Alex.

Who would have thought it? I try to imagine Alex's thin lips saying the words "dick pig." My hard-on throbs, leaks, and jumps untouched. My balls are like rocks. My ass is aching, imagining those lips against my quaking hole. And his cock, thick and slick with my juices, burying itself deep inside me, then sliding out to the crown before slamming back in, turning every inch of my chute into raw nerve endings. Alex's cock. Alex's cock?

"You like me pounding your tight pig pussy?" his words flash at me.

Yeah. I love it. Alex. Goddamn it. Not Alex. Fuck, why did it have to be Alex? I hate that fucker for doing this to me, but...Jesus...just keep doing it.

"I fucking love it!" I scream out loud. And keep screaming, "Yeah, fuck me harder, Alex! Fuck me harder!"

The screen stays blank. Then footsteps in Alex's room. I turn toward the door, legs spread, dick standing straight and proud, my hands dangling by my sides.

His door flies open. The first thing I notice is the tattoo. A snake stretches from his cock to his chest, coiling around his left pec, its mouth open over his nipple. Its sinuous body accents his own lithe muscularity. Long flat planes of muscle stretch over his chest and stomach, sinewy cables over his arms and legs. A patch of dark hair nests between his tits then narrows to a thin line over his belly before spreading out again into a dense patch of black curls between his legs. Following this trail, my eyes are riveted on the pole of flesh pointed almost straight up, curving slightly to the right at the head. His hand grasps it along with his heavy, hairy balls, pointing them directly at me. Without saying a word, he turns back to his computer, his hard ass flexing as he walks.

With his eyes locked on mine, one hand gripping his cock, slowly massaging it, his other hand types, "Show me your asshole."

Silently I lift my legs and spread them, scooting down in my chair until I feel the cool air of the room against my throbbing pucker.

Alex types more: "Stick your finger in."

I put my index finger in my mouth and suck it slowly. A thin strand of saliva stretches and breaks as I lower it between my legs and rub it against my fuck hole, slipping a tiny bit in, and then with a quick twitch all of it.

I can't believe I'm doing this. That I want to do this. That I'm looking at Alex, pale and hard, staring at me with those reflectionless, dark eyes, his hand stroking himself as he watches me finger-fucking myself.

"You want me to fuck you?" he asks aloud.

Not trusting my voice, I type, "Please!"

He spits into his palm and slicks it over the length of his twitching cock. "I'm fucking you," he says as if he were telling me the weather.

Dry-mouthed, I watch his hand travel the length of his dick, pulling the skin tight as he drives toward his bush. My finger matches his slow rhythm. Adding a second finger as he picks up speed, I drive into my hot center, finding the hard knob of my prostate.

He spits again, pounding at his prick as his balls pull up, jerking inside their sac.

"You like my thick cock, pig?" he asks conversationally.

"Jesus, Alex." I gasp. I want him inside me. To fuck me for two days and then shoot gallons of Alex spunk all over me. I want to swallow his cock and massage it with my throat until he fills me with come.

"Are you my little fuck pig?" His voice hitches slightly.

"Yes." I breathe, transfixed on the blur of his hand on his swelling muscle; the purple head looks primed and ready to blow.

I drive another finger into my hole, and my body spasms as if hit by 10,000 volts of electricity.

"You gonna take my hot load?" His eyes bore into me, impaling me.

"Fuck. Oh, fuck, Alex, I'm gonna come. Oh, God, Alex, please let me come."

His hand stops, and his toes curl. Then his legs shoot out, and every muscle in his lean body pops as his cock fires a white stream that hits him in the throat.

I'm frozen, my fingers pressed tight against the throbbing knob at my center as jet after jet of sperm flies from the flaming crown of his shaft, abstractly painting his abdomen as his body jerks and a sound like grinding machinery fights out of his clenched teeth. I imagine it shooting into me, burning my guts, filling me until I overflow, and it pours out of me.

I lose it. I can't stop to save my life. My ass ring clamps down on my fingers, the velvety muscles inside clench, and the room disappears in blackness. The first blast never hits my body at all, but I feel it coursing up the length of my cock, ripping the hole open, and flying into space. My balls seize and release, and a flood of come pours out of my cock, burning my skin, and bringing a scream from my throat that I have never heard before.

I come back into my body, shivering and trembling, the funk of jism in my nostrils, the cooling slickness of it covering me from nuts to neck.

Alex rises from his chair, his own load running in rivulets into his dark bush, and walks toward me. He stops, and the corner of his mouth jerks upward in a half smile.

"Pig," he says, and then with one foot kicks the door shut.

Date Rape

By Jerry Prince

I wasn't really looking for a hole—he just happened on me. I was in the Eagle as usual, sitting at the bar, drinking my beer, and smoking my cigar. He'd been sitting on the stool to the right of me, talking to the guy on his right side, and pretty much ignoring me. I knew that because I'd been watching him in the mirror, and he was really interested in the other guy and not too excited about me.

But his interest in the fellow on the other side wasn't enough to keep the guy there when a better-looking man came up and started chatting with him. Those two left together, and then it was just the two of us, so he began to talk to me. I'd had enough drinks that I was a little looser of tongue than usual, so I kept up with him, and the raunchier he talked, the more I talked. He was a pretty good-looking fellow. I'd guess mid to late 30s, light beard, sandy-brown hair, dark eyes—but kinda sad-looking. He wasn't too heavy but could stand to work out. Of course, who am I to talk? I'm a real bear of a man, hairy all over with salt-and-pepper hair and beard that show my age.

Basically he gave me the condensed version of his life story, how he'd had a lover but was now alone. He'd been practicing safe sex even with the lover, but after that was over he'd hooked up with a guy one night who was into raw sex, bareback sex. He said he'd never had a guy shoot his load up his ass before and was unsure if the guy was HIV-positive or -negative, but that one night changed his life. He told me it was the most incredible sexual experience he had ever had.

Now, you understand, I'm a poz bareback top, so he was really preaching to the choir, but I wanted to hear his side of it, so I didn't say anything. I just listened and asked enough questions to keep him talking so I could find out more.

Luckily this guy had been at the bar quite a while, so he had inhaled enough beer to make his tongue very loose, and he was telling me a lot more than he would or should have. His name was Tom, and he'd lived in the area all his life; in fact, he lived in an apartment building not too far from the bar. I didn't tell him I lived just a few blocks farther away—I let him do the talking.

Anyway, the guy he had been sitting next to and talking with earlier he had met online, and they had agreed to meet that night at the bar to see if they liked each other. The reason Tom had picked this particular guy was that he was poz. Tom wanted this guy to for sure plant the bug in his ass so that he could get over the hump and have bareback sex without any more worry. But he was so uptight about it that he wanted whoever gave him the bug to also give him the date rape drug so that he wouldn't be able to resist. He was afraid that he might chicken out at the very end and kick the cock out of his ass before it delivered the dirty load.

When Tom had told the guy he had met online what he wanted, it had turned the guy off. He just wanted to fuck raw—he didn't want to have to rape his date. So Tom was crying into his beer, confessing his warped desire to a stranger at a bar. Now what Tom didn't know was that I was feeling like the luckiest man in the world. I had been over to visit a friend just before I hit the bar. The point of my visit was to pick up a little of the above-mentioned drug. It has to be refrigerated, so I had it all wrapped up in a padded freezer container like you see on TV, and it was in my coat pocket. So I began to wonder how I could make the dreams of two men come true. I had been looking for a guy to use it on, and I thought I had one lined up a few days later. But when life deals you a card like this, you play it.

I was so excited, I was having trouble concealing it. I was beginning to get drunk, so I concentrated more on smoking and less on drinking. Tom was very loose now, so I'd have to stay ahead of him and keep him at the bar; otherwise, he'd realize how drunk he was and go home to sleep it off. So I did my best counseling, putting my arm around his shoulder, telling him he wasn't crazy or weird; he had normal urges like everyone else; don't worry about it; relax; you're an OK guy—the things you say to a guy you want to get in your bed.

All the time I was doing that I was very carefully peeling open the wrapper in the pocket of my coat that hung over the back of my barstool. I had been able to get my left hand into the pocket while working Tom's shoulder with my right arm. Every time I was about to move or make a noise with the wrapper, I'd squeeze his shoulder or hug him tight so he wouldn't notice. And soon I had a very cold bottle stuck between my legs. I had to do some fancy work to keep Tom looking over at the pretty boys who had just come into the bar and not at what I was doing: trying to push down and turn the cap to get the damn thing open. And then I had to spin him around to look at the hot man playing the pinball machine while I leaned over, pretending to tap the ash off my cigar, when I actually had the bottle in the same hand, and I poured just enough of the drug into his beer.

Then I closed the bottle and eased it back into the wrapper while urging Tom to tell me more about what he wanted out of his rape scene. Tom was almost running off at the mouth, so glad he was to finally have someone he could talk to about what he wanted. He was describing a scene that had my cock so stiff and dripping precome that I was sure I had a big wet spot on my pants.

I got the bottle put away just as Tom was finishing up his beer. I knew I had to act quick, so I advised Tom that he needed to go home and get some rest, he'd had too much to drink, etc. It worked. He was so drunk that he couldn't think straight, and the drug was beginning to take effect. I had to help him put on his coat and help him count the money out to the bartender as he paid his bill. The bartender gave me that look that said, *You are gonna see that this drunk gets out of here safely, aren't you?* I was all smiles and helped Tom to the door since he was in that listing stage—that is, just before the staggers. I knew exactly what was happening. He didn't.

When we got out in the night air, it sort of sobered him up a little, and he began to search for his keys and to try to remember where he parked his car. That was the time to tell him that I lived just a little beyond him, and I offered to drive him home, since he was in no condition to be driving, as drunk as he was. Did he want to risk a ticket or an accident? No, sir, I could take him home safely, and he could easily come back in the morning to get his car. The fog was settling in—I could see it in his eyes. Tom could do little but agree, and I led him to my van.

My van is basically a rolling bedroom: two seats up front and then a huge empty back with nothing but packing pads. No windows. Curtain between the front and the back so no one can see what's going on. I opened the back and helped Tom in, and I told him to lie down and rest till we got home. He was having trouble keeping his eyes open, so he just climbed in, lay down, and flopped like a wet washrag. He was out, gone. I had timed it perfectly. Wonderful!

I locked up the back and got in the front and got my cell phone and called my buddy, Rudy, who had given me the drug. I told him, "I got a live one, Rudy. I've already used the drug, but I need some help getting this guy into my apartment." Luckily Rudy was about as far from the bar in the other direction, so it didn't take him long to get there, just long enough for me to get to my place, open it all up, get it ready, and have a smoke.

When Rudy pulled up, he helped me get Tom out of the back and into my place. I have a first-floor apartment with a door on the street level, so it wasn't too obvious what was going on; it looked just like two friends helping a drunk friend home. While I got Tom stripped and into my bed, Rudy set up the video equipment and the digital camera. We were going to document the experience for Tom so that he had some proof. I made a pot of coffee, since I needed to be up and sober, and Rudy had some, though he spiked his with a little whiskey. Rudy would be the photographer, I would be the rapist, and Tom would be the victim.

I figured with all the beer and the drug, we had a good two hours before he came around. I sucked Tom's dick to be sure he was out, and there was no response, so he was gone. Rudy connected the video cam to the TV which was on the chest of drawers opposite the bed so I could watch what he was taping and be sure we got it all set up correctly. He put the video camera on the tripod and used the digital cam to get several shots of Tom passed out on the bed, naked, face down. After we got all the preliminary stuff done, Rudy aimed the video cam at me as I stripped, taking a few flash pix as well as some of me getting naked and working my cock up good and stiff.

You know how sometimes it's hard getting your cock into a guy when he's tight? Well, try it sometime when he's dead to the world. There was no telling him to lift his ass a little. I just had to keep lubing up the hole and probing it. Once I had my cock head in, I just eased down and in, and as I did I began the narration of the event, facing into the camera and addressing it mainly to Tom to show him what had happened.

We got some excellent shots of my cock popping his ass open, me sliding in, and finally of me fucking him. As I was getting close to the point of coming in his ass, I stopped to tell the camera that this was it—the moment of conversion. Rudy got an excellent shot of my ass muscles puckering up when I fired the first shots. And I didn't realize how much I was talking till I saw the video, I was really telling him what was happening, that I was shooting my dirty load up his hot hole, etc. Soon there was sweat dripping off my nose onto his back, and we got a beautiful shot of a come-creamy cock pulling out of his hole and the come oozing out of his open asshole. He never moved during the whole fuck; it was like fucking a dead man.

Then Rudy and I shut off the video cam and had a smoke break. Rudy had his cock out jacking it while I was coming, and I asked him if he wanted to add his load, but he said he wanted to wait and see what the guy thought—if he wanted it—because he was always up for a hot fuck in another guy's come. I had some coffee while I smoked and thought about what we should do next. It had been over an hour, and I had given Tom a light dose, so it was about time for him to be coming around soon.

I began jacking my cock, trying to get it up, and Rudy was kind enough to give me a light blow job to get me started. I was about to start undressing him so I could return the favor, when he stopped and got up and turned the camera and TV on again. So it was time for Act 2.

We had flipped Tom over on his back, and he was sprawled all across the bed, arms out, legs spread, ass still drooling a little of that first load. I got on the bed, and it really took a lot of work to get him into position. I had to put his legs on my shoulders and try to hold them there while I raised his ass enough to get my cock in. He was nice and juicy with my come load this time, and I had lubed up, so once I got the angle right, I could get in, but getting there was difficult. His legs kept falling off my shoulders, and it was rather funny when we watched the tape later—but not during my efforts.

I finally got him all wadded up, holding his ass up with my knees, his legs over my shoulders, so I could fuck hard enough to get a come shot without any assistance from the bottom. I was working into the fuck, getting up steam, when Tom began to moan and move a little. I held my head right against his ear, and I told him, "Tom, you need to wake up now, lover, can you hear me?"

He opened his eyes and blinked a couple of times and looked at me. I rose up a little so he could see me through the fog in his brain. I kept fucking him. I was getting close, and I wanted to be right at the edge.

"Tom, remember me? Jerry? From the bar? Remember how you told me you wanted to be fucked poz?" He wiped his face and eyes and seemed to become aware of what was going on. His ass tightened up real hard around my cock. Then he looked at me, and I could tell he was feeling the fuck and beginning to understand what was happening.

"Jerry, what's going on?" His legs began to straighten a little, and I had to hold him tight to keep my cock in his ass.

"You told me you wanted a poz load up your ass, Tom, and if you just relax, feel it now when I come in your ass. You're getting that poz load you wanted so bad." I started fucking him hard again, and as I got to the edge and began to go over it, I stopped and held real still so he could feel my cock spasm in his ass.

"Oh, God!" His legs went straight up over his head. "Do it, man! I can feel it! Oh, God! Fuck me poz, man! Fuck my ass!"

I started fucking him hard again as my cock unloaded the second dirty load into his fuck hole. He grabbed me with his legs, his heels in my ass cheeks, forcing my cock in even deeper. I pumped that load in as deep and as hard as I could, and I kissed him hard. He had his tongue in my mouth, and his hands were all over me, hugging me, messing up my hair. He was in a fuck frenzy, doing everything a bottom does when he wants that load deep, and I was doing everything a top does to plant it deep and heavy. He was really spurring me on. It took a long time for us to wind down from that, but finally my cock deflated, and I fell out of his ass. I gave him one last kiss as I climbed off him, and I sucked his cock clean of the strings of precome that had dribbled out during the fuck.

That was when he finally noticed Rudy with the video camera and saw the TV showing us the scene. I could see him realizing exactly what was going on. Rudy shoved his cock back in his pants and zipped up, then he turned his attention to the equipment as I explained to Tom what had happened and that we had the whole scene on tape. I introduced Rudy to Tom, and Tom was both embarrassed and excited. He wanted to see, so we had to rewind the tape and show him the whole first rape scene, and then the second, and he kept saying, "Oh, God, it was just what I wanted, man. It was just what I wanted!"

Watching the tape had gotten Tom's cock stiff as a poker, and Rudy had gotten his cock out and was stroking it up, so when the tape ran out, I leaned over and began to suck Tom's cock, and Rudy came over and offered his cock to Tom. He took it in his mouth greedily, so excited by what had happened and what he had seen on the tape. After a minute I asked Tom if he wanted to guarantee his conversion. "What do you mean?" he asked.

"Let's put a different strain in on top of the two loads you just got. Rudy's poz too and a great fucker."

Rudy smiled at Tom, and Tom said sure and spread out on the middle of the bed as I got out of the way and Rudy quickly stripped off his clothes. Rudy is tall, about 6 foot 1 or so and thin. He's got a nice long cock with a big head on it. His dick's not as thick as mine, but it's longer. He's got black hair and isn't too hairy, just a little bush around the crotch, but he has nice hairy, juicy balls that hang down low and slap a bottom's ass while he fucks.

Rudy had Tom suck him up stiff and juicy again, and I got the video camera and TV going again so we could get their fuck on tape too. When Rudy was ready, he pulled Tom up, though Tom was a little shorter than he was. They kissed, Tom working Rudy's cock and Rudy feeling up that juicy ass he was after. Then Rudy turned Tom around and centered his cock on Tom's hole. He held Tom tight against him and thrust in. Now Rudy is not as thick as me, like I said, so he slid in easy on my loads, but he hit bottom, and it took a little work to get that long fuck pole of his past Tom's second sphincter. There was a lot of moaning, and Tom had to bend over a little and work his ass with a lot of wiggling to let that meat all the way in. And I got it all on tape. It is one of the most exciting sequences.

Then they moved as a team, joined together. Rudy stood on the floor, and Tom got on hands and knees so Rudy could fuck him doggy-style. I moved the tripod around to the side to get all the action. Rudy's cock is so long you could easily see it pistoning in and out and his balls flapping against Tom's ass. Once I had it set, I just stood there, naked, jacking my cock, watching as Rudy held Tom's ass and centered that pistoning fuck rod.

Tom looked over at me, smiled, and said, "Join us!" So I went over to the other side and let Tom suck me up while he got fucked. Rudy fucks long and hard before he shoots, so I knew it would take a while for him to get off, even in Tom's juicy ass. After Tom had sucked me up stiff, I reached under and found Tom's hard cock dribbling precome and about ready to blow. So I pulled my cock out of Tom's mouth, lay down on the bed on my back, and crept under Tom, slowly getting into a sixty-nine position.

As soon as Tom realized what I was doing, he raised up to let me situate and then lowered his cock into my waiting mouth and took my stiff member in his. It was difficult to suck Tom with Rudy slamming into him so hard, but I moved down so that the force of Rudy's fuck strokes would shove Tom's stiff rod into my mouth. Tom was really going to town on my dick. I didn't have much come left, if any, so he was sucking my shaved balls and licking me all over, just having a wonderful time with that long rod up his ass and a hungry man sucking him off.

Rudy said he was getting close, and Tom said something, but he had my cock back in his mouth, so it was just a muffled grunt. When Rudy began to fuck him furiously, I knew he was shooting his load into Tom's ass. Then I suddenly got the biggest mouthful of come I think I've ever had, and it took me a long time to be able to swallow it all with that stiff cock constantly being pounded down my throat. I thought I was gonna gag from it.

Rudy made one final hard thrust and stayed in deep and hugged Tom real tight. On the video you can see the sweat all over him, dripping from his chest onto Tom's back. Tom was sucking my cock, hoping to get something, but there was nothing there. His cock was deflating in my mouth, finally, and I was sucking the last strings of heavy, gooey fluid out; it had obviously been a long time since he'd shot his load. It tasted wonderful, salty and spermy. Rudy finally pulled out, and there was a string of his come from Tom's ass to his cock head that shows up beautifully on the tape. He gave Tom's ass a parting slap, which knocked Tom's cock out of my mouth. Tom gave up on my cock, and we began to disentangle.

We all had to have a cigarette and watch the tape, and it was just great. Tom kept telling me how wonderful it felt to feel Rudy come in his ass just as he was shooting in my mouth. You can't see much of when Tom comes in my mouth on the tape; by the time he climbed off I had swallowed it and licked his cock head clean.

Rudy got dressed and packed up his equipment, leaving the videotape for me to duplicate on my machine. Tom was on the bed, spread-eagled, trying to recover from what had happened. After Rudy left we sat on the bed and talked for what seemed a long time. I offered to get dressed and take Tom back to his car, but he said he was too tired. If I didn't mind, he asked, he'd just spend the rest of the night with me.

I didn't mind, and we had a good time just talking. Tom just couldn't get over that it had actually happened. It was just what he wanted, he said, in fact, even better. He had two poz tops seed his ass with dirty sperm, so he was really high. I'd had so much coffee that it took me a while to run down, but eventually we ended up kissing, and that led to the final fuck of the night.

This one wasn't the fireworks kind—it was a long lovers' fuck.

First we started doggy, then faced each other, kissing as we fucked for a long time. We eventually got on our sides, and my third load oozed up his ass very slowly, though he said he could still feel it when I shot—even with his ass as worn out as it was. We fell asleep with my cock inside him, and when I woke up very late the next morning, I was able to fuck him awake and give him a small load to start the day.

About four weeks later he called me. He'd had a cold and gone to the doctor and gotten tested. He invited me to go over to his place and spend the night with him again—to celebrate.

The Hard Way

By Larry Fuller

He had the straight-boy look: half shaved head, hemp necklace, no socks. An hour ago, online, I hadn't believed him, but watching him rock back and forth on the balls of his feet and bob his neck around while he checked out my apartment, I could smell heterosexuality hanging on him like bad cologne.

"How old are you?" I asked.

"Twenty-three," he said without hesitation.

"Yeah? Let's see the ID." I wasn't going to jail just to get a nut off.

He pulled a battered wallet out of the pocket of his baggy basketball shorts and flashed his driver's license.

Richard James Ellicott. Born 1977.

So I had five years on him.

"Do you want to come in, Richard?"

"Rick," he replied a little nervously.

"OK, Rick, you want to sit down?" I offered.

He hadn't gotten up the nerve to move off the linoleum in my entryway.

"What?" He looked startled. "Oh, yeah, sure."

I waved toward the couch, and he headed in that direction, darting nervous looks over his shoulder like he thought I might be trying to stick my dick up his ass without his knowing.

Actually I was checking out his butt as he walked, his long, ropy arms swinging awkwardly as if he wasn't quite used to their length. He belonged in a Saturday afternoon pickup basketball game down at the high school, not here. But he was here. He had wanted to come. He'd been hanging around the chat room, and I guess I was the one who scared him the least.

He sat down, long legs spread wide, blond swirls of hair on his thighs disappearing into darkness. I sat next to him and put my hand on one of those thighs, feeling muscles jump and quiver. He jerked his head to the side as though he couldn't stand to watch.

"Rick," I said.

"Yeah?"

"You want me to do this, right?"

"Yeah. Yeah. It's cool."

I slid my hand up under the shorts, drawn toward the heat radiating from where his legs met. My other hand went under the tank top, feeling the ridges of his abdomen, hard from youth, not exercise.

He didn't move. Just closed his eyes.

I slid his shorts down over his hips; he wasn't wearing anything under them.

His breath hissed, and he jumped slightly as my tongue made contact, first circling the base of his balls, and then moving upward, more roughly, rasping against the underside of his lengthening shaft. He shifted his hips and clamped both hands on the back of my head, starting a savage rhythm as he fucked my mouth.

Unprepared, I jerked my head away, coughing.

"Sorry," he said. "I guess I don't know what I'm doing."

"It's OK, man. I don't mind. I just wasn't ready."

He stared at me, unblinking for a moment, his rod pulsing against his stomach, and then he stared down at it like it was a complete stranger. I stood and pulled my shirt over my head. Half seducing, half unveiling, stripping for a waiting lover is a ritualized performance, played for maximum effect and heightened anticipation.

Rick stared at me as I unbuckled my belt and the top button of my jeans. His eyes grew wide.

"No way," he muttered, standing and pulling his shorts back

into place. "I can't do this." He started for the door.

"Rick, wait, what's wrong?"

"Nothing. I'm sorry. I guess I'm not ready to suck dick or whatever."

"Wait. We don't have to. There are other things..." My voice sounded desperate, and I hated it.

"Sorry," he said. "I shouldn't have done this."

"You didn't do anything." I tried to soothe his nerves.

"Look, man. I'm sorry. I said I was sorry. I thought it would be cool, but this is fuckin' freakin' me out. I gotta get out of here."

That pissed me off. "You thought it would be cool? What, to let the faggot suck your dick? Fucking gamer asshole."

His face was raw, his eyes desperate as he spoke. "It's not a game. It's not. It's just, fuck, I don't know...it's so weird. I mean, you're a guy. You're all hairy and shit." He whirled and yanked at the door.

I leaned around him, my chest touching his bare shoulder, and undid the dead bolt. We stood like that for a split second, which seemed longer. Our eyes locked, our noses almost touching. Then I yanked the door open, pushing him out of the way. "Get the fuck outta here."

"I'm sorry, man."

"Sorry fuckin' ass is what you are," I said and shut the door.

All hairy and shit. Goddamn. There I was, practically flexing, preening, giving the boy a show, and the whole time I was making him sick.

"Freak show," I said to my reflection in the mirror just inside the door.

Wandering into the bedroom, I saw my computer monitor glowing in the darkness. I slapped it openhanded like it was a puppy that had shit on the rug. I felt like crap. Like chicken-hawk crap. Fuck that. I was only five years older than him. But still, I felt like a creepy predator lurking in the corner of a bus station men's room waiting for some kid from Kansas to disembark.

Well, guess what. Fuck him. Fuck him and his little nocturnal experimentation with the dark side. I sat down heavily on the bed.

All hairy and shit. Jesus.

⌨ ⌨ ⌨

He came back. Four days later.

The knock came around 9. I opened the door, and there he was. Khakis and gray T-shirt this time. Gap model look.

"It's Rick," he said, mistaking my dumbfoundedness for lack of recognition.

"Yeah, I know."

"Can I come in?"

"No," I told him, still not happy about our previous encounter.

He shifted from foot to foot, glancing down the hallway, obviously taken aback.

"Please. Just to talk?"

"About what?"

"The other night. I..." His voice trailed away.

"Yeah?"

"I need to talk to you." His voice came out as a scratchy whisper.

The desperation in his voice was startling enough for me to step aside and let him in. He brushed by me, smelling clean and windy like autumn, blond hair adorably ruffled, nipples poking tantalizingly through his T-shirt. I wondered how much of that was deliberate.

I, on the other hand, was anything but tantalizing in baggy sweats and an old, ripped Lollapalooza T-shirt. I was happy about that. I was dressed to distress, and I hoped it had the desired effect.

He turned suddenly, a ferociously determined look on his face. Then his lips were on mine, his tongue forcing itself into my mouth, his hands clutching at my back, his whole body pressed against me. I got my arms between us and shoved him away, wiping my lips with the back of my hand.

"Get off me. Jesus. What's your problem?"

"I want to do it."

"What? Fuck me?" I laughed. "Forget about it."

"I couldn't stop thinking about it." His eyes were locked on mine. "I kept seeing you, and I was so close, and I blew it. I need to do this."

"Well, I don't," I let him know plainly.

He stared at me. Shocked. This was clearly not how he had played the scene out in his mind. To him, his plan must have seemed pretty smooth.

"Look, Rick," I said in a nicer, older-brother voice. "I don't think you know what the hell you want. And I'm not really into being your big gay experiment. I kind of like the guy whose dick I'm sucking to want me to be sucking his dick. You know?"

"I want to. I mean, I want that. I do." He was almost begging.

"No, you don't. Remember. We already tried that."

"I wanted to. I was just too chickenshit. But I wanted to. I *want* to."

It was time to call his bluff and get him the hell out the door. I stepped toward him. "You do? You want me to suck your dick?"

"Yeah," he nodded vigorously. "Yeah, I do. I liked it. Do it."

I smiled and walked right up to him. Putting a hand on his shoulder, I said in a voice as cold as I could make it, "Then suck mine."

"OK," he said, moving toward me, cocky and defiant.

I didn't move, just stood there, one hand resting on his shoulder as a suggestion. Like a penitent, he went to his knees in front of me, his hands sliding my sweats down over my hips, my dick bouncing into view, soft and startled.

He paused, his hands resting on his knees, then leaned forward and gulped me into his mouth, his eyes looking up into mine as if to say, "See, I did it."

Then something shifted behind his eyes, a strange groan drifted from him, and he began to devour me. I felt myself growing longer and harder inside his hungry mouth, saw myself expanding as his lips bobbed up and down, taking a little less with each downward gulp. He nipped me with his teeth, coughed, choked, his total lack of experience obvious. But watching him—blond hair falling in his eyes, lips stretched, long-fascinated fingers playing over my length, his hunger and enthusiasm—it all brought me close to the edge.

I pulled him to his feet, meeting his wet lips with my own in an openmouthed kiss. I ran my hands down his back, feeling his muscles contract and expand against my palms, moved lower to cup the hard curves of his ass, drawing him tighter against me, the hard length of him throbbing against my own exposed manhood.

I pulled his T-shirt over his head and consumed the fresh, clean taste of him, gently taking one of his tiny hard nipples between my teeth, running my tongue along the ridges of his stomach, through the soft line of hair that disappeared under the waistband of his pants. I unbuttoned them and let them fall away, my hands dragging his boxers with them. And then he was in my mouth again, long and hard, skin tight and unbelievably hot to my tongue, the sweet tang of his excitement tingling my taste buds. I sucked him in slowly, burying my nose in the curls of his crotch, both hands clutching the smooth hardness of his ass, one finger traveling between his muscled cheeks to his tight, hot, pulsing center.

"Shit. Oh, shit, man. Oh, God. Yeah. Oh, man." His hoarse whispers drifted down, urging me on.

This time he pulled me up, into another kiss, clutching at me and whispering in my ear, "I want you to fuck me."

"Are you serious?" I laughed out loud.

"What? You don't want to?"

"Well, yeah, but I don't think you're ready."

"Yeah? Well, I think I am." His tilted chin was defiant as he tried to stare me down.

What was with this guy? His eyes blazed with some sort of mixed-up lust; I couldn't figure out what he was all about. Jesus, yes, of course I wanted to fuck him. I just didn't want to fuck him up.

He turned away from me and bent over, his pants bunched around his ankles, demandingly inviting. I moved in behind him, running my hands over him, gently, then more firmly, riding him, letting him get used to the feel of hard cock against his skin. He bent farther over until his hands grabbed his ankles, his long frame bent nearly in half.

"Don't move," I whispered as I kicked off my shoes and jiggled out of my sweats. I hurried to the bathroom and returned with lube and a condom.

"Turn around, Rick." He turned, eyes wide and nostrils flaring. "Put it on me."

He fumbled with the foil packet, finally tearing it with his teeth, and placed the ring against the head of my dick.

"Lube me up first," I said, handing him the bottle.

His slicked hand ran the length of my shaft, squeezing and stroking, his eyes never leaving mine.

"Now put it on me."

Silently, he rolled the condom onto my cock, pinching the reservoir gently. He had obviously used one before, but not like this, I was sure.

"Now bend over." This wasn't the easiest way to take it the first time. But something told me he didn't want it easy. "Spread your legs a little wider."

Snorting with impatience, he kicked one leg out of his pants and moved his legs apart.

Jesus, I wanted to be inside him so bad, but I took my time, teasing him with my thumbs, pressing deeper, then slipping the tip of my index finger inside him as he sucked in his breath.

"Breathe, Rick. Breathe, and keep breathing," I coached him.

I wiggled my finger in a little farther, searching for the hard knob inside that would give him the pleasure he was seeking. Finding it, I massaged it gently, then more insistently as his hips began to buck against my hand. He didn't say a word, but I knew he was getting close to blowing. That was good because once I started fucking him, I wanted him right on the edge, since I didn't think I could last long.

I got another finger inside him, readying him for what he couldn't possibly know was about to come next. His hips were rolling now, his breath coming fast. Then I positioned myself behind him.

"Rick, are you sure you want to go through with this?"

His yes was a gasp.

"All right. But if you want me to stop, just say so. Now listen, when I push in, you need to push out, OK? Push back. It'll be better that way."

"OK," he gasped.

I leaned in, pressing my hard length into his tight heat. Gritting my teeth, I clamped my hand hard around the base of my cock to keep me in control as I slid into him.

"Shit! Fuck! Fuck!" The words exploded raggedly from his mouth in bursts of breath.

I reached my hand around his middle and grabbed his cock. He had gone soft, so I stopped, buried halfway inside, and brought him back to life. Within seconds he was stretched to his full length and his hips had resumed their rocking motion, taking a little more of me each time. I continued to stroke him, feeling him get harder, the skin get tighter, as he rode close to the edge. The tiny bit of friction against the head of my cock combined with the hot fist of muscle locked around it had me just as close. I wrapped myself around him, sweat pouring from my body, fucking him, stroking him, both of us going to our knees, never separating. It lasted maybe a minute.

His body went rigid, his head was flung back, and liquid heat exploded in my hand. Deep inside him, where I was buried, his explosion wrung pleasure from me in a torrent that almost broke me in half. One of us, maybe both of us, screamed in jagged bursts, timed to the convulsions of our climaxes. Together we slumped to the floor, glued to each other with sweat, curling into a heap, my softening dick still buried inside him, his still trembling in my fist.

As my shaking subsided, I felt his continuing. He convulsed in my arms as the first sob rocketed from his throat. It was a quiet sobbing, a choking sound, violent in its restraint.

"Rick?"

"Shut up," he whispered between sobs. "Please don't talk now."

I tightened my arms around him and buried my face in his wet hair, feeling like a dumbfuck. A blind dumbfuck. *Straight boy. Oh, sure. Try gay virgin—or at least until now.*

I let him cry. I stroked his back and smoothed his hair. I lifted his face and kissed his eyes and tear-stained cheeks—and finally his mouth. His sobbing died away, his muscles relaxed, and he slumped against me, his cheek resting against my chest.

"You OK?" I asked.

"Yeah. Yeah, I think I am," he said. I felt a sense of relief in his words.

I bent down and kissed the top of his head. "All hairy and shit," I said under my breath, half chuckling.

"What?"

"Nothing. Nothing."

Better to Have Lusted and Lost...

The One

By Raymond

June 1999: The summer heat took its toll with Atlanta's older citizens. Every day a report was broadcast about a victim fallen to the heat. It's best to stay inside, they recommended. Well, with nothing really to do, I sat down to play on the Net. A reason I bought the computer in the first place. The video and card games, the chat rooms, and the adult sites that turn me on.

As day fell into night I found myself sitting in my chair with a bag of Tootsie Rolls by my side. I'd checked all my E-mails, played a round of DigDug, and it was time to cruise a couple of sites. I usually started with a search engine, but this time I went right into a site through a link someone sent to me. It didn't have a title, just the address. Once I was there, I scanned all the info and graphics to find the chat rooms. I clicked inside, searching for a local room to kill some time. Once I found the room, I signed in using my DickinMe handle. A handle I sometimes use just to see what kind of reaction I can get.

Well, there were five private messages sent to me within minutes of signing on. While I checked the senders' profiles, my eyes were caught by one in particular. It read: "BM seeks another BM, DL for fun." I thought, *Well, let's see how much fun one can have with another.*

I returned his private message, asking for a description, ignoring all the other guys. He sent me his description: dark-skinned black male, bald head, some facial hair, 31 years old, clean/healthy, single, and 8.5 inches. Well, a description we would all drool over if there ever was one, right? Well, my curiosity was at its highest. I had to find out more so I could determine if he was taking me on a trip or if he wanted to really go as far as we both could. I asked him where he was located in Atlanta and if he only wanted a little fun on the Net.

To my surprise he was just 15 minutes away from my home. He said he wanted to get out of the house for a minute and maybe have a drink or something. Well, I don't drink, and I wasn't thinking about leaving, and, besides, Mom always said never to bring a stranger to your home.

He asked if I would meet him somewhere, just so that we could see each other and decide if it was something to pursue. Well, I was having fun just chatting with the image I'd made from his description. I thought it would mess everything up if we were to meet. We continued chatting for a while. He asked me what I enjoyed doing with a guy, what turned me on, and if I would ever consider meeting him. The words he used, the way he carried the conversation, increased my attention.

I don't know if it was me being in summer-heat drive or if I was just plain curious because this guy was saying everything I wanted to hear. I answered all his questions and posed a couple to him. I wanted to know if a guy was so good-looking and had all the qualities a guy is usually looking for, then why was he single?

"With work and all," he replied, "I can't find a guy that's willing to be trustworthy and there for me while I go off and make a living. So I've resulted to just dating when I have time."

Hmm, I thought, this could be The One. But we were talking in an environment where you could be anyone or anything. For all I knew, that guy could really be a 12-year-old girl or a 50-year-old man. It angered me to know that he was just 15 minutes away from me and was able to communicate with me in a chat room but would not give me a minute of his time while passing me by on the street. So I asked him for his number, thinking maybe we could talk offline and see if it was worthwhile to meet. He agreed and gave me his number.

I ended my chat session and reached for the phone, not knowing how he would sound or if the number he gave me was even a working number. It rang, and it rang again. He answered my call with a hurried pace, as if he were running from another room in the house. I asked him if he wanted me to call back later.

He said, "No, it's cool now. I just had to use the bathroom."

I jokingly asked him if he forgot to wash his hands; we laughed, and I realized his voice was soothing. A voice that would be nice breathing down the back of your neck on a hot, summer night.

I asked him if it was cool if I asked his real name. He told me Stephon. I told him my name, Daryl, and the reason I chose the chat-room handle. He thought I was funny and had a great sense of humor. I thought he was the match from heaven—the other half of me that would make me whole. Yeah, I was premature in thinking that, but I felt as if I knew him. I told him we were only 15 minutes away from each other, that, in fact, he lives across the street from where I attended middle school—it is now a rehabilitation center and business park.

We talked for about 15 minutes more and decided to meet. It was around 8 P.M., and I was wearing only shorts and a tank top. He said he could be at the College Park train station in about 30 minutes. I went upstairs to jump in the shower just long enough for the stench to wash off, and then I jumped in something to wear. I was having second thoughts about what we were planning to do. I wanted more than just a hot night of man sex. I wanted the friend that I longed for. Someone who liked movies, bowling, card games, or just relaxing at home.

Stephon liked all those things, and he was waiting for me at the train station. So what was it? Why was I having second thoughts? Well, I knew he wanted to do more. Perhaps, if the situation permitted, we could end up at his house for a nightcap or something. I reached for my Calvin Klein underwear, thinking I would impress him by wearing such, but I opted not to wear any at all, hoping he would get a good laugh at my readiness.

I got into my truck, turned up the radio, and lowered the window. Trying to relax without the pressure getting to me. I made it to the train station before Stephon arrived. He pulled up soon after I turned my truck off. I knew it was him; he had given me a description of his car. And, besides, what other man would drive into a train station at that time and just sit around? It wasn't known as a cruising spot or something. He turned his engine off and sat motionless for a good minute or two. I sat in my car, watching him in my rearview mirror. I was thinking, *Now he knows what I'm driving.*

I heard a door open and the sound of footsteps coming near. I lay back farther in my seat, trying to give the look of coolness. He approached my door and said, "Daryl? What's up?"

I sat up with a grin and said, "We finally meet." We stared at each other for a while and began to laugh. I asked why *he* was laughing. He didn't respond; he just stood there with his hands in his pockets, head lowered. I stopped laughing, rose up from my seat to turn down the radio, and I asked again, "Why are you laughing like that? Huh?"

He looked at me and said, "I can't believe I'm meeting someone like this. In a train station parking lot, you know. I mean, I can't believe that someone is you. What are you doing in a chat room? You look too good to be doing something like this."

I replied with, "I can say the same about you. There should be many guys knocking down your door." He asked me to step outside my truck. I tried to adjust my shorts so that he wouldn't see my bulge when I stood.

He said, "Man, man, damn! You look good, and you know it. You're one of those guys that wants to play it off, but deep down, you know you look good."

I asked him if it was a problem—did I lie about my description?

He said, "Well, yeah, you did. You didn't tell me you look this good." We laughed it off for a while, until a security guard found our conversation interesting. We had to make up our minds about what was going to happen next.

He looked at me through his oval-rimmed glasses and asked, "If it's all right with you, would you like to come back to my place?"

I thought, OK, if I say no, he might think I'm not interested, but if I say yes, will he still think I'm more than the normal type found in chat rooms? I jumped in my truck and said, "All right, I'll follow ya."

We headed out of the parking lot of the train station. I was hoping for a lot from this encounter, but I forced myself to remember where we'd met. Can a guy expect more when the premise is all about fantasy and escapades? I had to find out, so we ended up across the street from the business park.

His lawn wasn't tended to; it had been a while since he last mowed it. We walked in the front door, leaving my car parked in the driveway. He escorted me to the kitchen area, where I noticed dirty dishes piled up in the sink, an old carton of a microwavable TV dinner on the counter, and stacks of unanswered mail. He reached for his refrigerator, trying not to open it so wide that I saw the empty racks. I did.

I asked him if he really lived there or if he just stopped by every once in a while.

He turned to me and said, "I have to apologize for this house. Man, I just got back into town last night from a business trip and haven't had the time to straighten up. I haven't even been grocery shopping."

I told him I understood. Although I would have never invited someone to my house if I knew it was unclean. He handed me a can of Coke and reached for a glass. I told him not to worry about the glass, that I could drink it from the can. "It'll be one less glass you'll have to wash, right?"

We walked into the living room, where the TV was on. I sat down on the couch, and he sat down on the love seat. He grabbed the remote control and asked what I would like to watch. Well, there wasn't anything really on TV that I had to watch. "Whatever you want, I will watch," I said.

He looked over his shoulder with a grin and said, "Be careful of what you say."

I was puzzled. I asked him why he said that. He said, well, you might find yourself watching the Turner Classics. I busted out laughing, spilling my Coke on his couch. He didn't notice; I asked for a napkin. I could hear him in the kitchen, laughing while I tried to dry off his couch before he noticed. He handed me the napkin, and I used it on my face until he turned around.

I asked him if he liked the old black-and-white movies. He said, "Yeah. There's a good one on now. It's *The Bad Seed.* Have you seen that one?" I told him I read the book years ago, but I had not seen the movie.

He said, "You'll enjoy the movie version—it's really good." So we decided to watch that. Thirty-five minutes into the movie, I was finished with my Coke and was very relaxed in the center of his couch, my bulge beginning to rear its head again. The way he folded his leg under him and casually leaned into the love seat made me think only about being under him. Yet there was no way I was going to make the first move. It was his house, his living room—I wasn't going to put myself in an embarrassing situation. So I waited, patiently, like the transient passengers at the College Park train station.

The phone rang in his kitchen, breaking the silence. He got up and excused himself. I wanted to reach for the remote control to mute the TV so I could hear the conversation. I sat there wondering what he would say when he came back. If he had just come back from out of town, his friends were probably hoping to find him home safely and to see if the trip went well.

I stretched my legs as he was walking back into the living room. He said, "Why don't you make yourself comfortable? Take off your shoes, man, get comfortable." That was the welcome mat I was waiting for. If a man wanted you to remove your shoes, there was no way he was gonna ask you to leave anytime soon—unless you had smelly feet or something. I took off my shoes, placed them over near the end of the couch, and stretched again.

He noticed the bulge that was very visible through my shorts. He said, "Hey, man, what's that? Hey, hey, what have you been looking at while I was on the phone, huh?" He had a smirk on his face.

Too shy or awkward to admit what he'd noticed, I said, "What are you talking about? What?"

We laughed and then laughed some more, and all the while I tried to adjust my shorts. He started to move over closer to me but stayed on the love seat. I looked at him, trying to see deep into his eyes to determine what was about to happen. He got up from the love seat and went over to the couch where he placed one leg behind my back and the other one across my lap. I asked him what he was doing.

He looked at me, grinning, and said, “Making you feel comfortable over here. This couch is too big for one person.” He lay back on the couch and asked me to take off my shirt. Well, I thought it was quick what we were doing. I wanted to find out how the movie was going to end, but I removed my shirt, holding in my stomach. I'm just so self-conscious about that part of my body.

I turned to him and said, “There. Now's your turn.” Without hesitation, he removed his shirt with ease, as if he had practice taking it off while keeping his glasses on. I didn't have to worry about that one—I was wearing my contacts.

I looked down at his chest. His pecs were rock-hard with a li'l peach fuzz making a pathway to his lower body. I reached for his stomach and began to rub it. I could feel him warming up. His nipples were pointing upward; they had to have been about an inch long. I reached down to lick them. I could hear him moan a little. It got me so hot. I could have been satisfied with just doing that.

I sat back up and said to him, “What's this? What is this you have in your shorts?”

He smiled and said, “Why don't you take them off and find out?” I was happy with that reply. He moved his left leg so that I could remove his shorts to find a dark, thick, 10-inch dick.

I said, “You lied to me. You told me it was only 8½ inches. Why did you do that?”

He replied, “If I would have told you the real size, you wouldn't believe me anyway, right? I know some people get scared of a guy with a hung dick.”

I didn't know how to respond to that. I didn't want to say, “Well, I can handle it,” nor did I want to appear afraid of it. I reached down and played with it while he watched. There was one huge vein running down it. It seemed to make a pathway to the hair surrounding it. My mouth was watering. I wanted to feel it inside my mouth, but I didn't want him to think I was a guy who enjoyed giving head to just anyone. But after close examination of his dick,

I couldn't resist, and I reached down and took it in my mouth. I could really hear him moan. His legs were tightening up around me.

"It feels so good," he whispered. We went on like that for 10 minutes or so. He reached for me, grabbing my shoulders, and said, "Come here. Take off your shorts."

I did so. We lay there on the couch, bumping and grinding, kissing while the credits of *The Bad Seed* were rolling by on the TV.

He said to me, "Let's go the bedroom." Without a second lost, I jumped up and started to follow him. He reached for the remote control and turned off the TV, making it too dark for me to tell where I was going. He grabbed my hand, got behind me, and started to walk to the bedroom. I could feel his dick up against my ass cheeks. It was the heaven I always wanted.

We got to the bedroom, but he didn't turn on the lights. The streetlights from the business park had the room lit enough for me to get around. We stood over the bed. He kissed me from the back and massaged my chest. I stroked his dick in a slow motion. I could feel him getting wet. I turned around and lay down on the bed. He stood there for a while then said, "Damn, man. Why haven't I found you earlier?"

I didn't say anything.

I got to the top of the bed and laid my head on the pillow, and he knelt below me and started to kiss my right ankle. I could see his image in the light that was coming through the blinds. The way the light beamed down on his body totally enhanced his muscular lines. He raised my leg a little more, trying to figure out how far he could go with me in that position. He kissed and licked my leg until he got to my hips. He massaged my hips, looking up at me, and then his mouth took in my cock.

It didn't excite me that he was doing that. He did it like a novice, but I didn't dare stop him. He continued up my body, getting to my chest. He made circular motions around my nipples with his tongue and then sucked them in. I reached for the pillow beside me and ended up grabbing the bottom of the headboard. He knew I was enjoying it. He did it with excellence. He ground into me with his mouth while my head was as far back as it could go, exposing my neck. He went up to my neck area and started to suck on it softly. My neck was a weak spot that I don't tell everyone about, but he figured it out, maybe because I raised my legs around him and held him tightly. We were entangled like that for about 15 minutes. Just bumping and grinding, kissing and massaging. It was enough to call it a night. A very good night.

He raised himself up over me, looking down, and said, "Can I have you? I want to feel you. The inside of you." With a statement like that, who could resist?

He reached for his goody bag, which was on the nightstand by the bed. He removed his glasses, and I tried to prepare myself for what was to come. He passed me the lube while he tore open a condom pack. I could see him in the light as he unrolled the condom over his cock. It had to have been a Magnum condom. I laid my head back on the pillow. He reached down to play with my ass, and I started to moan.

I could feel him move his fingers away from me as his cock touched my ass. I looked up to him and said, "Now, you gotta take it slow, man. It's been a while."

He replied, "Whatever you want, Boo. Just tell me when it's OK."

I closed my eyes, head back, still gripping the headboard. He started to make small pushes into me. I could feel him. I didn't think I would be able to take all of it in, but I didn't want to turn him off by saying stop. He leaned down to me and started to nibble on my neck again. I raised my legs higher, giving him some room to get in closer, which he did with great passion. It hurt. But I didn't want it to stop. I took deep breaths, trying not to give in to the pain of the moment, letting him know I could take it like a man. He started to grind back and forth with only about five inches inside me. It was enough, but I was sure he wouldn't be satisfied with just that. We had to lie there like that for a while.

While my body got adjusted to him, I could feel him moving farther into me. I reached for his shoulder, biting down on him to keep myself from hollering. He had gotten it all in me. I could feel his nuts up against me. He moved slow, staying in one place for a long time. I continued to bite him on his shoulder as he lifted my legs up and wider out.

I flung my head back into the pillow and released a howl. Thinking he would get turned off by that, I turned my face into the pillow, trying to muffle my sounds. To my surprise, his cock got stiffer and straighter. He rose up on his knees and started to go a little faster.

I said, "Hold on. Go slow, man. Just take it slow."

He slowed down a little, but it didn't matter. The pain was there, and I was in ecstasy. He held my legs apart while he thrust deep inside me. My cock was pointing straight up at my face. I reached down to play with it, hoping that it would bring some ease to the pain, but I had to stop because I was about to climax.

He said, "You might enjoy it more another way. You want me to stop and do it a different way?"

I said, "Yes. Um, let me ride it—that way I can control how much of it is going in me."

He released my legs and lay back on the end of the bed. I got up, trying to look cool, as if I were taking it like a man. I straddled him with my legs, seeing only the white condom pointing upward. I positioned myself as he said, "Yeah, boy, you can do it. This dick is yours, baby."

I could feel the head of it going inside me. I went slow. I could see him grinding with his hips, trying to force it inside me deeper, so I raised my legs, getting into a position where I could squat over him. I could see him looking down at his cock. He grabbed my cheeks and started to grind while I stayed above him.

Once he found his groove with that, he started to make those circular motions again. It felt so good. I could tell my body had adjusted to him. I was going farther down his cock. He started to moan. I reached down and grabbed my cock and started to jack off. He stopped me. I could hear him say, "Don't. You're gonna come, and I don't want you to right now."

I stretched my head backward and placed my hands on his chest while he moved my ass up and down on his cock. He started to say, "Yeah, that's it. That's it. That's what I'm talking about, boy."

"Damn!" I could feel him stretch the insides of me. I could hear the sound of the juices pop as our bodies came together, cock to ass. I had to stop him there. I had to.

I got off of him and took a deep breath. His cock was still throbbing. He got up over me, leaned down, and kissed me. I tried to tighten back up just so that I would know he hadn't broken me totally. He asked me if I'd had enough. I took another deep breath and said, "No." He started to kiss me on the neck, knowing what would happen with my legs.

Once they got into position above him, he moved in closer. He began by taking it slow, but he was soon pounding his cock into me again. It felt good this time. My body quickly invited him in, keeping him tightly comfortable. He began to thrust faster. He looked down at me and all my facial expressions while continuing to move his hips. It was art. He was making art out of two entangled bodies.

I reached down and grabbed my legs at the knees. I stretched them as far as I could. He noticed this and took heed. The sounds of our bodies colliding must have been a turn-on to him too. He raised his head back so that the light from the window was on his face. It was pure joy seeing him that excited with me. He started to move faster and deeper. I couldn't hold my legs much longer. I moaned and groaned until the sounds became a scream.

He said, "I can't hold it. I can't hold it. Damn, damn!"

I reached down for my cock and began to stroke it feverishly. Our sounds became unison. I could feel Stephon grabbing the sheets around me with every pounce his hips made on my ass. I knew he was there, about to come. And I was too. I stretched my legs as far as I could, grabbed my cock, held it tight, and stroked it with the rhythm of our bodies.

He looked down at me as I was releasing my creamy load onto my stomach. He said, "Baby, here it comes. Here it comes." I felt the hot come pour into the condom. I had a moment of reasoning, thinking he should pull out of me because the condom could break. He took one good thrust and pulled out.

I looked down, seeing the rubber still on him safely, and eased my head back to the pillow. He lowered his body to the bed as we tried to catch our breath. I sat there, no feeling in my legs, wet from the waist down, but full only with feelings of joy. Everything I wanted in a man was lying beside me. He reached over to me, laying his left arm on my chest.

"Damn! Damn! That was good," he gasped out.

I lay there for a while, then I motioned to get up. He asked, "Where are you going? What? What's wrong?"

I said, "Nothing, I just have to get up and clean myself." I found the bathroom without turning the lights on because I didn't want him to see me walk. Try walking with no feeling in your legs. The sex was worth it, though.

After cleaning up, I heard sounds in the bedroom. I wondered what he was doing. I walked back to the room and saw he had changed the sheets in the dark. Just like a pro. That guy had the experience of a housemaid, porno star, and best friend rolled into one. If only he would clean up the whole house. I fumbled around for my shorts and shirt.

He asked, "What? You don't want to stay? Can you spend the night with me?"

I stood there thinking, *OK, this is too good to be true.* I reached for the bed and lay next to him. He cuddled and spooned me.

Whispering in my ear, he said, "Are you OK? Does it still hurt?"

Not trying to sound like a wounded soldier, I replied, "I'll make it. It's all right." I lay there for about an hour. I could hear him snore and move around the bed as if he were still in ecstasy. All of a sudden, the phone rang.

He jumped up as if it were the alarm clock. He stumbled for the phone, and I tried to play like I was asleep. I could hear a guy talking to him. His answers were short and quick. Stephon didn't mention me, nor did he say he was in bed. He told the guy he would call him tomorrow; well, tomorrow was today. It was almost 1 A.M. What guy would be calling to make small talk at that time? I realized that it was a good time to get up and leave. I didn't want to be around when the "lover" made a surprise late-night visit. Stephon hung the phone up and lay back down on the pillow.

I turned to him and said, "Hey, I can't sleep. I have to go home."

He asked, "Why? What's wrong?"

I said, "I have on my contacts, and I can't sleep in them. If I do, they will get stuck to my eyes."

"You don't have your case for them?" he asked.

Like I knew I was going to spend the night. "I didn't plan on staying overnight, man. I gotta go." I got up from the bed and reached for my shorts and shirt before remembering that I had taken them off in the living room.

He got up behind me and followed. I could feel his limp dick pressed up against me. He said, "You know, I really don't want you to go. I want you to stay the night with me."

I didn't respond. I couldn't. I didn't know what to say. Maybe I had come to my senses and realized that he could be telling me all kinds of lies. That could well have been his lover checking up on him on the phone. I thought it would be best to spend the night at home in my own bed and recuperate. I got my clothes on while he watched me. He kept on moving his head from side to side, just murmuring that he couldn't believe what I was doing.

I couldn't believe what I was doing. I was leaving the guy who was heaven-sent. The guy that made a dream come true—if only for one night. I was about to walk out of his house with no plans for the future. In a way I was hoping he would explain the call and ask me one more time to stay. But he just stood there, chocolate muscles rippling, limp dick still throbbing with every breath, and a euphoric look on his face.

And I was walking away.

I got to the door with keys in one hand and the memories of our rhythm in the other. We kissed. We kissed again.

I said, "Well, it was cool to have met you. I hope we can see each other again," opening the door to an invitation or something.

"Man," he replied. "I can't believe you're leaving. But I understand. I will call you. Maybe we can catch a game or something."

His indecisive response gave me the answer I was looking for. I knew right then that he wasn't gonna call. I walked out the door and headed to my truck. I could hear him close the door slowly as if he were still watching me. I got into my truck and headed home.

The next day was a day for remembrance, a day spent near my phone. A day I will never forget. The night before had given me hopes, given me a dream complete, but that day gave me the realization that I would not hear the phone ring. Maybe I have high hopes for finding a particular guy to call my lover. Maybe a chat room is just that, a chat room. A place where you can be anything and find anything—but maybe not the one.

Neighbors

By Jm Tella

Men have more attitudes in San Francisco chat rooms than their real-life counterparts at the Midnight Sun. At least at the bar the video screens keep me entertained in between potential sex mates. But AOL is cheaper. So far tonight I've sent Instant Messages to 10 guys whose profiles got me hard thinking of the possibilities. If I'd bought each of those men a cocktail, it would've cost me more than AOL's $19.95.

Tonight it's getting late, and as I'm just about ready to call it quits on another unsuccessful attempt to find the fuck of the week online I walk downstairs to my kitchen for a glass of water. From downstairs, I can look out the window and see directly across the street into my neighbors' living room.

They never close their shades. But then neither do I.

Ever since the day those two moved in, I've watched them parade around their flat with shirts off and shorts that barely leave anything to the imagination.

Of course, tonight I can see the Bee Gee-looking one. Shit, just my luck! It's the other one who gets me hard every time I see him. He's short, muscular, tanned, and has a British accent that leaves a stain in my pants just hearing his hello.

I put my glass down, and right before I head back to my room, headlights illuminate the street. The garage across the way opens, and neighbor 2 pulls his gray Saab into the driveway.

I watch him get out of the car, his blue sweatpants like wet paint against his tight ass. The door closes, and two minutes later I see him in the living room. He peels off his shirt, kisses his lover on the cheek, and disappears. I look at my empty house and head back to my bedroom.

The only Instant Message on my screen is from Hotdad4u. I close the window, remembering the first time I saw his picture. Such a waste to have that flawless body—but a face needing a pillowcase over it permanently. I look to see who's new to the SanFranciscoM4M room. I click on the profile for HOTNHNKY:

Member Name: Later
Location: San Francisco
Birthdate: 31 years old
Sex: Male
Marital Status: In a long-term relationship but allowed to play
Hobbies: SERIOUSLY HANDSOME TOP, MUSCULAR, MASCULINE GUY, 5'7", 31w, dark hair and eyes, friendly with no attitude
Computers: HOT & MUSCULAR BOTTOMS (especially Italians). Into passion, kissing, and f***ing.
Occupation: PIC REQUIRED. Too often VGL means pretty ordinary. No time-wasters.
Personal Quote: I'm not a snob. I just know what I like.

With one last attempt of the night, I type an Instant Message to him: "Knowing what you like is good. Take a look at my Web site, and if it meets your approval, say hello."

A few minutes pass, and then to my surprise I get a reply: "Shit, you've got that right. You're fucking cute."

"Oh, thanks. That's nice of you."

His message flies back: "What are you up to tonight?"

"I was just about to call it in. It's been pretty slim on here for me."

"Damn. I just got home a little while ago. Thought it would be exciting."

"Now it is," I tell him. "You're talking to me. ;-0"

"Oh, shit. All these messages are popping up on my screen," he replies. "Hold on. I need to get rid of them."

Great. Only two seconds online, and he already has a million offers. I exit the room and then get ready to sign off when his message pops back at me: "So you don't mind guys with lovers?"

"Someone else's relationship is no concern of mine," I say. "How long have you been in yours?"

"Seven years."

"And you're 31? Damn. You started young. Where do you live?"

"Castro area."

"Imagine that. So do I." *Great,* I think. *A fuck at last!*

"Whereabouts?" he asks.

"It's a tiny street. You've never heard of it. Around the top of 19th. Eagle."

"You live on Eagle?" he says with a sense of surprise.

"Yep. You know it? No one has ever heard of it."

"Hold on a second. Let me look at your Web site again."

"OK," I say patiently. I tap my fingers across the keyboard before his message comes through.

"Can you keep a secret?" he comes back at me.

"Sure," I tell him. After all, we're only online. What could be so revelatory?

"I mean, really keep one? Not tell a soul?"

I wrinkle my face at the screen, then type, "Who would I tell?"

His words surprise me: "I know you."

"You do? Fuck. Have I just embarrassed myself? Have you been here before, and I can't remember?"

"Not exactly," he says, leaving me frustrated with his response.

I type back furiously, "??????"

"I live on Eagle."

"Get out! Really?"

"Yep. Just look out your window."

I push my chair back as the realization hits me. I grab for the keyboard: "Oh, shit. You don't drive a gray—"

And before I can finish, he completes my thought: "I have the gray Saab."

My fingers are so sweaty that they leave the keyboard wet: "I've looked at you for months."

"Small world, isn't it? I'm Gary. You're one hell of a cute guy. I want to fuck you."

"No problem with that," I tell him. I truly had no problem with that. "Come on over."

"Well, my lover's home."

"It's an open relationship, though," I remind him of his profile.

"Well, you're kind of close to home and all."

"OIC. Fuck around but not within plain view." I understand his concern, but I still try: "You could wait till he goes to bed."

"You live with people, though," he says. Obviously he's watched me through those windows as well.

"They're not my lovers. They're just housemates," I try to reassure him.

"But they know me. I don't want them saying anything."

"Ah! Well this is a problem."

"Shit, yeah. I so want my dick up your ass!"

"There's always a hotel room. Or I could just borrow a friend's house," I say, struggling for a solution. I've lusted for this man for so long, and I'm so close to him now that I can almost taste him.

"Can you do that?"

I think for a moment and then reply, "I can check around."

"Do it! I really want to slide my cock in you." Then he mails me his cell phone number.

"I will have something lined up by tomorrow," I let him know.

"So if I stand in my living room," he asks, "you can see me?"

"Every bit of you," I let him know with lusty memories popping into my head.

"Go take a look," he says.

I take the last sip of water from my glass and practically fly downstairs. Shirtless and displaying a package that even his boxer shorts can't hide from this distance, Gary is standing in front of his window. He winks, grabs his crotch, and then turns out the light.

"Jim, honey, you can use my spare room to fuck."

I could've jumped through the phone and kissed Dougie. "God," I tell him, "everyone's said no but you. You are my only decadent friend. Thanks so much."

"No problem," Doug says reassuringly. "Anything to help a friend. Yeah! *Anything* to help a friend have sex. Come over and get the key. I'll just go to dinner or a movie."

I call Gary on his cell phone and tell him it's all arranged.

"Great," he says. "I'll tell the boyfriend I'm off to the gym for a workout."

"Well, that's really not an entire lie, is it?" I urge him on.

He laughs. "Right you are, Jim. Very good. I'll see you at 7."

I'm at Doug's house at 6:30. I put a bunch of condoms and a bottle of lube on the dresser next to the bed and then watch for the gray Saab to pull into the driveway. The second I see Gary turn the corner, I'm outside.

He rolls his window down. "I've waited a long time for this," he says and then leans out and kisses me, slipping his tongue down my throat. I try to devour him right there, but the car door is a bit of a hindrance.

"Park it. Come upstairs," I say, taking my mouth away from his and wiping the saliva on my hand.

With my dick hard and straining against its prison in my pants, I can hardly walk up the front steps. Gary's right behind me and dressed in his office clothes—well-fitting office clothes. I can't help but think that if I even tried to wear pants that tight to my office, I'd be escorted out of the building for inappropriate attire.

We stand in the living room in front of the picture window, kissing and fondling each other until I reach down and unbuckle his belt. "I want you," I whisper. Not wanting to put on a show for the neighbors, I lead him to the back bedroom, holding his belt as if it were a leash.

My heart pounds, ready to rip itself out of my body, as Gary unbuttons my shirt. "Fuck, man," he says in his thick British accent. "I want to fuck your arse. I'm going to pound the living shit out of you!"

"Stop talking and do it," I moan as his hands reach down and cup my ass cheeks.

My mouth latches onto one of his nipples, and I suck as if I'm an out-of-control milking machine. My tongue traces down his belly, across his tight abs, darts in and out of his navel, and then follows the trail of hair to his groin. With one quick pull on his underwear, his dick juts out in front of me, and I swallow it to the deepest part of my throat. I push my nose into his crotch, and he moans as I feel his dick fill with heat. His cock is the perfect size—thick and about nine inches. I caress it with my tongue, flick its head. I grab his cock by the base and flick my tongue over his piss slit. Then I open my hungry mouth and let him fuck my face.

"Get on your back," he orders through his moans. I obey, shedding the rest of my clothes and looking into his dark eyes as he mounts me. "Suck it again like I know you want to," he growls, and then without waiting he shoves his cock to the deepest recesses of my throat. At the same time his finger finds my asshole. He plays with it slowly at first and then pulls his dick out of my mouth. "You are so fuckin' sweet," he says.

He reaches over to the nightstand and grabs a condom. Squirting the lube onto his hand, he rubs it into my hole, rolls the condom over his shaft, and then rubs his manhood against my ass. With a single thrust he's going to go for it, I can tell, and I stiffen as he starts forcing all nine inches into me. "Relax, baby," he coaxes, "let me in."

I throw my legs up and brace them against his square, muscled shoulders. He lets out a sigh, curls his lips over his teeth, and then starts to fuck me. Slowly at first and then harder and harder. I meet every thrust with a deep groan of pleasure. The sweat starts to drip off his body.

"Some goddamned workout, Jim boy," he mutters and then grips me by the shoulders. With his dick still deep inside me, he flips us over. With an air of authority, he tells me more than he asks,

"You like my cock inside you, boy?"

All I can do is nod my head.

"Then ride it, baby."

I imagine no cowboy could ride a bull any better. I lean down and kiss him full on the mouth. The trail of spit connects us as I raise my head and grind my ass onto his pole.

"Shit, man!" Gary says, trying to catch his breath. "I want to see you fucked by my friends. I want to watch and then have them all take turns with this sweet ass. But I get last dibs. You want that, baby?" he asks as he thrusts his hips upward. His cock seems to reach up to the back of my throat.

"Fuck, yes!" I gasp. "I'll take them all."

My ass presses down again, and Gary starts to pump, every shove of his hips being helped to batter my aching hole by the springs of the mattress. I moan even louder, not hearing the door downstairs open and close.

I look into Gary's eyes and bite my lip from the sheer pleasure he's inflicting on me. Gary throws his head from side to side and then grips my ass and pulls me closer to him. I think it impossible, but he pounds my ass even tougher, as if he were a boxer pummeling his opponent even after he's clearly won the round. Then Gary puts his hands behind his neck, displaying his perfectly round, vascular biceps, and with one move, he rolls us over again.

"Jesus," I utter. "How do you do that?"

I can't hold back any longer, and the first spray of come explodes from my dick.

"Shit, man!" he gasps. "Never has anyone come like that while I was inside him."

He reaches down, grabs my cock, and starts to jerk it, milking another shot out of me until my dick drips like a leaky faucet. His well-oiled dick pulsates inside me.

Then he pulls out, rips the condom off, and I feel his hot jizz splatter all over me. I rub it into my sweaty skin and then grip Gary close to me as his body continues to heave. I feel one more stream of juice hit my chest as he finishes unloading between our pressed bodies.

"You, neighbor," he sighs, "are one hell of a fuck."

Then I hear the phone ring and someone downstairs answers. "Looks like Dougie's home," I say with a smile. "Be sure to thank him for the room after you shower. Every good Jim workout deserves a nice hot shower, you know?"

I don't see Gary online for weeks afterward. Finally, one night around midnight I see his screen name in one of the San Francisco rooms.

"Hey, neighbor," I type.

There's a five minute delay and then finally a response: "Hey."

"Haven't seen you around lately," I say, trying to engage him in conversation. "How are you?"

"Fine."

"Not too talkative tonight. Am I interrupting something?" I ask.

"No, not really," he finally responds. "Hey, I wanted to tell you something."

"Don't tell me," I quickly type back. "Wracked with guilt that I live across the street and you haven't told your other half?"

"Sort of," is all he says.

"It's no big deal," I say politely. "I told you when we first talked, it's your relationship, not mine. I had fun anyway. If you want to do it again, you know where to find me."

But his delay in responding is even longer this time: "Thanks, handsome."

But I know the reality of the situation. Ever since that night before we got together, the blinds across the street have remained closed.

OK. . . Let's Do It!

By Michael Edwards

Oh, great. Now isn't this just the way it always works out for me. I'm out at the clubs with my friends, and I can't get another guy to even give me a glance back, much less to hold eye contact. I'm free, available, hopeful, but that's when it just never seems to be the right night for the other guy. Yet if I had met and been dating someone for a few weeks or months and was just out on the town to be with my friends, I'd often feel stares nailing me to the wall, or a guy would try to find some way to get one of my friends to hook me up with him. This just wasn't one of those nights, though.

Maybe there's some aura or glow that you give off when you're dating a guy and you're feeling happy. Men sense that happiness, and then they want to be with you, thinking somehow the happiness is going to transfer to their lives. It's got some kind of distorted logic to it. Distorted? Uh-huh. Frustrating? You're damned right.

But a few hours later, back in the comfort and safety of my home, the online world can be the great equalizer. As I sit at my computer in the faceless, expressionless expanse of a chat room my aura, my glow—or the lack of it—doesn't matter one byte.

B-r-r-ring.

What a magical sound that had come to be while sitting at my computer. A sign that someone wanted a conversation—at least—with me. An Instant Message had just popped up on my computer screen. Well, it was late spring and the time for love, I guess. How was I to blame a man for finding something attractive about my profile and wanting to have a chat with me? Even if he had a screen name like Gigante9_4U. I mean, yeah, that's pretty sexual and to the point, and I'm not usually attracted to guys who approach you online in an overtly sexual way. But, hey, it was late, I'd had an OK night out only, so what was wrong with a little titillating chat? A little teasing conversation. After all, my one-year relationship had just become no longer a relationship, at least that's what I told my "boyfriend" when I found out he had and wanted to continue to have a new, additional boyfriend on the side.

We began with the typical "hello" and "what's up?" while I checked his online profile to find out a little about him, since he had already read about me. Hmm. This seemed definitely harmless—he was on the East Coast, and I live on the West Coast. It wasn't likely that he was looking for a late-night booty call with me, I could assume right away. So the guy must have liked something else about my profile to inspire him to chat me up, or maybe he was just looking for some quickie cyber action. I was game for a little sexy talk; it could keep the evening from being a total bust. So, yeah, a little "bustin' " action could be just what the doctor ordered.

He sent me a picture of himself, and I sent a couple that I had of myself. Even though they weren't the greatest I'd ever seen of myself, they were all I had. And a pic, no matter how bad, I felt, had become required for surfing the online world. With a whoosh, the blood rushed to my cock when I opened the E-mail with his pic. I couldn't have asked for a better vision to light up my night. I already knew from reading his profile that he was Cuban, and I'll admit I have more than a slight attraction for dark-skinned men, but this guy...this guy...he was what defined the phrase "Ay, que guapo!"

He was tall, about six feet, had dark hair, brown eyes, and a great body. I could see that even though he was wearing clothes in his pic. I asked him if he had any juicier shots of himself, meaning I wanted to see some cock, but he said he didn't have any like that. He asked for the same, but I didn't have any. I wasn't that bold yet. But he said he liked what he saw from my photos and that he really liked my green eyes.

We engaged in some idle chitchat for a while. He was single but did have a fuck buddy for occasional fun. I told him about the recent revelation of my dating life. But eventually the three hours' time difference between the wee hours of the morning on the West and East coasts meant he had to get to bed, so we said some good nights and that we'd watch out for each other later.

For the next several weeks I stayed away from my computer. I'd been spending a lot of time online, and, although in theory I had a boyfriend during all that time, deep down I sensed that things weren't right between us so I had been spending too much time lurking around chat rooms, waiting for a potential Mr. Right to pop up. But I was pretty damned bored with it. In addition, I took a vacation back home to visit family. After developing a roll of vacation film and finding a picture of myself that I thought made me look decent enough to be proud, I headed out to the local computer-by-the-hour shop to get a scan made.

It was early July when I logged back on. I was just hanging around, scrolling through lists of chat rooms, looking at who was inside, and checking out the occasional profile on a screen name that sounded tantalizing.

B-r-r-ring.

My old friend Gigante9_4U had sought me out. I told him I had a little surprise for him. "A pic of that thick, white cock?" he asked. Well, no, I told him, but I did finally have a better pic of me.

Gigante9_4U: Send it over!
MyGreenQQs: OK, will send now. However, I was just at the store and picked up one of those disposable Polaroids. Gonna try it out this weekend...if you know what I mean. :-P
Gigante9_4U: Oh, yeah! Send the other pic anyway.
MyGreenQQs: Sent.
MyGreenQQs: With my Polaroid, I guess I'll have my hard-on shot before you!!
Gigante9_4U: Cute!
Gigante9_4U: Very cute!
MyGreenQQs: Thanks. I've been told "sexy" too, you know.
Gigante9_4U: Nice dick?

MyGreenQQs: Oh, yeah. Nice and straight and white with a pinkish head, cut. But I'm a big fan of juicy foreskin!
Gigante9_4U: You have to try mine, baby!
MyGreenQQs: Any day, papi. Any day!
MyGreenQQs: When I finally get your dick pic, I'll jack off to it and taste my own come—and pretend like it's yours.
Gigante9_4U: But you are too far, bud!
MyGreenQQs: Yeah, ain't life a bitch!
Gigante9_4U: Oh, well!
MyGreenQQs: Maybe when your buddy visits with you again, you can get him to take some nice shots of your hard-on, juicy foreskin, and tight ass for me.
Gigante9_4U: Why you want a pic of my ass?
MyGreenQQs: So I know what I am not getting to eat!!
Gigante9_4U: So why you wanna see it for?
MyGreenQQs: So I can dream about it. What do you think? You make me hard as a rock looking at you even with clothes on.
Gigante9_4U: Do you like to top?
MyGreenQQs: I'm pretty much just a top.
Gigante9_4U: I didn't know that!
MyGreenQQs: Sad?
MyGreenQQs: I figured you thought I was a big ol' bottom. LOL.
Gigante9_4U: Nope.
MyGreenQQs: I assumed you did.
Gigante9_4U: And I don't know why.
MyGreenQQs: Because I'm a white guy chatting up a hot Cubano stud with a screen name of Gigante9_4U. A lot of times Latinos will assume a white guy who is into sexy Latino studs is a big bottom. And I surprise them.
Gigante9_4U: That is a good surprise!
MyGreenQQs: Really? Why?
Gigante9_4U: I'm versatile!
MyGreenQQs: I remember! You told me about your hot times with your buddy. Trust me, when you told me how you liked him to work his face into your ass, I was really turned on!

Gigante9_4U: Why?
MyGreenQQs: The way you describe yourself in your profile...thick legs and ass. Made me dream!
Gigante9_4U: LOL. You look masculine in your pic. Are you?
MyGreenQQs: Claro que si! You thought I was some fem?
Gigante9_4U: Not really, but one of the reasons I don't like blond guys is because the majority are feminine! At least here where I live!
MyGreenQQs: Well, I'm not a blond—it's dark blond—and I'm especially not like one of your typical blonds, obviously! LOL.
Gigante9_4U: So which pic of mine do you have?
MyGreenQQs: Just that fuzzy one of you in your clothes.

After a pause my E-mail alert went off. When I checked it, I had another blood rush to my cock. He clearly hadn't been truthful about having a naked picture of himself when we talked before. When I opened my E-mail I saw him lying back on his bed, naked as the day he was born. Staring me in the face was that thick, muscly pair of legs, and they were wonderfully hairy. His cock, although soft, truly must have been nine inches, as he advertised in his screen name, because it was so long that it sort of slunk down in the middle from its own weight as it stretched from his balls over to where the hooded head rested against one of his legs.

Gigante9_4U: It doesn't show any part of my ass, right?
MyGreenQQs: Let me check closer...LOL!
MyGreenQQs: I can see a bit of your ass, just below your balls. It's hairy. Looks damned hot.
Gigante9_4U: You horny dog!
MyGreenQQs: For you? You know it!
Gigante9_4U: You look like you can be a good husband!
MyGreenQQs: No, no. I know I can be. That's why I'm so pissed that I ain't one yet.
Gigante9_4U: You wanna marry me?
MyGreenQQs: And we can commute back and forth between coasts? Sounds very '90s! Hell, yeah, I'll marry you!

Gigante9_4U: Nah, you have to move to here with me, papi!
MyGreenQQs: What you got for me there?
Gigante9_4U: Me...a nice husband too!
MyGreenQQs: You know that you're probably only days from being married...all those men you probably meet online. You told me before that this month is your birthday, and you said it is always lucky for you.
Gigante9_4U: Know what? Honestly, I can change all that for the right one! I like to be married and in love, but in the meantime, what else should I do?
MyGreenQQs: OK, you got me there. Wild, exciting sex is great. But be happy that you are a good person. You have a good, well-rounded life. Live it to the fullest, and one day a man will see that and will die to share it with you.
Gigante9_4U: I do, but sometimes I feel sad that I don't have anybody to give all the love I have in my heart to!
Gigante9_4U: I know how you feel. OK, let's change the subject!
MyGreenQQs: When do I get to taste your hot culo? LOL!
Gigante9_4U: What! Do you like to eat ass?
MyGreenQQs: Love it...on the right guy.
Gigante9_4U: Mmm, I love it!
MyGreenQQs: Doing it or getting eaten?
Gigante9_4U: Getting!
MyGreenQQs: I got the two probing tools that you need, papi.
Gigante9_4U: I think if my lover did that to me every day, I'd let him fuck me every day!
Gigante9_4U: What is that?
MyGreenQQs: What is what?
Gigante9_4U: Probing tools?
MyGreenQQs: My stiff yet tender, warm, wet tongue...and my stiff and rugged white-boy boner.
Gigante9_4U: Are you well-hung?
MyGreenQQs: Well, it's not as big as yours! But about a little longer than six—but nicely thick! I may not hit bottom, but I can sure give the sides hell! LOL.
Gigante9_4U: LOL. Don't worry. I'll hit your bottom!

MyGreenQQs: Ay, dios mio. Hee hee. You really packin' nine?
Gigante9_4U: I guarantee you that, and it is a piece of art!
MyGreenQQs: I'd really like to see a good hard-on shot...without the foreskin retracted. I want to see the foreskin over the juicy head! Ah, I'm getting a raging hard-on here.
Gigante9_4U: My cock head looks like a juicy fruit!
MyGreenQQs: Lick, lick, slurp, slurp, suck.
Gigante9_4U: So when are you gonna come over and give me some maintenance? At least change my fluids!
MyGreenQQs: Day-um. You talk hot.
Gigante9_4U: Do you like kinky sex?
MyGreenQQs: With the right guy I would. Never met many guys who do. What kinda stuff you talking about? (Get me harder!)
Gigante9_4U: Not too kinky, like toys, etc.
MyGreenQQs: I would love to have a husband who would want to play around for hours: toys, videos, all over the house. Not just a guy who wants to come so he can roll over and go to sleep!
Gigante9_4U: My ex-lover had a small dick, and sometimes when I needed something bigger, we used to have a toy to play with!
MyGreenQQs: How small is small?
Gigante9_4U: Small=1 to 6, medium=7 & 8, and large is 9 and up!
MyGreenQQs: Well, if I thrust really pounding-hard, maybe I could make mine feel like a full 7!
Gigante9_4U: LOL. You are a funny guy!
MyGreenQQs: Funny is sexy too, you know!
Gigante9_4U: I know.
MyGreenQQs: My sexiness comes from my passion in love, my desire to give love, my ability for intimacy, and my green eyes!
Gigante9_4U: OK, OK, OK, I'll marry you!
MyGreenQQs: I knew you'd see it my way! LOL.
MyGreenQQs: But even though I talk about passion and love and intimacy, sex is a strong, important component of a rela-

tionship. My ex, he only liked to jack off and have me come on his chest. Then he would take a shower, hop into bed, and go to sleep.

Gigante9_4U: He didn't like sex? Boring!

MyGreenQQs: Very, very boring.

Gigante9_4U: Anyway, baby, I have to go. It's Friday, and I'm going out.

MyGreenQQs: Yeah, me too. I'm going out with some friends tonight. Well, at least I've got that pic of your dick...the work of art...to dream about later tonight. But of course the real thing is always best.

Gigante9_4U: And it's so tasty too! Just like candy!

MyGreenQQs: The kind with a cream-filled center, right?

Gigante9_4U: Yup!

Even though our talk had been very sexual, it was light-hearted and no more than a couple of guys having some fun. I was pretty clear in my mind, so I thought, that I was just having a good time idling the hours away with a good-natured new friend. It seemed for sure that there was no way I was going to be moving to the East Coast, and he had made it clear that he would never leave his family behind there. Although the idea had a romance-novel ring to it—me packing it all up and moving 3,000 miles to be with a man who I'd fall madly in love with—I was pretty sure that I was too rational to think that could truly happen. So the next day when I logged on and saw him online, I felt no qualms about continuing a friendship, and I sent him an Instant Message first this time.

MyGreenQQs: Hey, I got lucky last night!

Gigante9_4U: With a friend?

MyGreenQQs: With a friend? No! Some guy I met at the club.

Gigante9_4U: You are too easy!

MyGreenQQs: Uh, excuse me, please. It's been a long damn time since I've had sex! I told you how my ex was. LOL.

Gigante9_4U: LOL. So what did you do?

MyGreenQQs: With him? Fucked him hard and long and had a lot of really good kissing. My ex wasn't a very good kisser either. Man, I had missed that.

Gigante9_4U: How I wish you did that to me!

MyGreenQQs: Well, I think it was that you got me so revved up—so hot thinking about you with your talk and your pic—that I just picked him out so I could fuck him and fantasize about being with you.

MyGreenQQs: ;-)

Gigante9_4U: Liar! LOL.

MyGreenQQs: Mi amor…I wouldn't lie to you…yet. LOL!

Gigante9_4U: Fucking bitch!

MyGreenQQs: What? Who? Me?

Gigante9_4U: No, not you. If it couldn't be me, at least you fucked her hard!

MyGreenQQs: I know he had a good time 'cause he moaned and oohed and aahed and said "Yeah, baby" and "Yeah, papi" plenty of times.

Gigante9_4U: Sounds like you fucked him right!

MyGreenQQs: You betcha, papi.

Gigante9_4U: You have to show me how you did it! ;-)

MyGreenQQs: Oh, I thought of you a few times.

Gigante9_4U: You better do a good job with me, papi!

MyGreenQQs: Oh, don't you worry!

My social life was null and void pretty much, so I was spending a lot more time online again. I was still pining away over the ex despite how wrong it had all gone, so I was finding my comfort in hanging out with these faceless strangers who I didn't have to commit to. But by this time I was having a lot of fun talking with this guy. So I was really disappointed when I didn't see him online for a while. But after four days, my heart went thump (Oh, no! Did I say "my heart"?) when I saw him log online.

MyGreenQQs: Hey, where have you been?

Gigante9_4U: LOL. Just fine, you?

MyGreenQQs: I'm fine. I said *where* have you been?

Gigante9_4U: Horny like hell, but surviving! So how is your sexual life after the last event?

MyGreenQQs: Well, for some reason I got more sex last weekend than I had planned on. But none of it was great, like the kind you described with your fuck buddy. On Saturday night this guy who I met online wanted to meet.
Gigante9_4U: And?
MyGreenQQs: Well, I usually don't meet up with guys I talk to online right away, but this seemed innocent enough, so we had dinner. He was a bit pushy, too touchy. Well, I guess it wouldn't have been so bad if I had liked him better. He's very handsome, but he was a bit too effeminate for my taste.
Gigante9_4U: I can't stand that!
MyGreenQQs: He ended up coming home with me after dinner, and he kept on being so touchy that I just gave up and fucked the shit out of him that night. And Sunday morning. LOL!
Gigante9_4U: Oh, hell!
MyGreenQQs: Yeah, and I guess I got a good compliment out of him. On Sunday morning when I started playing with his ass, he said, "Careful, it's a little sore after you had it last night." Ha ha. I guess I put it to him pretty good.
Gigante9_4U: Maybe he was lying? LOL.
MyGreenQQs: Ay, que malo!
Gigante9_4U: I'm bad, yes…to make you feel good!
MyGreenQQs: Oh, papa. Trust me. He felt me.
Gigante9_4U: What did you do? Did you hit it with a chair or something? LOL!
MyGreenQQs: No, papa, just my big ol' man meat.
Gigante9_4U: Mmm, you are making me horny!
MyGreenQQs: Hee hee, yeah, right. I bet you were already horny!
Gigante9_4U: Well, even more now!
MyGreenQQs: I took him from the top, from the side, from the back. You name it, he got it. And go-o-od!
Gigante9_4U: Hey, I'm looking for a husband just like you!
MyGreenQQs: *Like* me? I thought I *am* him!
Gigante9_4U: Well, I don't see you knocking on my door yet!
MyGreenQQs: What happened with your fuck buddy? How's it with him?

Gigante9_4U: I need a husband who can sleep next to me and fuck every night and morning! I can't stay at his place overnight.
MyGreenQQs: Por que no?
Gigante9_4U: I have a dog living inside my house.
MyGreenQQs: Oh, then I'd stay at your house and sneak out of our bed early in the morning and take the doggy for a walk and get him some food, then cook you some breakfast to give you back your strength before I hopped back into bed with you.
Gigante9_4U: Papi, you *can* be a perfect husband!
MyGreenQQs: I told you I am. Haven't you figured that out yet?
Gigante9_4U: Yup, but not 100% perfect!
MyGreenQQs: I can be 100% perfect husband for the right husband. Como tu, papa!
Gigante9_4U: Not 100% because you are not here!
MyGreenQQs: Hmm. How do I fix that?
Gigante9_4U: Fix what?
MyGreenQQs: How to get there—with you.
Gigante9_4U: You have to move here.
MyGreenQQs: Oh, but I guess you'll say I'm not the perfect husband when you see my hard-on pic. I know you like them eight-plus inches. ;-)
Gigante9_4U: Not really, my buddy is just seven—but he knows how to use it!
MyGreenQQs: Well, I believe I know how to use mine. But maybe you could always give me some extra pointers! LOL.
MyGreenQQs: Oh, and then there's my other flaw. :-(
Gigante9_4U: What?
MyGreenQQs: I'm not a beautiful Cubano stud, and I know how you like them Cubano and as sexy as you.
Gigante9_4U: Well, you're not Cuban, but in that pic you are very handsome and look masculine!
MyGreenQQs: Thank you for saying I'm very handsome. Most Latinos here don't pay much attention to me.
Gigante9_4U: So when did you say you are moving?
MyGreenQQs: Hmm, let me check my calendar. LOL.

I was beginning to take myself seriously. We were having really good chats with each other, and we obviously had an attraction for each other, but we were too far apart. Still, I found myself wondering about taking that trip to visit him just to see what the in-person chemistry would be like. I wondered what it would be like to leave my great job and my great friends behind...if. And that was unlike me. I wasn't an impetuous person. Right? Well, right? And I was thinking that he was beginning to consider "us" seriously.

When my E-mail alert sounded, I just assumed it was some spam. But it was from him. Another photo. A much better photo.

MyGreenQQs: I can see your face so much better in that one! How come you never told me that you're so damn handsome?
Gigante9_4U: Because I don't feel like that!
MyGreenQQs: Oh, all guys say that. OK, then...how come you never told me that I'd be so fucking hot for you?
Gigante9_4U: I guess that's just the way it works out, but I also didn't know *you* were *that* hot, papi!
MyGreenQQs: Ay, muchas gracias! I think I'm in love now!
Gigante9_4U: LOL. Really?
MyGreenQQs: You bet.

But as luck would have it, his fuck buddy had logged on and started taking some of his attention away from me. I couldn't help but realize that I was feeling a bit jealous at the thought of having to share him in conversation. I mean, he was supposed to be focusing on *me*.

MyGreenQQs: So is he coming over to play with you?
Gigante9_4U: When? Tonight?
MyGreenQQs: Si.
Gigante9_4U: Nope, he has never come to my house. I always go to his place!
MyGreenQQs: "Always"! So many times, huh? Were they all as hot as the first?
MyGreenQQs: Damn, I can't stop looking at your pic. So damned hot!

Gigante9_4U: Yup, we always do something different.

MyGreenQQs: Hmm. Can I hear? I wanna know what kind of hot times you are having. And what about the videotape you were going to make for me?

Gigante9_4U: Last night he invited me over and told me, "I'm going to leave the door open. Just go inside my room, get in my bed, and pretend you are there to force me to have sex with you." And guess what. I did!

Gigante9_4U: No! No videotape! LOL.

MyGreenQQs: Life is not fair. Why is this whole stinking continent keeping us apart? I should be the man in your bed, damn it!

Gigante9_4U: You could always get a job here too just like the one you have!

MyGreenQQs: So, tell me, what's so hot about this buddy of yours—who you don't want to be your husband?

Gigante9_4U: He is very masculine, and he likes to wear leather stuff!

MyGreenQQs: Ah! So you get a turn-on for that? You know I'd do whatever I have to do to keep you turned on.

And even though it made me even more jealous, I had asked for details about his sexcapades with his buddy, and he detailed them. He gave me explicit details of some action that they got into at a bar together one night. The fuck buddy had him wear a pair of leather shorts, T-shirt, and a collar for the night. The scene sounded pretty hot to me, so I know it was definitely hot for the other guys in the bar who had formed a crowd around them while they kissed, groped, did a little nipple sucking through unbuttoned shirts. Generally, it sounded like the kind of action where someone usually chimes in with a "Get a room" comment. But apparently the crowd at this leather bar was digging it.

MyGreenQQs: So you were his leatherboy?

Gigante9_4U: I feel wild while I'm in leather, and, hey, I'm single and like to play. But when I'm married, it's a different story, and I'm not gonna marry him for sure!

MyGreenQQs: That's my papa!
Gigante9_4U: He makes me feel so good sexually and like a man, but I want my man to be faithful to me, and he can't do that.
MyGreenQQs: You know I would be faithful to you.
Gigante9_4U: I'm not too sure about that.
MyGreenQQs: Hey, once I give you a ring, I'm only yours. :-)
Gigante9_4U: If I find my man shitting on me, I'll wait until he is sleeping and cut his dick off!
Gigante9_4U: But it's so fucking hot being with this guy.
MyGreenQQs: I hear you. It sure sounds like it was. I am very jealous of him for now. Be sure to let him know that.
Gigante9_4U: He wants to take me to a leather festival coming up.
MyGreenQQs: Hey, that's how we can meet. I'll have to talk you into coming out here so that we can go to San Francisco for the leather street festivals, then I can parade you around with your leather collar and shorts!
Gigante9_4U: Yeah, I look great in my shorts. It's from all the racquetball I play.
MyGreenQQs: Well, how about you and I get up early in the morning once we're together. You'd take me out to the courts to teach me some racquetball. We'd play for a few hours, getting all hot and sticky, and then we'd go back home and jump right into bed. I'd tie you up to the bed with some leather straps, and then I'd lick all the salt and sweat off your body and have my way with you for the next 20 hours or so?
Gigante9_4U: LOL! If you can have sex with me for 20 hours, I *will* marry you for the rest of my life!
MyGreenQQs: LOL. Well, jeez, I'd hope you'd marry me for life!
Gigante9_4U: If you can keep that dick hard for 20 hours, I don't know how I'm gonna do it, but you're gonna be in trouble.
MyGreenQQs: In trouble? No, papa. Contigo...en el cielo!!
Gigante9_4U: So what is your fantasy?
MyGreenQQs: I told you. I only came up with the one so far. It was you and me getting all sweaty and hot from you teach-

ing me racquetball. And then us going home and having hot, sweaty, sticky sex.

Gigante9_4U: I thought you had another fantasy, but that was hot too.

Gigante9_4U: Papi, I got to go.

MyGreenQQs: OK, you have a good night.

Gigante9_4U: Nice dreams...with me!

MyGreenQQs: Claro!

Gigante9_4U: Just dream that you are eating my ass all night.

MyGreenQQs: LOL. I would love that. I hope I just don't wake up with a mouth full of pillow feathers in the morning.

Gigante9_4U: I'm gonna dream too, but I'm going to put a pillow between my legs, thinking it's your head! LOL. Nite.

MyGreenQQs: Muchos besos para ti.

Gigante9_4U: Donde?

MyGreenQQs: All over your body, of course, where else? Eyes, lips, neck, chest, cock, ass, legs!

Gigante9_4U: Good. Very relaxing.

MyGreenQQs: Except for when I wake you up in the middle of the night. Then you're gonna have to work!

Gigante9_4U: I don't care. I will! You already know me well enough for that!

OK, maybe it was just my horniness reacting. I was very physically attracted to this guy, I liked the way he talked—casual chat and sexy conversation—but he was getting to me. Each day after work I found myself logging on, or I'd get up on weekend mornings and look for him or wait around for him to show up. And the gods were behind us: It was never long before he appeared, and I'd always jump right into conversation with him. I'd started giving my full online attention just to him.

MyGreenQQs: What are you up to?

Gigante9_4U: Just buying some racquetball clothes online.

MyGreenQQs: Online? Aren't you worried they won't fit?

Gigante9_4U: Don't you wanna see me handsome when I play?

MyGreenQQs: Sure, I want you handsome, but I'd rather have you play naked for me.
Gigante9_4U: LOL. Horny dog!
MyGreenQQs: Just in love...
Gigante9_4U: When you gonna send me your naked pic? What happened to that Polaroid you bought?
MyGreenQQs: Is that all you care about—by bod and my dick? What about my heart? LOL.
Gigante9_4U: I have that already! ;-)
MyGreenQQs: Oh, you said the perfect thing!
Gigante9_4U: It's true! You have mine too!
MyGreenQQs: I'm gonna have to try again, babe, to get those cock shots of me. It didn't work. I used the whole roll of 10 pics and couldn't get a good one of my cock. :-(
MyGreenQQs: I have your heart too! Ay, mi amor...I'm more in love now than I realized!!
Gigante9_4U: LOL.
MyGreenQQs: What? That I used the whole roll?
Gigante9_4U: Nope, that you are so in love! And you haven't tried anything yet!
MyGreenQQs: I haven't tried what?
Gigante9_4U: The real thing!
MyGreenQQs: But, baby, whatever you have, that's what I want!
Gigante9_4U: Once you try a piece of me, you're gonna be hooked.
MyGreenQQs: I'm already hooked.
Gigante9_4U: That's nothing compared to how you're gonna be.
MyGreenQQs: How could I be any more in love with you than I already am?
Gigante9_4U: You will. I guarantee you that.
MyGreenQQs: You don't have to convince me, papi. I'm sure it's true.
Gigante9_4U: So how are we gonna get married?
MyGreenQQs: Hmm. You're not going to move here are you?
Gigante9_4U: Nope. You have to move.

MyGreenQQs: OK, I've got to start figuring out how to get us together.

Gigante9_4U: Well, you get here somehow. Because you will have to meet my mom.

MyGreenQQs: Oh, the mom test!

Gigante9_4U: Yup, but your zuegra doesn't speak English. So you're gonna have to speak Spanish with her.

MyGreenQQs: "Zuegra"?

Gigante9_4U: "Zuegra" is your mother-in-law!

MyGreenQQs: I have learned a lot of Spanish the past 2 1/2 years from my friends. And I've always been hoping to find a lover who would care enough to help me learn.

Gigante9_4U: You will learn.

MyGreenQQs: Ay, mi amor. You make me fall for you even more. I wish we didn't live so far apart. I'd like to meet you very much.

Gigante9_4U: Yeah, me too!

MyGreenQQs: Es verdad, papi?

Gigante9_4U: Si, senor. It's the truth.

MyGreenQQs: So you've never dated a white guy?

Gigante9_4U: Dated one for a little while, yes. Lover, never!

MyGreenQQs: Why do you say "never!" with an exclamation point?

Gigante9_4U: Because never had a white guy lover. I am too picky with white guys! He'd have to be a very attractive guy!

MyGreenQQs: I guess that leaves me out.

Gigante9_4U: No, by that picture you sent, I think you are!

MyGreenQQs: Now, you, you are very attractive.

Gigante9_4U: That's your opinion.

MyGreenQQs: It's what my hard-on is telling me.

Gigante9_4U: You don't have a hard-on!

MyGreenQQs: When I first got that pic I did have one. I couldn't believe such a handsome man was being so nice to me like you were.

Gigante9_4U: Nice? This is me!

MyGreenQQs: Well, you were talking to me a lot more than you used to. And you were asking questions, trying to get to know about me. And seemed genuinely interested.

Gigante9_4U: You sound like a nice person. I want to get to know you better.

MyGreenQQs: I am the nicest person in the whole wide world. And I will make some man the best husband someday. I just need to find the right guy to give me the opportunity to show him!

Gigante9_4U: You're too far away for that!

MyGreenQQs: Well, I'm working on a plan to fix that.

Gigante9_4U: Well, I'm sleepy baby. I've got to go.

MyGreenQQs: OK. I wish I could hold you tonight while we sleep. I feel like I want to be that close to you.

Gigante9_4U: Keep working on that plan then!

True to our regular meetings online now, the next day I got my *b-r-r-ring.*

Gigante9_4U: Papi!

MyGreenQQs: Mi amor! I didn't see you here. I was just answering some E-mail. How was your day?

Gigante9_4U: Boring.

Gigante9_4U: So when are you gonna visit me?

MyGreenQQs: Papi, believe it or not, as each week goes by and I get to know you better, I'm thinking about it more and more seriously.

Gigante9_4U: Good!

MyGreenQQs: Would you really like that?

Gigante9_4U: Yes!

MyGreenQQs: But what if we really like each other? I live all the way across the country, have really good friends and a really good job here.

Gigante9_4U: Friends can come and visit you here and the job, well, get a better one here. It's not that complicated.

MyGreenQQs: Stop talking like that. You're going to make me fall in love with you over this computer!

Gigante9_4U: That would be nice!

MyGreenQQs: Uh-oh, you're not going to keep on trying to

make me fall in love with you, are you? ;-)
Gigante9_4U: If we meet and we really connect, I'll make you move in no time!
MyGreenQQs: You make me smile…inside and out.
Gigante9_4U: How is it inside?
MyGreenQQs: Well, it's like not only my mouth smiles, but sometimes you say things that make my heart smile. Because they are such considerate and nice things that you say. Things that make me like you more and that make me think you would treat me right if we were together.
MyGreenQQs: How do you perceive me to be like?
Gigante9_4U: Masculine, gringo, sweet, hot!
Gigante9_4U: Smart.
Gigante9_4U: Nice husband for the right guy. For me!
MyGreenQQs: Sounds like you have me figured out completely. I like that.
Gigante9_4U: Mmm, more or less. LOL!
MyGreenQQs: Sounds like you are supposed to be my papi!
Gigante9_4U: This is crazy, but, yes, it sounds good!
Gigante9_4U: Tell me, what do you think is the most attractive part of your body?
MyGreenQQs: My chest is pretty attractive. Nice amount of hair. I could stand to pump up my pecs a bit, though. And Latino guys always go crazy over my green eyes. And my calves aren't so bad.
Gigante9_4U: In hairy chest range 1 to 5, what is your number?
MyGreenQQs: 4
Gigante9_4U: Really?
MyGreenQQs: Yup.
Gigante9_4U: I like a lot of hair on my man!
MyGreenQQs: Well, I've got plenty on my chest and stomach and legs and arms and ass.
Gigante9_4U: I wanna see that!
MyGreenQQs: LOL!
Gigante9_4U: Hey, baby, I have to go!
MyGreenQQs: OK.

<B>Gigante9_4U: Talk to you soon!
MyGreenQQs: I will miss you.
Gigante9_4U: Me too, papi!

I hated the three-hour time difference between us. He was always having to go to bed so much earlier than I was. But fortunately or unfortunately, it just made the suspense for our next chat build to a pitch. And the jokes and innuendo about our making plans to meet were becoming more and more real.

Gigante9_4U: Mi amor!
MyGreenQQs: That's me! I'm da one!
Gigante9_4U: You are the only one!
MyGreenQQs: What's been going on?
Gigante9_4U: Hey, do you rent or own your place? Live alone?
MyGreenQQs: Rent. Why?
Gigante9_4U: No reason.
MyGreenQQs: Oh, I thought you were getting at something.
Gigante9_4U: You are too smart, babe!
MyGreenQQs: Ha ha, why do you say that?
Gigante9_4U: Just a question!
MyGreenQQs: Did you wanna come visit me and have a place to stay? :-)~
Gigante9_4U: I wasn't thinking quite that.
MyGreenQQs: Oh. :-(
MyGreenQQs: You were wondering if I'd have to sell a house before I moved to spend the rest of my life with you?
Gigante9_4U: You are smart. I was thinking that if you move you won't have to sell a property, just finish the lease.
MyGreenQQs: You have really sweet thoughts, babe.
Gigante9_4U: I know! But they're devilish too.
MyGreenQQs: You're the best thing I've met in years, even if it's not in person yet!
Gigante9_4U: Not really! One of the best!

Well, another Friday night had rolled around, and I was as horny and wishing to be connected with a man—this man?—more so than usual. So when I was surprised to find him online so late that night after I'd been to a club with my friends, I was ready for no-holds- and no-holes-barred. If I couldn't be there with him in person, I was going to find a way to make his night. We'd been having a lot of teasing talk, but my sex drive was on the rage, and my brain was tainted with vodka. He had no idea what was in store, and, honestly, going into it, I really didn't either.

MyGreenQQs: What are you up to tonight? It's so late there.
Gigante9_4U: Bored and getting sleepy. Where have you been all night? I've been waiting for you.
MyGreenQQs: Waiting for me in bed so we can spend the entire weekend kissing and relaxing?
Gigante9_4U: OK, baby, I'm clean from head to toe. What you wanna do to me?
MyGreenQQs: I don't think you're clean enough, so after I give you a long passionate kiss, I'm gonna give you a tongue bath from head to toe.
Gigante9_4U: But, please, stop in the right place for a while!
MyGreenQQs: Well, I'd like to stop for a while and hold my face against your ass. Give your cheeks a lot of soft little kisses. Then slowly dig my face between your cheeks and eat at your hole to my heart's delight.
MyGreenQQs: Tonguing, licking, tasting, kissing your beautiful, tight hole.
Gigante9_4U: Mmm, hot papi!
MyGreenQQs: And then digging my tongue inside you, tasting every bit of your sweaty hole.
Gigante9_4U: Very tasty!
MyGreenQQs: Will you moan and talk to me and call out my name and beg me for more?
Gigante9_4U: Oh, yes, baby!
MyGreenQQs: And after I get your hole all juiced up with my mouth, I want to ease my way up onto your back...sliding slowly so that every inch of my hairy chest scrapes as it rides up...over your ass...over your back. And I want to lie on top of you. Slide my arms down around you and under you.

MyGreenQQs: Then I'll put my open mouth on the back of your neck and shoulders and place my rock-hard cock against the crack of your ass.
MyGreenQQs: Can you feel me, papi? Can you feel the hot hardness of my cock resting on your ass?
Gigante9_4U: Yes, papi. Let me catch my breath!
MyGreenQQs: I wiggle my hips so that it wedges my cock between your ass cheeks. My cock feels the dampness that my mouth left on your ass, and it's mixed with the beautiful hair between your ass cheeks. And it turns my cock into rock-solid, throbbing hardness.
MyGreenQQs: Your ass ignites a fire in my cock. And it grows even hotter.
Gigante9_4U: Oh, that's the best part! I feel you there!
MyGreenQQs: I slide my tongue up the back of your neck, kiss your ear, and say, "Te quiero mucho, mi papi. Te quiero."
Gigante9_4U: Te quiero mucho, papi, tambien!
MyGreenQQs: I tighten the grip of my arms around your chest, squeezing you, holding you tighter and closer to me. I grab your nipples at the same time and work them between my thumbs and forefingers.
MyGreenQQs: Then I feel you move under me...your ass wiggles, and you spread your beautiful, thick, hairy, manly legs apart. You push your ass up into the air, and it causes my cock to slide down farther between your ass cheeks.
MyGreenQQs: My cock is lubed and slippery from the spit that my mouth left on your ass.
Gigante9_4U: Yes, papi, that is so damned good!
MyGreenQQs: Without me touching it and without you touching it...because we are so in sync, so perfectly made for each other...my cock head is set right at your tight, sexy hole.
MyGreenQQs: The moment is here—so ready, so perfect, so right for our first time together. It's everything we've been waiting for. Every nerve in both our bodies is tingling.
MyGreenQQs: I whisper in your ear, "Eres listo, amor? Are you ready, my love? Do you want me to make love to you?"

Gigante9_4U: You definitely are ready to be my husband! I want only to be with you, baby!
MyGreenQQs: Are you ready, babe? Ready for our first time? Do you want me inside you?
Gigante9_4U: I've been ready. Ready for so much longer than you know. My body is in shock!
MyGreenQQs: I hold on tight around your chest, and I slide my hips in toward your body. My cock head breaks into your hole, and I slide in just until the head is surrounded by your fiery hole.
MyGreenQQs: Then I wait and ask you if you're OK. I don't want it to hurt you...unless you want it to hurt good. How does it feel, baby?
Gigante9_4U: Oh, papi, feels g-o-o-od! Mas, amor!
MyGreenQQs: I slide my hips into you more, and my cock squeezes its way deeper inside you. Your ass is steaming. It's like the heat of a million fires wrapped around my cock. I can't help but moan out loud because the sensation is so fucking intense. The pleasure is so great that I am finally with my babe. Inside mi papi.
MyGreenQQs: And I lose control.
MyGreenQQs: I slam my cock in the rest of the way and hold onto you tighter for better leverage and wiggle and grind my hips so that I can get my cock into you even deeper. I want my whole cock, balls, and body inside you!
Gigante9_4U: Ay, que rico, papi!
MyGreenQQs: Then I clamp my mouth down onto your neck and suck and kiss for all life. I take the first slide of my cock out from your ass and then plunge it back in. The pleasure is so intense for me that I can't control myself.
Gigante9_4U: Give me the poppers, baby!
MyGreenQQs: They're right here for you under the pillow. I'll open the bottle and give you your hits and then take mine.
MyGreenQQs: Ah, the poppers push me over the edge. Now I'm a wild man. Fucking and pumping and humping and sliding in and out of your hot, tight, juicy, hairy hole. The hole of the man that I've been dying to be with.

MyGreenQQs: After pumping for a while, I start to tease...
MyGreenQQs: Pulling my cock all the way out of your hole and bouncing it right against your hole.
MyGreenQQs: I give you another hit of the poppers, and you start to beg me to fuck you.
Gigante9_4U: After pumping for a while, keep pumping!
MyGreenQQs: You want my cock inside you forever?
Gigante9_4U: You are fucking hot, papi!
MyGreenQQs: So I dip my cock head in like I'm getting ready to go for it, but I quickly pop it right back out. Holding it right against your puckered little hole again, teasing, making you want it even more.
Gigante9_4U: N-o-o-o! Don't stop, amor!
MyGreenQQs: And I do that a few more times just to drive you mad with passion.
Gigante9_4U: Damelo! Damelo! Give it to me!
MyGreenQQs: I want your Latin blood boiling to a high heat.
MyGreenQQs: When I know you're ready, I lick and kiss and bite on your neck, and I slam my cock deep into you again and start pumping my cock again with all the gusto that I can manage.
MyGreenQQs: Your ass sets me on fire like I never knew anything could. The emotion of being with you finally is so incredibly intense. I can't believe we've been apart for so long, but now we're together forever!
MyGreenQQs: I pump away at your ass with all the intensity that I can give it. We can hear my balls slapping against your ass with each pounding thrust. I work away, pounding, grinding, slamming into my papi's ass. His beautiful, sexy, manly ass.
MyGreenQQs: In your ear again, I tell you, "Ay, babe, I love you. It's so fucking perfect and hot in your ass. This is better than I ever imagined for us."
Gigante9_4U: Come on, baby, keep going!
MyGreenQQs: We keep going, bodies connected, minds connecting, passions colliding, cock and ass, ass and cock, your juices, my juices, the intensity, the passion, the heat, the amor is flowing.

MyGreenQQs: I work my entire hairy chest and stomach over your back so you can feel the heat of my body as much as you can feel the heat of my cock as it pounds and slams and grinds inside you.
Gigante9_4U: And we keep going and going and going!
MyGreenQQs: But the intensity of our first time together overwhelms me more than I realized, and I grow close to coming. My cock swells inside you as all the life in my body prepares to burst out of my cock to meet with your juices and your passion.
MyGreenQQs: But I don't want to come inside you!
Gigante9_4U: Oh, it's gonna be too late, baby!
MyGreenQQs: I pull my cock from your ass, and you beg me, plead with me to put it back in so that you can feel the heat of the juices of my love inside you, coating you, making you feel all warm so that you know how much I do love you. But it's too late! My cock jerks and shudders, and the first shot hits right between your ass cheeks. All over that tight, beautiful hole that I had longed to have and be inside forever.
MyGreenQQs: Then come the following shots. Spurts of hot, juicy threads of sticky, white come pour out onto your asshole. It's thick and clings to your body. And I push myself up on my knees to see. "It's beautiful," I tell you. "So beautiful, babe."
MyGreenQQs: Then I bend over your ass again with my face, and I lick at your hole, suck at your hole, licking up all the juices that my body let flow onto you. I clean up your ass, licking up every drop of come that I unloaded.
Gigante9_4U: I can't believe this!
MyGreenQQs: Then I turn you over on your back, and you look into my eyes, and I can see the passion and desire and love in your eyes again for the first time. You reach out your arms and pull me on top of your stomach and chest. You grab my head with both hands and pull my face to yours, and you give me a long passionate kiss, probing your tongue into my mouth, getting as much and as good a taste of my come from my mouth as you can.
MyGreenQQs: As you lick and suck the last drop of my come

from my mouth, your body begins to shudder. You shake and moan and clamp your mouth onto mine. Suddenly I feel the come spurt from your cock between us against our stomachs as they rub together.

MyGreenQQs: I slide down your body and lick all your come from your stomach. I suck it clean from that beautiful juicy foreskin that I've been waiting to taste. I lick and suck and devour your foreskin, getting every drop of your come.

MyGreenQQs: Your body is still shuddering as you reach down and grab my head and pull my face back up to yours, and we kiss passionately again as you suck—this time—your come from my mouth.

MyGreenQQs: We lie together and kiss forever.

Gigante9_4U: I still can't believe this!

MyGreenQQs: What can't you believe?

Gigante9_4U: The way you are talking!

Gigante9_4U: You made me come! A big load!

MyGreenQQs: How was that?

Gigante9_4U: You've got to stop! That is too much for one night!

Gigante9_4U: Now I know that you *will* be my husband!

MyGreenQQs: Really, papi? You came a big load? I was simply telling you what I want to do with you.

Gigante9_4U: You could be a writer for a porno magazine.

MyGreenQQs: So you were playing with yourself the whole time, jacking that Giant9, working your foreskin?

Gigante9_4U: Yup!

MyGreenQQs: I had no idea. OK, I'm really flattered now. So you liked everything?

Gigante9_4U: Oh, yes! O-o-oh yes!

MyGreenQQs: I was afraid you would not like it. I didn't know how kinky, even as soft as this was, that you might like to get.

Gigante9_4U: That was just perfect!

MyGreenQQs: I'm glad. You don't know how long I've wanted to tell you what I want to do with you.

Gigante9_4U: It was great!

MyGreenQQs: I wish it had been in person! OK, how big was your load?
Gigante9_4U: I wish it was in person too! Like more than a week's load!
MyGreenQQs: Cool, then I've ruined you for all other men. My job is done!

Almost a week of a busy schedule at work kept me away from the computer regularly. Or at least kept us from being online at the same time. But every night I logged on looking for mi amor Cubano. I couldn't get our cybersex session out of my mind, and I was intensely turned on by the fact that everything I wanted to do, everything I said to him, turned him on completely as well. It wasn't until late the following Saturday that we got to "see" each other again.

Gigante9_4U: Papi, I was looking for you!
MyGreenQQs: Hola, mi amor. Looking for me?
Gigante9_4U: I've been missing you.
MyGreenQQs: It's only been a few days. I've been taking a break from the computer. Right now I'm just trying to cook dinner.
Gigante9_4U: Cooking? Nice! Another point in your favor!
MyGreenQQs: I love to cook.
Gigante9_4U: Wow, you impress me with something new every day!
MyGreenQQs: Why were you looking for me?
Gigante9_4U: Because I like to talk to you. I miss talking to you.
MyGreenQQs: You are too sweet to me.
Gigante9_4U: It's the truth.
MyGreenQQs: Muchas gracias, amor.
Gigante9_4U: Welcome, papi.
MyGreenQQs: Did you do anything fun tonight?
Gigante9_4U: Nope. I was planning to go out after a nap, but I woke up too late, and I decided to stay home!
MyGreenQQs: Me too. Hmm, two lonely men staying home on a Saturday night. Que lastima!

Gigante9_4U: Yup, it is sad. You should be here with me in bed, hugging me and watching some TV.
MyGreenQQs: Ah, that sounds like a perfect Saturday evening to me.
Gigante9_4U: To me too.
MyGreenQQs: :-(
Gigante9_4U: Oh, well.
MyGreenQQs: OK, let's not be sad.
MyGreenQQs: (Evil grin)
Gigante9_4U: Horny again, papi?
MyGreenQQs: I would always be horny if I was with you.
Gigante9_4U: And I would please you.
MyGreenQQs: Papi, even just hugging in bed and watching TV with you would please me.
Gigante9_4U: Very nice!
MyGreenQQs: Just sharing time together can be just as good as hot sex.
Gigante9_4U: I agree.
MyGreenQQs: I think we were supposed to be in the same city!
Gigante9_4U: I know. One of these days...
MyGreenQQs: I hope! I do.
Gigante9_4U: What are we gonna do about it?
MyGreenQQs: I don't know. Need time to think.
Gigante9_4U: Think fast!
MyGreenQQs: OK, I'll try...LOL.
Gigante9_4U: When's the cooking going to be done? I'm hungry.
MyGreenQQs: Soon. Half an hour?
Gigante9_4U: Come on to the room; we have time for a quickie!
MyGreenQQs: LOL. Que rico!
Gigante9_4U: And then after dinner, I'll give you the dessert!
MyGreenQQs: Umm. Can I have whipped cream on it?
Gigante9_4U: I'll supply the cream again!
MyGreenQQs: Ay! I just looked at your nude pic again!
Gigante9_4U: And?

MyGreenQQs: Forget dinner! I wanna suck on those balls and lick that furry ass!

Gigante9_4U: LOL...but that is the dessert, papi!

MyGreenQQs: Hey, haven't you heard? Life's short...eat dessert first!

Gigante9_4U: Once I have a ring on my finger!

MyGreenQQs: OK, OK, I get it. I guess I'm starting to have too big a fantasy, wishing you were mine.

Gigante9_4U: Who knows!

Gigante9_4U: Papi, I'm going to bed!

MyGreenQQs: OK, amor. Get some rest. It's really late there.

Gigante9_4U: Nite, baby!

MyGreenQQs: Te extraño.

Gigante9_4U: I miss you too and wish you were here, but, anyway, 'night!

The rigors of work took precedence, and I was forced into late nights at work. Every night it was almost right to bed when I got home for about a week. I knew there was no use in logging on to look for him. The time difference had him sleeping away by the time I got home each night—or at least I hoped that was what he was doing. It was the first week of August, and I was thinking about this man almost every day. It had been a summer of some intense interaction, and I couldn't get him out of my mind—especially how to bring us together for a meeting. It was late in the week, Thursday, so I took a quick sneak to log on while I was at work to see if I could find him.

Gigante9_4U: Hey.

MyGreenQQs: "Hey"? I haven't seen you for several days, and all I get is a "hey"? Where's my big hug and kiss?

Gigante9_4U: *Mwah!*

MyGreenQQs: Wha's dat?

Gigante9_4U: A kiss.

MyGreenQQs: Oh! Muchos besos para ti tambien, papi!

Gigante9_4U: I miss you, papi! Moving yet?

MyGreenQQs: Did you make room on one side of your bed for me?

Gigante9_4U: Yes.

MyGreenQQs: Really? You would share your bed with me?

Gigante9_4U: If you married me, of course.

MyGreenQQs: You have the most delicious, kindest, warmest, sweetest thoughts in the world.

Gigante9_4U: You have not seen anything yet!

MyGreenQQs: You make my heart break over the fact that I am not there with you.

Gigante9_4U: That's true for me too! Don't you realize?

MyGreenQQs: I do, but I have to get back to work now. I was just hoping to find you and say hi, since it's been days since we've talked. I hope to see you later.

But I don't find him online again until Saturday evening, after a party he'd been looking for a date to take to. Despite our intimate conversations, my jealousy tells me that I can't compete with the tons of sexy, available men that he has living all around him. And he's just too unwilling to go to a party—even among his friends—without a date. So I have to keep telling myself that we're most likely not going to meet, and so he's allowed his flings to keep up good appearances.

MyGreenQQs: Hola! How was your party the other night?

Gigante9_4U: Great!

MyGreenQQs: Really? That good? And you made it sound like it was going to be an obligation when you talked about going!

Gigante9_4U: I know!

MyGreenQQs: You must have found a really hot date online after all.

Gigante9_4U: You know me, a party animal!

MyGreenQQs: You are? No, I thought you were a stay-at-home-and-cuddle sorta guy!!

Gigante9_4U: When I'm married...when I'm married!

MyGreenQQs: I see. So did you find a date?

Gigante9_4U: Yup.

MyGreenQQs: Well, that's good. I knew you didn't want to stand around all alone at the party.

Gigante9_4U: We left almost at the end, and everybody was getting horny!

MyGreenQQs: Was it about to break out into an orgy?

Gigante9_4U: I guess so!

MyGreenQQs: So why didn't you stay?

Gigante9_4U: Because those guys are my friends only.

MyGreenQQs: But were they all going to have sex with each other?

Gigante9_4U: They wanted to get into the Jacuzzi naked at 2 A.M.!

MyGreenQQs: LOL! So was your date a new guy that you met?

Gigante9_4U: Yup.

Gigante9_4U: A Cuban guy!

MyGreenQQs: Wow, you're really good at finding dates online!

Gigante9_4U: Yup.

MyGreenQQs: I'm glad you're having a good time.

MyGreenQQs: Well, I'm leaving between 3 and 3:30 to go to a concert with my friends this afternoon. This Spanish rock station here throws a big concert one night each summer. Tonight we're going to see Fey, Nek, Elvis Crespo, Javier, y mas!

Gigante9_4U: Live! Wow! Can I go?

MyGreenQQs: You don't know how much I wish you could.

Gigante9_4U: I would love to go with you!

MyGreenQQs: I would love for you to go with me too.

MyGreenQQs: Finally I would be able to steal you away from all your hot blind dates!

Gigante9_4U: LOL!

MyGreenQQs: I'm drinking a homemade margarita right now to get loosened up for all the fun!

Gigante9_4U: I have another party next week!

MyGreenQQs: And one tonight too, right?

Gigante9_4U: No, it was canceled.

MyGreenQQs: Was your date last night very hot?

Gigante9_4U: Not really.
MyGreenQQs: Yay! LOL!
Gigante9_4U: I know you are jealous, though, aren't you?
MyGreenQQs: Yeah, a bit.
MyGreenQQs: All I want is my Cubano papi's dick and butt…and heart!
Gigante9_4U: When are you gonna have it?
MyGreenQQs: I don't know. I might not ever.
Gigante9_4U: I'm waiting!
MyGreenQQs: Did you have sex with the guy from last night?
Gigante9_4U: Nope.
Gigante9_4U: He just sucked my…
MyGreenQQs: Your what? Tu pinga?
Gigante9_4U: You know!
MyGreenQQs: Y tu?
Gigante9_4U: Nope. Just he did it.
MyGreenQQs: Did you take him home or go home with him?
Gigante9_4U: In my car!
MyGreenQQs: I've been thinking. Do you have vacation time?
Gigante9_4U: In September.
MyGreenQQs: Really? There's a big leather street festival in San Francisco—in September, I think. I was wondering if you'd be interested in coming out for a long weekend, and I could take you.
Gigante9_4U: LOL, thanks, baby, but we are gonna have to work that out.
MyGreenQQs: What's to work out? It could be our chance to have some fun together.
Gigante9_4U: I mean, talk more about it.
MyGreenQQs: Don't you want to meet? Well, I understand. Of course we would have to talk about it. Try to make plans and see if it makes sense or would work out.
Gigante9_4U: Yeah, sounds good.
MyGreenQQs: You know you wouldn't want me now anyway. You're meeting too many hot Cubano men there! LOL.
Gigante9_4U: What are you gonna do if we take it all the way and we fall so in love that we cannot be apart no more?

MyGreenQQs: Are you scared of that? Wouldn't that be a good thing? Then we'd just figure out what to do! You keep inviting me there. The same thing could happen if I visit you. I just don't have any vacation time available to travel right now.

Gigante9_4U: It's an option.

MyGreenQQs: Just think about it. I'll find out when the leather festival is for sure. I thought you might like to come and go as my leatherboy! LOL.

Gigante9_4U: Let me know.

MyGreenQQs: OK, mi amor, I gotta run. Time to leave for the concert. I'll bring back a souvenir for you, OK? (But then you'll have to give me your address so I can mail it to you!)

Gigante9_4U: OK!

Gigante9_4U: And a picture. I want a naked picture of you!

MyGreenQQs: Bye, papi! Miss me! 'Cuz I'll miss you!

And believe it or not, that's the end. That was the last extended conversation we ever had. The next time I saw him online, I sent him an Instant Message that it took him a very long time to respond to. Finally, he simply replied "Not tonight" to my attempts to engage him in conversation. I tried a few more times over the next few days, but he never responded to my Instant Messages.

I sent him an E-mail a few days later, just hoping that he would give me an explanation of why he wouldn't talk with me anymore. He read my E-mail, but I never got a response, and I never found out why he so abruptly cut me out of his life. Maybe it was becoming too real once I asked him to consider making a trip to visit me. Maybe it was too real for him emotionally, and he didn't want to risk falling for someone who lived so far away. Maybe he found some new online friend to play with. Maybe, maybe, maybe...

Even though it's been seven months since we last chatted, I saw him again online tonight. I sent him an Instant Message, hoping the past had changed his attitude toward me and that I might get some clue as to what went wrong—some revelation of what happened to us. But still, no reply. My Instant Message to him just sat staring me in the face on my computer screen unanswered.

One Sunday Night

By Cameron King

Like many gay men, I have had a fantasy over the years to seduce and have sex with a straight man. Like most of my other fantasies, though, I never thought that that one would actually come true. It certainly did not come about at all like I had expected, nor was I the one really doing the seducing.

It all started nearly three years ago as I was innocently playing a card game online. I wasn't one to go searching people out to chat with, but if by chance someone sent me a message, I always happily responded. One fall day I received a message from this guy named Alex. He had read my online profile and had a similar interest in one of the obscure musical artists I had mentioned liking. We began discussing this musician while I checked out his profile. There was nothing in it that would have led me to believe he was gay, but he soon mentioned he was married.

It seemed he and his wife were having some difficulties, and I believe he just needed someone to listen to him. I attempted to be supportive and offer him encouragement that everything would work out. He seemed to appreciate it and seemed to genuinely be a nice guy. I thought to myself how the cliché seemed to be so true: The nice online guys were always taken or thousands of miles away. We talked for maybe an hour that time before he signed off, and I did not really have any expectations that I would hear from him again.

A few days later, though, I noticed he had signed on, and sure enough, he sent me a message. He was in a much better mood and said he and his wife had had a nice talk and were working things through. He was excited also because he was about to leave on a business trip to Hawaii. It was this discussion and the one following his return from Hawaii that led me to believe Alex may not have been as straight as he had first seemed. He freely began discussing his sex life with his wife and how she liked getting his big cock as much as possible. He was 26 and could not get enough sex, it seemed. He even alluded to having an affair with a coworker while in Hawaii. He also described to me how tan he had gotten and what good shape he was in. I had not told him yet that I was gay, but my obvious interest in his physique certainly should have given him a hint. Furthermore, he was never turned off or uncomfortable with my somewhat innocent flirting.

As the months went by, we continued to chat online every few weeks. Most of the time it was normal talk about work and music, but there was always some sex talk thrown in. We never had cybersex at all; it was usually just him bragging about how much sex he got and how good he was at it.

Eventually, I did come out to him. As always when revealing my sexual orientation, I was a little worried about how he would react. Though we had never met in real life, as anyone with online friends can tell you, there's still a special bond that forms. He was a nice, interesting, funny guy, and I wanted to continue this online relationship with him. When I told him, he didn't seem too surprised, and it wasn't long before he started asking all kinds of questions.

Mostly, he wanted to know what it was like to have sex with another guy. I told him since I had never been with a woman, I couldn't give him a comparison, so I just explained that it was pretty damn good!

He said that he had never been with another guy, but thought it would be cool to be worked on by one. When he said things like that, he usually followed it with the online symbol for a smile :) so I never could tell if he was serious or just trying to make me feel comfortable. When his travels brought him to my area of the country, though, I sure found out.

I hadn't seen Alex online for a month or more, then one day I received an E-mail message from him saying he was going to be in my area and he wanted to know if I'd be interested in meeting. Always hesitant to meet online people in real life, I told him I'd think about it.

He assured me he wasn't crazy and would not harm me in any way. He even sent me his picture to make me feel more comfortable. It turned out he was my perfect type: blond hair, blue eyes, adorable, tall, stocky build. So I thought, *What the hell?* I had met a dozen or more people from online with no problems whatsoever. Alex and I arranged to meet in the parking lot of a local mall on a Sunday night. He finished the conversation by saying, "Sorry, but no sex" and again ended with a smiley face.

As I pulled up next to his rental car, my heart was pounding. Though it seemed safe, you just never can tell. We got out of our cars, shook hands, and chatted a few minutes just about the area and such. We agreed I would drive us to a local restaurant after dropping his car off at his hotel. It was nearly 9 P.M., and the restaurant was fairly deserted. The hostess took us all the way to the back and sat us at a cozy little table for two, saying, "Sorry, this is a table we usually save for couples."

Alex said, "That's OK. We'll be a couple tonight."

Both of their comments had my mind reeling. Did the hostess think we were a couple? Then why did she say it apologetically? What did he mean by what he said? Just an innocent comment or something more?

We ate our meals and just had normal conversations about normal topics. There was no mention of sex at all. He was absolutely adorable with a great smile and broad shoulders and back. There were times when I did have to pull myself back to reality and stop thinking about how I'd like to have my arms wrapped around those shoulders.

We finished the meal and I drove him back to the hotel—with still no mention of sex at all. I was surprised that he didn't even make one of his little comments about it. As we pulled up to the hotel, he pointed out to me in great detail where his room was located. I didn't think anything of it until I pulled to the front of the hotel to let him out. I told him it was great to finally meet him and that I had had a nice time. He agreed, shook my hand, but then without letting go said very hesitantly, "You can park the car over there and come on up if you want."

Still holding his hand, I stared at him for the longest time with my mind totally racing. Was he just being nice and asking me up to chat some more, maybe have a drink? Or was this a proposition? If so, do I run with it? He was a married man after all. A lot of people in such a situation would probably just back away and excuse themselves politely, but not me. Thinking his intentions could be completely innocent, I said, "OK."

He went into the hotel and up to the room as I parked the car. When I walked into the lobby, I avoided eye contact with everyone. I was filled with mixed emotions—the main ones being shame and excitement. As I passed a mirror in the lobby, I looked at myself and thought, *What kind of mess have you gotten yourself into this time, Cam?* I had an evil little grin on my face, though. I knew all reasoning was out the door at that point. My carnal instincts had taken over completely, and there was no turning back.

I went up to the fifth floor and started down the hall. I hesitated briefly before knocking on the door. My heart was pounding in my chest, and I already had an erection. If he did just have conversation and drinks in mind, I could end up being pretty embarrassed, so I certainly was going to let him lead the way. Somehow I had convinced myself that if I didn't encourage him, then I wouldn't be responsible for what happened if something did. He opened the door, flashing his big, beautiful smile, and beckoned me in. I walked in with my eyes downcast and stopped inside the door.

Once he'd closed the door, he walked up to me, lifted my chin delicately, and stared into my eyes like no one had before. He nodded and then leaned over and placed his soft lips on mine. Initially I did nothing, but soon I parted my lips and allowed his tongue to penetrate my mouth. It was only a matter of seconds before we both let loose and began kissing with unbridled fervor, our hands exploring each other's bodies. He reached around me and pulled me close to him, running his hands up and down my back soothingly. I reached up under his shirt, over his taut stomach and up to his well-developed pecs. For one brief second it flashed through my mind that I was making out with a straight man, a married man, but any shame I should have felt was washed away by the pure ecstasy I was experiencing in his strong arms.

We moved farther into the room, where I got my first glance of the huge, king-size bed. How I hoped those sheets would get more messed up than they had ever been! We pulled off each other's shirts, and then I pushed him down gently onto the bed. We continued kissing and letting our tongues and hands explore each other for at least 15 minutes.

In that time he never came close to touching my crotch, and I avoided his out of fear of scaring him off. I had to be very careful how I proceeded. I wouldn't settle for just kissing at that point, but I didn't know how much further he would willingly go.

After straddling him on the bed awhile, I pushed myself up and away from him. At first he resisted, but I just held both his hands in mine and smiled at him. We stared into each other for the longest time. I tried to judge if I should make the next move, and seeming to read my mind, Alex smiled bigger and nodded his head once again.

I slid down farther, over the top of his knees, and ran my fingers down over his abs to the top of his jeans. I could see he was hard under them, and judging from the size of the bulge, he—unlike most online guys—had not lied about his endowment. Still staring into his eyes, I slowly unbuckled his belt and the top button on his pants. He showed no sign of resistance and instead put his head back, closed his eyes, and softly moaned. I wasted no time at that point and unzipped his jeans and gently pulled them down over his hips.

The bulge in his briefs was even bigger than before and was throbbing. I slowly bent over and kissed his hard cock through his briefs. Still with his eyes closed, he began rocking his head from side to side and breathing heavily. I removed his briefs, finally exposing his full eight-inch cock in all its erect glory. I began to lightly lick around the head and kiss it softly. He lifted his head, opened his eyes, looked at what I was doing, smiled, and said, "Oh, man, I knew this would be the best." He was all mine at that point, and I took full advantage.

I continued to work on his cock, taking it all repeatedly down my throat. I sucked on his balls and worked my tongue all around the area between his legs. He began thrusting his hips up, fucking my mouth like a pro. I could tell from the look on his face, no woman had ever blown him like this. I continued working him while running my hands all over his nice body. I even ran my fingers gently along his ass crack, but he was too oblivious, lost in pure ecstasy, to even notice. I wanted to probe his virgin ass so badly, but again, I did not want to chance him stopping me. I thought I had a better chance of getting his dick up my ass, so that's what I started concentrating on.

He pulled his torso up, resting on his hands, and said he was close to coming. That just made me suck on him all the more vigorously. I pulled his dick out of my mouth when I sensed he was ready, and as I stroked him, he blew a huge load up in the air and all over his stomach.

All flushed and sweaty, he crashed back on the bed, breathing heavily. I slid up on top of him again and went to kiss him. He willingly opened his mouth to me again and then told me how he had never, ever been blown or shot a load like that before. He thanked me for giving him the best he had ever had. I said it was my pleasure, but with a wicked smirk on my face, I'm sure, I told him I wanted more.

He said he was exhausted and couldn't possibly do any more. I just smiled and began working my tongue and hands back down over his body—licking at his armpits, his nipples—bringing moans of delight from him. By the time I got back down to his cock, it was once again rock-hard. I continued down, though, exploring every part of his body from head to toe. I still had my jeans on at this point, but I was as hard as I had ever been and needed to pull them off. He watched me as I started removing them and made no objection.

I straddled him one more time and took his hand and guided it to my cock. He was tentative at first, but I told him to just pretend it was his own. He soon began giving me a great hand job, but I couldn't resist that big dick of his any longer. I reached back and began yanking on it with one hand while I reached over to my jeans pocket with the other.

Though I hadn't really expected anything to happen, I usually carry a condom with me just to be safe. It was a last-minute decision to put one in my pants that night, and I was glad I had made it. I'm ashamed to say that even if I didn't have a rubber, I think I would have continued on.

I ripped open the package with my teeth and placed the rubber over his still fully erect penis. He looked at me inquisitively but made no objection. I quickly reached around and fingered my hole a few times to loosen it and then kneeled down onto his pole. It had been a while since I'd been fucked, so I eased on top of him slowly. The pleasure I had been missing roared through my body as I took all eight inches of him up my hungry ass.

He again tossed his head back and began moaning over and over, "Oh, my God!"

I stayed rock hard the whole time as I bounced up and down on his cock, first slowly and then in a pig-bottom frenzy. Soon Alex began thrusting his hips up to meet my downward motion. I was in pure heaven! Not only did I have a straight boy's dick up my ass, but it couldn't have been a more perfect fit. The length was just right, and the girth stimulated me to the max.

We continued fucking for what seemed like an hour, and then I blew a big load all over his chest and stomach. That just made him thrust upward all the harder. I knew he was loving it more than anything else at that point. Suddenly, though, he got a very determined look on his face and without notice grabbed me and tossed me to the side. He quickly slid around behind me, pulled me up on my knees, and stuck his dick all the way in my ass again. I had to make some quick adjustments, since he was clearly in a sexual frenzy at that point—but I wasn't about to stop him.

He continued to pound my ass relentlessly for another good 10 minutes, then he began moaning, and I knew he was coming again. He collapsed on top of me, and we lay there, entangled and connected, catching our breaths. When he pulled out of me, I saw he had filled the condom with another huge load of man juice. He tossed that aside and we just lay next to each other, staring at one another again.

We gently caressed and kissed each other some more until he

fell asleep in my arms. I knew I wasn't going to get any more out of him, but that was fine. He might have sucked me off or let me fuck him, but that might also have ruined the fantasy. I kissed him a few more times, whispered how much I loved what had happened, and silently left his room

The next morning I had an E-mail from him saying how much he had enjoyed meeting me and getting to know me better. There was no direct reference to what had happened the night before. He just said he had some work to do that day and would be flying back home that evening. In the months since then we've chatted with each other online but have only made vague references to that meeting.

There's been some talk about meeting up together somewhere again, but I think it would be best not to. One of my major fantasies had become a reality, and it was perfect. There was no use in risking spoiling it.

Boys. . .and the Men Who Make Them

Christmas Topping

By Rob Fucci

As I saw his online signature on my screen, I quickly typed out my own.

NYBoy: Hi
AMASTER: Hello
NYBoy: Great profile, Sir
AMASTER: That's "Master" to you, slave
NYBoy: Yes, Master

Thus started a Christmas Eve and Day I would never forget…nor repeat.

About one year ago this same man, under a different online name, tried his best to get me under his control, sweet-talking me into an online buddy type of friendship. He asked me if I was "ready to be topped by a real man." Being somewhat of a top, I found myself both repelled and drawn to this crass proposal. This was my first Christmas alone. Having recently been dumped by my lover of 25 years, I was naturally at an all-time low—both emotionally and sexually; perhaps that's why his invitation got the best of me. I knew something was missing in my life, but I wasn't sure just what it was.

MASTER4U: Are you ready for it, Slave?
NYBoy: I think so, Sir.
MASTER4U: Then be in front of the Sears store at the mall at 1 A.M. sharp. No socks. Just boots. No underwear. Only jeans. No shirt at all.
NYBoy: How will I know it's you, Sir?
MASTER4U: I will pull up next to the curb. You get in and go down on my cock immediately and remain that way the entire time it takes me to drive back to my place.
NYBoy: Ok, Sir, I will be there.

I quickly logged off, shutting down my computer. My heart was pumping wildly and so was my growing cock. Swiftly dressing accordingly, I called a friend to let someone know something about what I was going to do. As a good friend, he tried desperately to convince me not to go. I thanked him for his concern, and as I was hanging up the phone, I could still hear him yelling that I was a crazed, sex-perverted fool.

At 2 in the morning I was still standing in the designated spot, now sure he was not really coming after all. I returned home, still sporting a hard-on, feeling even more dejected. As soon as I calmed down I sent him an E-mail, telling him he had missed the best piece of ass he would ever have the pleasure of not getting. I hit the SEND button very aware that I still was sporting that pulsing hard-on.

It had been a few weeks, and while I was online in my usual chat room, he returned under a new name: AMASTER. In the weeks ahead he tried many times to get me to go over to his place, telling me about all the sexually perverted things he wanted to do to my body. He fantasized about how he wanted to tie me to his bed and slowly attach clamps to every part of my body, drop hot wax over my dick and balls till I screamed for him to stop, yet really wanting more. The final episode would be to shove his nine-plus inches of dick up my virgin hole.

I told him, however, that I was no longer interested in his plans, since there was plenty of entertaining of guys going on at my place anyway. And I was not interested—at least until that fateful Christmas Eve.

I returned home that evening after having attended to some family obligations and found myself once again glued to that damned computer while the rest of creation was celebrating. As the screen came into focus I saw:

AMASTER: Is this the night, Boy?
NYBoy: Could be, Sir.
AMASTER: I will pick you up within the hour. You know the drill.
NYBoy: Like last time, Sir?
AMASTER: No. This time I will really come for you.
NYBoy: Yes, Sir. Thank you, Sir.
AMASTER: I will be in front of the movie house at 2 o'clock. Count on it, Boy. Don't keep me waiting.
NYBoy: Yes, Master. It's raining. Shall I wear my leather jacket and hat?
AMASTER: Jacket open. Lose the hat.
NYBoy: Yes, Master.

Again, I quickly dressed as instructed, arriving at the movie house at exactly 2 A.M. I had no idea how desolate the area was going to be at that hour on a Christmas morning. The theater was of course closed, but the music of the season was still playing as the festive Christmas lighting showered the parking lot.

There I stood, no shirt on, bare chest showing, in leather jacket, jeans, and boots, looking like a hustler and feeling the part too. He was right on time. Even in the semidarkness I could see he was more handsome than I had imagined. Dark hair, blue eyes, and perfect white teeth. As he was lowering the glass, I hurried to the window on the driver's side.

A steady stream of blue-white smoke drifted out as I put my face into the dark void to listen for instructions. "You getting in or what?" is all he said.

Going around the car, I quickly entered and sat quietly, wondering what would come next. My entire body was shaking with anticipation. Some time passed, and he reached over, clasping my hand in his, then moving it to cover the rapidly expanding mound between his legs. Taking this as a cue, I quickly undid his zipper reached into the warm, inviting folds of underwear to search for the much-anticipated prize.

Finding what I was looking for, I slid closer to him, lowering my head into his crotch, smelling the stale urine and sweat that clung to him, waiting for the hot throbbing manhood to show itself. His cock was enormous, perhaps nine or more inches and very thick from base to head. Placing his hand to the back of my neck he slowly pushed me down onto his shaft. I opened my mouth as wide as I could, but it was a lost cause. Not content with that, he continued to put pressure at the back of my neck till I started swallowing his cock to the base, feeling his coarse, curly hair tickling at my lips. Gagging all the time, I was sure I would upchuck at any moment. It was hard to breathe, and I was salivating like mad.

The trip took 45 minutes, all of which I spent in this position. In the meantime, he had his right hand firmly attached to my ass cheeks, kneading away, working closer and closer to my virgin pussy hole. Soon he entered, one digit at a time, till not one but two fingers were working my hot hole. My ass was aflame with anticipation. I'm sure it was wriggling about out of control.

As we approached his condo, he told me to get out. My clothes were all but off at this stage, but it didn't seem to matter to him. I stepped out. There I was, without my jacket, with a now-naked upper body, my jeans almost down around my knees, standing in a chilling, steady rain with the light from his car shining off my slick, wet, smoothly shaved body. What a Christmas morning this was turning out to be.

"Open the garage door, Boy, and stand there till I'm parked," he bellowed. "I should make you wallow in that puddle over there." He pointed to the ground with his free hand.

I took a quick glance and noticed a shallow pool of muddy water just to the side of the car. "If that's what you want, Sir," I whispered so low I hoped he wouldn't hear.

"Well, no time for that. Follow me closely, Boy. I don't want too many of my neighbors to see you entering my place." I did as I was told.

Upon entering the foyer, he turned to me very calmly, saying in a voice more fatherly than masterly, "Here. Take this towel and go in the bathroom. Take a warm shower. We don't want you catching a cold now, do we?" Again, I did as I was told, taking my time to both warm up in the hot spray of the shower and to take stock of my situation, wondering how I had gotten myself into this and what would happen next.

As I exited the bathroom, Shade (he had introduced himself to me by the name) said, "Here, enjoy this glass of wine before we get started. You had mentioned that it is your favorite, I think."

As I sipped the wine, Shade took both my legs, spreading them apart as I lay face up on his bed and securing each to a corner, then doing the same to each arm. First the left, giving me time to finish my second glass of wine, then attaching the right.

Thinking what a great adventure this was turning out to be, I was not prepared for what came next. Having firmly tied me to the bed, Shade leaned over my warm smooth body and placed a blindfold over my eyes.

Shit, I said to myself. *What the fuck?* I was no longer in any control, and I knew it. Every sense I had screamed for me to stop, but I couldn't. I wanted it no matter the consequences. I wanted it with every pore of my body, right down to the core of my soul.

He started slowly, twisting my nipples, first lightly, building to a hard, painful sensation that sent pulsing waves of shock through my body that caused me to let out a guttural gasp while twisting my torso from side to side. "Good." His voice betrayed a smirk. "Like that, Boy?"

"Yes Sir," I replied quickly.

"Sir?" he yelled. "I told you in the past to call me 'Master' when in a session. Seems you need to be taught a lesson." There wasn't much I could do as he started to slap at my exposed ball sac, striking me over and over as I writhed in pain. Finished at last, he leaned close enough to my face for me to feel the heat of his breath against my cheek. "Did you like that, Boy?"

"Yes, Master," I whimpered.

"Hot enough in here for you, Boy?"

I had no clue why he would ask such a question, since there were many candles lit around the room that gave off a pleasant rose aroma along with a pervasive heat. "Plenty warm enough for me, thank you, Sir," I answered.

"Not nearly as warm as it will be soon, Boy," his deep voice whispered in my ear.

"A-a-ah," I screamed over and over as my body seemed lit afire. Not sure exactly what he was doing, I started to panic.

"Whoa, calm down, Boy," he said as he placed his strong hand on my chest. "It's just hot wax. It's not burning you. It won't leave any lasting marks. Take it easy."

I tried hard to relax. Feeling his hand firmly planted against my body was a great calming factor.

Shade slowly made a trail with the wax from my chest down to my shaved crotch. I was straining against the ropes as the stinging droplets rained down closer and closer to my cowering cock and balls. Covering my cock with his hand, he splashed wax liberally over my ball sac, my body straining in every direction, wanting him to stop, but hoping somehow that it would never end. Finally when I thought he had finished, he shifted his body as if getting up from the bed and all of a sudden a flow of hot wax descended upon my now-erect cock, sending me into another emotional dimension.

Shade placed his hand over my mouth, leaning his hot, wet, nude body against mine. "I can't wait any longer, Boy," he breathed. "I need and want your ass *now.*"

Turning me over onto my stomach after freeing only my hands, my legs thereby crossing, made my ass even tighter. As he hovered over me, I could feel his hot, short breaths against the nape of my neck and the sweat rolling off both of us. Slowly he lowered his body onto mine, pushing his cock into my tight asshole with only our sweat as lubrication. If I thought the hot wax was pleasurable pain, this was both heaven and hell.

Shade slowly entered me an inch at a time, his solid, massive body starting to pump in and out with a gentle, quiet rhythm till his entire manhood had firmly—incredibly—stretched my hole.

Suddenly all hell broke loose as he started pumping with a ferocity I thought a human being incapable of. My ass was on fire. I was sure I was ruined for life, my ass a gaping piece of meat never to be of use again. Yet my body ached for even more.

In a few moments I started bucking back, trying to match his every forward motion with a backward motion of my own. "Ride me, Master!" I yelled from some resounding depth of my soul. "Ride me harder!" I yelled even louder.

Shade was pumping at a rate a fine-tuned engine would have trouble keeping up with, pushing his cock deeper and deeper—ever harder and harder—inside me time after time. Finally, with all the flourish one would expect during a High Mass he yelled out, "Jesus Christ, I'm co-o-oming!"

I swear till this day, I can still feel the explosion of his cock juices within the bowels of my body. We both shook violently for what seemed an eternity, each gasping for his fair share of the available air. His body collapsed heavily onto mine, our sweat melding us together on the outside as his come flowed into me, mine running onto the sheets below us.

Withdrawing his cock from my body, with the decorum of a flushing toilet, he sat up saying, "Wow, you are as hot as I thought you would be...maybe better. I want you to stay with me forever as my boy."

I was in heaven. I was sure of it.

We made small talk until I fell asleep in his arms, my legs still tied to the bed. A life with this man was all I could think of as I awoke often during the night not sure it wasn't a dream.

In the morning he made love to me for real, and I cried in his arms. We were pretty quiet over breakfast, and he said he had to take me home because there was an important meeting he just remembered he had to attend later in the day. We drove in silence—him pensive, me still all bubbly, reliving every intense moment.

As we approached my home and pulled into the drive, the quiet of our ride became apparent. His last words to me were, "This was great, but you're too labor-intensive. Since you don't drive, I'm not coming down here just for a hot fuck, no matter how good it is. Have a good life. Bye." He drove off, leaving me standing there, stunned, even long after his car was far out of sight.

That was the last I saw of him but not the last I heard from him. The epilogue is that for months after, he would appear online begging me to move in with him. He would even write this plea on the chat room screen for all to see, telling anyone who would listen what a mistake he had made letting me go.

Hell, now I'm having a great time finding new online Masters every night. What in the world would I do if it weren't for being an online pussy boy? Hee hee!

23 Hours

By slave mike

"The only way you'll know is if you actually do it. Come down for a weekend or something—find out."

Be a slave for a weekend? It was something out of a jerk-off book or some dark, intense club scene, not the life I was living—holed up in my dorm room, avoiding a big paper. I looked back at the screen. He was waiting, and I didn't know what to say. Well, I was already typing an excuse. But this offer wasn't like the usual kind I got when chatting online. This time my excuse was not a politeness to some guy I'd never see anyway, not wanting to lead him on.

"I don't think I can get away—not even for a weekend." *That ought to piss him off enough to drop it,* I thought. "It's getting close to finals, and I have tons of work on papers before then."

He didn't give up: "If you want to know if this is what you really are, you need to try it. No book...nobody can tell you if this is who you are. You have to find out for yourself, through real experience."

"I don't know if I can," I responded. "I'm scared." The less self-assurance I showed now, I felt, the less he'd want to waste his time.

"Come down and try..."

My Korean civilization paper was due in a few days, but only one page out of 10 was on my screen. Staring at the blinking cursor was only emphasizing how slow the words were coming. I launched Ircle, my PowerBook's Internet relay chat program, and signed on to the Undernet network as "newboy."

Undernet had one of my favorite IRC channels for finding the type of man eager to chat with a shy, less experienced boy. I looked through the channel list for "gaydads4sons," searching for some promising nicknames—anything referring to wanting "young," "kink," or "leather." That night, one name caught my eye: SMBear4cub. Bears, generally larger and furrier guys, were usually fun to talk with, and this particular bear was on some other, more revealing channels. Usually, I could get a guy talking if I played up my naïveté and asked about whatever interests their channel choices revealed. This SMBear wanted a son but also was on channels like "gayslavemarket," "gayleather," and "gayasian."

I actually got on "dads4sons" publicly for once and several private messages immediately popped up on my screen—probably because they saw some fresh young meat on the channel. But I wanted to message SMBear to see if I could get him talking. I sent off a quick "Hi...hope i'm not bothering you, but i saw your nick on dads4sons and am curious" to him and waded through the channel traffic to pick out some other chat prospects. After responding to a few of the guys who had messaged me already, I sat back to see who would bite first.

All of this probably sounds like I was trolling for cybersex, like most computer geek stories. But I never ask for it anymore. I've tried it enough times to forget about sex by remote control. Pretending that text on a screen—even with a vivid imagination and descriptive words—never stopped me from dreaming about hot skin against mine. Still, I go online and chat up guys, hoping to talk—not "talking dirty"—about one kink or another.

I flipped back to my still-open, still-mostly-blank civ paper, hoping to fill in a few lines while I waited. Before I could continue my comparison of 19th-century China, Japan, and Korea, a loud ring in my dark and locked dorm room made me straighten up in my chair and glance around. I realized I had forgotten to turn the volume down on my computer from the last time I listened to a recording. Someone had messaged me back, and I switched to the IRC window. SMBear4cub was waiting.

Like most of the other nicer folks on the channels, he said I wasn't bothering him and asked what I was curious about. A promising opening. Any response deserved some kind of follow-through; maybe he would be someone fun to talk with. I said, "You've got an interesting nick...a bear looking for a cub, huh?"

":-) u bet. u a cub then? where are u?"

"Yeah, I guess so. Chicago. I'm a student at Northwestern."

"i'm in Milwaukee. what brings u online tonight?"

"Been trying to work on a paper, but it's not going well."

"what's it about?"

"It's for a class on Korean civilization. I'm trying to compare 19th-century Japanese, Chinese, and Korean politics and society."

"sounds like a lot of work. so u always go online when ur having a hard time—at homework anyway?"

"[Laugh] Yeah, some of the time. But I also like to talk with guys about stuff; stuff that I can't talk about with most people."

"like what?"

"Well, like a lot of those channels you're on. Stuff like being a boy and interested in 'dads' and leather and even slaves."

"u think ur a slave?"

"I dunno. I'm curious about it. I think about it a lot but didn't really think it existed for real. You know, just something for porn stories or some secret society."

"it's real. my name is marco. i'm a slave."

"Seriously?"

"yep."

"But why are you in the slave channels? Looking for a boy for yourself?"

"no. but Master wants to build a family. He uses this nick most of the time. if u have questions about being a slave, asking Him probably would help more than talking to me."

I did talk with marco's master that night, and he didn't posture about who he was and what he wanted. Instead of listing what he would do to a novice curious about slavery, he talked about how he and marco met and lived. No "Get on your knees, bitchboy, and suck" or "You won't need anything else" for once!

Never mind all that, though; I had a civ paper to finish.

After my paper was complete I went to classes, sat around watching TV, and anything else to take my mind off what we talked about. During the next two weeks, I made myself write to SMBear twice—just to be polite, I told myself. I wrote in circles, asking the same questions: "What do you expect of a slave?" "What would I do if I was your slave?"—and making the same excuses—"I don't know if this is what I really want." SMBear never listed all the hot, nasty things he would do to me in his dungeon, like every other leatherman I met had done. And unlike most of the IRC trolls that kept in contact after chatting one night, he didn't suddenly reveal he was coming to Chicago in a few days and ask to meet.

But as I kept E-mailing, I still signed on to IRC to talk to whomever and beat off when I needed a break. After almost a month since we first met, SMBear lost patience with my messages. I wasn't really trying to build a closer relationship with deeper questions or more personal revelations. He finally came through with "The only way you'll know is if you actually do it. Come down for a weekend and be a slave." It had a strong undertone that it was time to act or stop wasting his time.

I used my parents' credit card to buy a plane ticket, leaving O'Hare for Milwaukee the next Saturday morning at 7:20 and returning the next morning. I'd be there for almost exactly 23 hours.

After civ and French classes and dinner in the dining hall, I stood in front of my mirror, alone in my room again. I couldn't sit down; all I could do was pace my room or grab my dresser with both hands. I only had a few hours until I left.

What the fuck was I doing? Flying to another city without

telling anyone. I never even met these guys. Who ever heard of a real, full-time Master and slave? That's only something people play at on the weekends. Nobody *lives* that way!

I let go of my grip on my dresser and dove onto my bed. My stomach wasn't taking my obsessing very well on top of a dining-hall dinner. I couldn't even sit up straight. *But people do this all the time,* I said to myself. *How else do they meet? They go off and find someone, make small talk, and fuck. Well, I won't; this is a first date—even if it's a $60 ride away, even if it's with a Master and his slave. No way. Even if they're hot.*

I did have their picture, E-mailed the day I bought the tickets. A big Latino slave in tit clamps, kneeling between the legs of a man in leather chaps with a flogger over his shoulder and a huge cock. They were staring right out at me. They got what they wanted.

A Master and a slave...and me. I got up to look in the mirror again. I'm not the cute boy I can be online. I can talk up a nice picture—but not the skinny-armed, hairy-chested, fat-thighed kid I see in the mirror. I don't know what to want, but I'm going out to play with adults in the real world. What could happen with these two well-built guys?

I wrote out my fears, feeling the words as they went on the paper: "His body, cut and beaten, was found in a Dumpster or a Motel 6 room with a fake name on the register. The drying leather straps held him spread on the bed. The needle was still in his arm, his ass oozed bloody come, and there was vomit and more blood on the pillow."

Actually, letting my nightmares go stopped my stomach cramps and let me focus on more practical things. I sat down at my computer—I didn't get online to avoid distraction—and typed up a letter addressed "To whom it may concern" with my flight information and that I was trying to figure out what I wanted in life. To cap off the drama, I put it in an envelope and handwrote, "To be opened in case of my disappearance."

I planned out Saturday morning to the minute: 20 minutes for a shower and getting dressed, 15 to walk to the train, 20 to downtown, 45 to the airport. I checked the train schedules and packed my backpack with a fresh shirt. Then, after all my fussing, I tried to read a book on political theory (*Man, the State, and War,* a prescription for insomnia) for yet another paper. But with images of me kneeling in a dark dungeon, hands tied behind me, in front of Master, the origins of war couldn't hold my attention.

I gave up on schoolwork and went to bed early. I set my alarm for 4:45 A.M., giving me enough time for the schedule I came up with earlier. Trying to sleep turned out just as impossible as working. I turned to face the wall and my leather-filled dreams. I flipped over and watched the clock. For almost six hours I dozed, then opened my eyes to the wall, then back to the clock, and then dropped off again.

I woke up at 4:30. I got in the shower, got to the airport, got on the plane, but I didn't feel excited or nervous—nothing at all. I had gotten my breath earlier as I'd snuck into the bathroom, trying not to wake anyone, and then walked to the train station alone. I was independent, on my own, and doing something crazy. But I was numb. On the almost-empty plane I had the same honey-roasted peanuts and ginger ale I always got when I took trips with my dad. That's when the panic began.

What was I doing? I wasn't with Dad on some business trip. I was going to a strange city to meet two strange guys who were into strange sex, and no one knew I was doing it. By the time we landed, I had to put my fist in my mouth to keep my teeth from chattering as my stomach tightened. As people got off the plane, I reached down under the seat for my backpack, but I couldn't make myself get up. Everyone had left before I managed to move, and then I bolted straight to the nearest bathroom in the terminal.

Sitting on a toilet, I realized I still had a choice: I could stay here until SMBear left, leave him a message that I missed my flight in Chicago, and hang around the Milwaukee airport until tomorrow. I sat, remembering both my fantasies and fears about meeting a real leather Master. I don't know why I didn't just stay in that bathroom. But I walked to the baggage area and found the information desk where SMBear said he'd meet me. I saw a man facing the outside doors, his back toward me. He had mid length brown hair and wore a leather vest. I knew it was him.

"Hi," I said. Great first line. "I'm Mike."

He turned, and his eyes brightened. "Hey. Glad you made it."

He looked at my face, which apparently showed my fear more than I felt it. "Need a hug?" I nodded, surprised that the butch guy from that picture would hug a potential slave in the middle of baggage claim. He felt solid, secure.

I followed SMBear across the street in front of the terminal and into the parking structure, looking for his car. After walking back to the terminal, a car—a tinted-window Cadillac just like in all those rich Master stories—pulled up. I got in the backseat, and the driver turned around and said, "Hey!"

If I focused on my fears, maybe I would've heard a sinister hello just as the car screeched off to God-knows-where, but I didn't. marco, the slave I first talked to, who started everything, looked happy and glad to see me.

The less said about the car trip to SMBear's house, the better. I wasn't completely panicked, but I couldn't think of anything to say. marco, probably noticing how different this was from my online personality, actually said, "Pretty quiet back there." All I could do was nod.

We drove behind SMBear's house just as he asked if I had any problems with dogs. Two panting creatures, one named George and the other Irving, bounded up the stairs as soon as I got in the door. They jumped and sniffed but didn't bark—not their usual reaction to most visitors, I found out. Actually, I wasn't scared of them either—an unusual reaction for me too. SMBear took me upstairs to drop off my backpack before going out for lunch.

The first thing I saw was a large wood-framed bed with four posts and a chain arcing over it. A bondage bed. "Oh, I've heard about those," I said, trying to sound used to sex. SMBear laughed and pulled me close. We kissed. Many times online people asked me if I was gay, and I had always answered that I thought so but wasn't sure. That kiss settled the question.

Stroking my growing bulge, SMBear sat me down on the bed and eased me back into his arms. "Someone likes this," SMBear said. SMBear told marco as he came into the room to take off my shoes. SMBear asked the standard safe-sex questions about if I had an STD or had had unprotected sex or had used drugs. Yeah, right. I'd barely ever touched another guy.

I stretched out on the bed and SMBear and marco each got on one side of me. SMBear took out my cock and pulled his slave's head down to it. His mouth was hot. He sucked as his Master tweaked my tits.

Nothing amazing, right? Except I didn't come. Only my second full-on blow job, and I didn't come. They took turns stroking for a while. Nothing. Not that I wasn't mostly enjoying it. In the end, my body told marco what was going on before I knew it myself: "He's shaking, Sir." I was still afraid.

Eventually they gave up on me, and marco sucked off his Master. We got up from the bed, reassembled our clothes, and went back downstairs. SMBear said, laughing, "We were just going to get rid of your bag and get some lunch!"

We went out to a little diner, and I started learning about slavery in practice. SMBear ordered for marco, who took the bill to the register and opened doors for his Master. I found out that calling SMBear "Sir" was proper. All the same, though, I didn't know why I was attracted to doing this. When we got back to the house we went down to the basement, which was lit only by a few red bulbs in the ceiling. SMBear sat me on a barstool and asked why I was curious about slavery. I couldn't give any better answer to him than I could to myself: Leather, service, and sex turned me on, but I hadn't ever done anything about it, and I didn't know why.

SMBear spoke about what leather books and stories left out. That Masters and slaves helped complete each other. That a slave, owned by a Master, was an equal who chose to surrender his will to another as an act of love. That a slave had no control over events in his life or over his body, but that a Master made decisions with the slave's best interests at heart. In surrendering everything, he said, a slave gains a freedom not easily found in this world.

I didn't understand much of what he said. I still don't. But, as SMBear explained it, Leather isn't just sex but a spiritual journey—led by a Master and followed by a slave—and spiritual matters aren't for the mind to understand but the soul to know. He revealed why Leather meant more than hot outfits and dark fantasies. With the right people, Leather meant growth and freedom.

Sir and marco talked for most of the afternoon and evening.

Maybe to demonstrate what they were saying, Sir took us down into the dungeon again—this time naked. He tied marco to an X-shaped cross, putting a leather strap under his cock and around his balls, and told me to stand between his legs and twist his nipple rings. marco both winced and got harder; they weren't joking about feeling pain as pleasure! Sir had a small device with two electrical leads connected to two pads. As he brought the pads close to marco's nuts, both his body and his cock jumped against their bonds. I stood off to the side, occasionally squeezing marco's tit but mainly watching the dance, numb. Growling, marco, still tied to the cross, came in three huge spurts, and Sir kissed him.

I had only a few more hours to go. We went upstairs to the same bed where we started the day. I didn't exactly sleep, lying between SMBear and marco. I turned from one to the other, too hot and too close to another person to sleep. What would I do anyway? Dream? I was living in a dream.

We woke up around 5:30 A.M., drove out to the airport, and said goodbye. I said I'd see them again, but SMBear just said to stay in touch. They didn't expect me to come back. I got back to Chicago and stopped off downtown for lunch at a Burger King. For the first time I saw the Michigan Avenue bridge go up—and then realized I couldn't tell anyone about it or anything else I had done. Even though no one saw me all Saturday, I didn't have any messages asking where I was. No one noticed I was missing.

In my first E-mail to Sir after I got back, I said I was smiling the whole walk back to my dorm as my newly sensitized nipples rubbed against my shirt. marco thought maybe they were telling me something. Whatever they were saying, I didn't want to be a slave. It was too extreme. What about all the things I wanted to do in life? What about living how I wanted? Sir said that independence was an illusion, that everyone follows someone. A slave chooses a Master deliberately instead of society or a corporation forcing one on him.

I couldn't stop thinking about Milwaukee. What now? School was almost over. I couldn't get away for another weekend, and, besides, we needed more than just two days. Sir suggested that I tell my parents that I was going to a friend's end-of-year party and staying a week in Milwaukee. I didn't like lying, but what could I do? I had only their credit card to buy tickets, and I wasn't really out as gay to myself, let alone to them.

After Dad came to Chicago to help me move out of the dorm, staring at me the whole time, trying to figure out why I was doing something so different, I left for the airport.

As i flew toward Milwaukee, i sat up straight and relaxed in my seat. i could ignore the whining kids and irritated businessmen around me. i was going back, back to Master, back to a different way of life. And i was looking forward to seeing marco at the airport and kneeling in front of Sir when i got to the house. Maybe...maybe i was finally going where i needed to be: where i could be myself.

But when i walked to the baggage area this time, no one was there. i had left a message about a flight delay with Sir, and i guessed he didn't want to wait for me at the airport. I decided he must be waiting for me to call. But no one answered when i phoned. i dropped into a plastic airport chair. Alone.

What was i doing?

marco got to the airport 50 minutes later and took me home. i've been with Master for almost two years now. i don't have many answers, but, then, most of my questions have changed.

Bear Cub

By Jerry Prince

We met on the Internet. I had purchased my computer to keep track of expenses and pay bills but discovered the fun of cruising the Internet Relay Chat groups to the point that it occupied much of my time. Early on I had done a listing of the gay IRC channels and discovered lots of fun places to chat and trade pictures, which cut down on the expenses of renting videos and buying magazines. Eventually I found a fellow who said he was as hairy as I was, and he recommended that I try the Bearcave channel. This was a real revelation to me; guys that were hairy and liked other guys that were hairy. I was not alone!

I had picked up copies of *Bear* magazine and imagined myself in the company of other hairy men, but I had no idea of the number of men who were online and had the same fascination with body hair. Another surprise was the number of really young guys there. I had imagined myself finding a young guy, a son to whom I could be Dad, but never imagined finding a hairy young son.

When I cruised the bars, which was rare, I could usually hook up with a guy about my own age, but I usually found guys with only a little body hair, and seldom were there any who were much younger. The whole scene was not enjoyable: a lot of time spent drinking and smoking and occasionally getting lucky—maybe having a fun roll on the sheets, but never finding just the guy I wanted. So I was very excited to find a place where I felt at home, a channel on the Internet devoted to body fur and filled with men of all ages, including what I would call "boys," even though they were over 18.

I never left the comfort of my own home yet got to know many guys very well—all by their nicknames, of course. A few traded pictures with me of masculine men who were naked or engaged in exciting fucking or sucking action, and some even sent their own personal pictures, simply naked or engaged in sex. When I was fortunate enough to receive a picture labeled youngbear.jpg, I was in ecstasy. There was a furry young guy, rubbing himself, getting himself excited—but me even more so. This became my fantasy: a young bear; a furry kid; a hot, hairy young stud. On the Bearcave channel, they called themselves bear cubs. Finding a bear cub became my challenge.

There were so many men and boys on the channel, but all were in Europe or in states far away from me. At first I despaired of ever meeting one face to face. I spent my time looking at all the bear pictures I had accumulated: Kelso and Ryker and other well-known figures from the gay videos. I even found AVIs, tiny bits of movies, I could watch on my computer. Getting to watch these bears in action just made me pound my meat more often and fantasize about finding a bear cub of my very own, to love and to love me.

One night while I was online one of the guys called for an age/location check, where we all say how old we are and where we live. I was excited when one of the cubs listed himself as 20 and not over an hour's drive from me. I sent a private message to him, and he accepted. We chatted for a long time: about what we did for a living, what we liked about sex, body type, facial hair, etc. I'm 48, and I have a mustache and goatee; I'm kinda heavy at 210, sorta feel I need to lose weight. But this kid said he was a little taller than me (I'm 5 foot 8, and he was six feet), and he said he weighed 220 and wouldn't want a man less than 200 pounds. He loved men with some love handles to hold onto while he was giving a terrific blow job, he said.

Well, by this point I was about to cream my pants; I had to pull my cock out and stroke it good. My mind was just running everywhere, trying to imagine sex with a guy young enough to be my son, a bear cub who liked older hairy men—men with a belly and tits. It didn't take long to get me stiff and leaking precome as I chatted with him. He had to leave and cut me off kinda abruptly, which was a great disappointment, but I knew his nickname and knew that he was usually online about the same time I was, so I also knew I would see him again.

Work the next day was awful; I couldn't keep my mind on anything. I nearly walked into walls, and I kept finding myself in odd places and wondering why I was there. That bear cub was in my head and would not leave. I didn't want him to leave—I wanted him. The more I thought about him, the worse it got. I finally went into the bathroom stall and beat off, looking at a copy of the young bear picture I had folded up and put in my pocket. I wanted him so bad that it didn't take long to have a come fountain shooting. It took me a while to clean up the mess, but it was worth it. At least I got a little work done after that.

That evening I made supper fast and ate it fast so that I could settle down in front of my computer. I stayed online for hours, it seemed. My back hurt from sitting in one position. I was tired of trading pictures, and there was no one around worth talking to. I had finally decided to give it up, when up popped his nickname on the screen. I immediately messaged him, and he accepted. I pulled my cock out and began the familiar motion to bring it to life. It made typing difficult but was worth it; I needed this cub so bad that it hurt.

After a while he was willing to talk on the phone! Wonderful! We both got off the computer, and soon I was dialing; I was so excited I was shaking. When he answered, he was smooth and relaxed, a college kid home for the summer, working a job he hated in order to get money to go back to college. We talked about all sorts of things until I finally got up the courage to ask him if we could meet.

"Sure, no problem," he said. "In fact, my parents are going on vacation next week. How does next Tuesday evening sound? I'm free then."

I was about to come just thinking about it. We set the date and time, and he promised to send me directions to his house by E-mail.

Well, if work had been hard before, it was worse now. People were waving in front of my face and saying, "Hello, anyone home?" I was embarrassed. Jacking off didn't help now; it just seemed to make it worse because I kept imagining him sucking me or me sucking him. Finally I decided to keep my come in my balls. I was hoping I was gonna need it.

Tuesday finally arrived, and so did the E-mail with directions to his house. Work dragged on forever. I was waiting by the door with my time card in the clock when it changed to 4 P.M., which was very unusual for me. I told the other employees I had to hurry home to meet a repairman. I did have something that needed work, but it was not at home. Luckily no policeman stopped me on the way because I was definitely exceeding the speed limit to get to this kid.

His directions were fine; I had printed them out so I would be sure to find the house. It was far back in a subdivision, an older part, lots of trees around it. I ran up and rang the bell. He quickly opened the door, and there he stood, a perfect example of young bearhood: six feet tall, close-cropped hair, and a young-boy beard, fuzzy.

"Hi, come on in," the same masculine voice I had heard on the phone said. I walked in, and when I turned around, he kissed me. He had to bend down a little, but he enveloped me in a bear hug that I quickly returned. As our tongues explored our mouths, he began to explore my body with his hands, and I quickly followed his lead. He had told me he was a bottom, but he was taking the lead.

I was a little unsure how to proceed; I had never been with such a young boy before, but he was perfectly at ease. He gave me a great massage that turned me on; my cock was straining to get free. He was wearing a knit shirt and a pair of shorts; it turned out he wasn't wearing anything under the shorts, as my hands found his young cock when I lifted them a little. He was trying to unbutton my shirt as we kissed, and I had one hand under his shirt trying to find his nipples and the other playing with his cock.

After what seemed like a long time of kissing and fondling, he broke it off and pointed me to the bedroom down the hall. I practically ran to it, unbuttoning my shirt as I went. When I reached the bedroom and turned around, he kissed me again, another strong manly kiss, this time forcing my shirt to partly fall off. I shrugged it off the rest of the way as I tried to undress him. We finally had to break off the kiss so I could unbuckle my pants and let them fall. My cock was sticking out of my shorts, and before I could do anything, he bent down and took it in his mouth. I was in ecstasy once again. A kid was sucking my dick! A beautiful, hairy young guy was bobbing up and down on my prick; I hoped I could hold back the come, but I was getting too excited. I had to reach down and pull him up so I could kiss him. The taste of my cock was still in his mouth.

After more oral and physical exploring, I pulled back, dropped to my knees, got his dick out from under his shorts, and went down on him. It was delicious, that wonderful young-boy taste! I wanted him so much! I took him deep in my throat; all six inches disappeared quickly. My nose was planted in his pubic hairs as he ran his fingers through the hair atop my head.

"Like that cock, Dad?" he asked. "I sure like having you suck it!"

I gave him what I thought was an excellent cock sucking, but he seemed nowhere near as excited as I was; he just stood there and took it, fondling my hair. He must be more sexually experienced than me, I thought, to take this and not show any excitement; I was shaking with lust.

I finally pulled off and released his shorts, and they fell to the floor, letting me finally see his full manhood. His cock was sticking straight out at me, a nice sac of balls hanging below it. I immediately went down on him again. I wanted to devour that delicious cock. I wanted him to shoot in my mouth, but he was nowhere near ready.

When I sensed I was wasting my time, I pulled off, stood up again, and experienced another of those wonderful boy kisses! This kid could kiss better than any man I had ever been with. He was just the best at kissing! We explored each other with tongues and hands. My shorts soon were on the floor, and I stepped out of them as he took off his shirt. Two naked men, looking each other over. He was beautiful! Looked like he was 18 but furry all over, his back hair just kept going up to his head. (I kept my fur trimmed at the collar.)

And that boy beard; it made him look so hunky! I couldn't resist—I just had to kiss him again. All over. He seemed appreciative and soon began to kiss what he could reach, while our two stiff cocks rubbed against each other.

Soon he pulled me to the bed and laid me gently down. Then he laid his body in the opposite position so we could be on our sides and sixty-nine. My cock disappeared into his mouth, and I took his dick in mine. This was heaven, watching his head bobbing up and down on my cock while I had his in my own mouth! I put my tongue down his piss slit as far as I could while he deep-throated me, his nose rubbing my balls. I tried to think of anything, everything else to keep from coming too soon.

It was so hard not to unload my come, watching my cock disappear in that wonderful, warm mouth, seeing that boy beard working. I put myself into a great cocksucking effort, fondling his balls, putting a finger up his ass; he did the same for me. I was close and knew it wouldn't be long. I just couldn't hold it back any longer.

"I'm coming!" I shouted, having to let that delicious cock of his fall from my mouth. He pulled off and jacked my cock a few strokes, and the come shot like a Roman candle over both of us.

"Nice shot, Dad," he said. "Thick and creamy." He rubbed it into his chest and smiled; I returned to his cock, determined now to get him off as well as he had me.

It took a long time, a lot of determined cock sucking to get this boy to let loose, but when I tasted the precome, I pulled off and jacked him, cupping his balls in my other hand.

"That's it, Dad. Jack my cock, beat my dick hard, rub my balls! Come on, Dad, you can do it!" Short spurts of boy juice squirted all over my face and beard. I rubbed it in. Then I gently massaged the head of his tender cock with my thumb; he flinched and took a sharp breath.

"Oh, Dad, that feels so good on the end of my cock!"

I didn't stop—I wanted to keep him stiff for the next round.

Instead, he rolled me on my stomach and gave me a great massage and back rub. What a pleasure it was, having a son to service me like that! I was having the sensual experience of a lifetime. Then he rolled me over again and lay down on top of me. Two cocks were rubbing together, stiffening. Nipples were rubbing against nipples, stiffening. Then his lips were on mine again, and I was enveloped in a huge kiss and an incredible full-body bear hug. I was about to lose it again. What a terrific, sexy bear cub! I just could not believe my luck.

He got off of me, sat up a little, and went down on me again, sucking me to full stiffness. It sure didn't take long despite the relatively short time since I had shot my load. Then, just when I was really getting into it, he stopped, dried my cock with the sheet, and produced a lime-green rubber, which he rolled down my staff.

I was gonna get to fuck him! I couldn't believe it. He put a dollop of K-Y Jelly on the very tip, then got up on his knees and got over me, facing me. I thought maybe I'd get to suck that wonderful boy cock again, but instead he took my cock and steadied it as he let his ass down on it slowly.

I was lying there, watching myself fuck this magnificent boy! He was doing it all, wrapping his ass around my cock slowly; I could see the muscles working in his legs and thighs. I felt the pop when my cock head parted his asshole, and then he just slowly descended—stopping when it hurt, then raising up a little, then going back down—until finally he was resting on top of me, smiling at me.

"Like it, Dad?" he asked, smiling wickedly.

"Love it, Son!" I replied.

"Well, Dad, what does this feel like?" He didn't move, but my cock could feel his ass muscles moving. It was like a hand was on my cock, jacking me off. He was not moving much, just sort of rocking, but each time he was clenching his ass muscles and then letting go. He was fucking himself with my cock! This was just the most incredible sexual experience, lying there watching and feeling it all happen.

As he got more excited, he began to raise and lower himself on my rod, and I, of course, assisted by slamming it as far as I could up his ass on the downstroke. Oh, this was a fuck! This was the most unusual fuckin' great fuck! He must have done many leg lifts to have the strength to be able to sex me so thoroughly by hardly moving. The sweat was forming on his brow, and I could see it through the fur on his chest. He was fucking harder now, trying to milk the come out of my balls, and he was doing a great job of it. I was fighting like mad to fuck him back, but there wasn't much I could do, just try to meet him with my thrusts each time he slid down.

"Like this boy fuck?" he said between grunts.

"God, you are one hot fucker. This is just the best fuck!" I panted. "I love it how you grip my cock with your ass muscles."

"Give it to me hard, Dad," he urged me. "I want you to come deep inside me. I want to feel your man cock fire a big load up my boy ass!"

This was so exciting it really didn't take long. I could feel my cock get hot and rigid and my balls tighten up, ready to spew their load. "I'm gonna come!" I shouted. "Goddamn! What a great fucker you are! This is one hot boy fuck!"

"Slam it to me, Dad," he yelled, gasping for breath. "Heave it up inside me. Let me feel it when you come. I want to feel it!"

Well, we both felt it. The come spewed from my balls, up the length of my rigid fuck pole, and into his hot ass. It was marvelous! I shot and shot, and it seemed like I would never stop coming, and he just kept fucking my dick with his ass. Finally the come stream became a trickle, and he sat down heavily on me, sweating and smiling. His muscles continued to squeeze my cock, milking the come out as he held my dick prisoner inside him. Sweat was rolling down his nose, falling onto my stomach.

"You're a damn good fucker for an old man, Dad," he said, smiling.

"You are the damn good fuck, Son. I was just here under you, and you did all the fuckin' yourself. God, you are the best thing I ever saw!"

He smiled and rubbed my tummy where the sweat drops had pooled and then lay down gently on top of me, still with my cock impaled deep inside. We kissed again for a long time—a great, sweaty, man-boy kiss. He was wonderful. I was enveloped in his smell, a sweaty locker-room smell. I licked the sweat off his face and beard.

When he finally rolled off, I was able to return the favor by giving some solo attention to his cock. I had one hand on his nipples and one on his balls, and I tried my best to do him as well as he had done me.

"Suck that cock, Dad," he said in a wail of pleasure. "Let me feel that tongue again—down my piss hole—that's it. Now finger my ass good."

I licked his ass, licked my finger, and tried my best to find his prostate; his cock got stiffer with my finger in his ass. I was sucking like a madman; my head was bobbing up and down, my strong suction about to pull his cock down my throat. The more I wiggled my finger in his ass and played with his balls, the more excited he became.

"That's it, Dad! You're doin' it!" he yelled. "Suck that cock. Let me feel it. Suck it hard. Pull the come outta my balls! Do it to me, Dad...let me feel it. Come on, Dad, suck your son...suck that boy cock!"

His hot talk really got me going too, and soon I was rewarded with the taste of precome, so I pulled off and stroked him as hard as I dared. He thrashed his legs, and I stuck my finger farther up his ass. Then he stiffened, and the come flew again—all across my face and chest. I kept stroking till he was empty; he took my hands and drew me toward him. We embraced again, rolling on the bed, the come smeared on our bodies as we kissed and rubbed each other.

We finally collapsed and just lay there, breathing heavily. I just could not believe it: I had been sucked by this beautiful cub; I had fucked him; and I had sucked him off twice. This was just incredible. I had never had such a great sex experience with such a young man, such a beautiful young bear cub.

Afterward, we showered together, and there was a little sex play, but neither of us was up to a full erection after our balls had been so thoroughly emptied. I hated to let that boy cock go, though, so I kept holding it, stroking it while I kissed him with the water washing over us, washing all the sweat and come away. We toweled off, and he swatted me with his rolled-up towel, just a kid playing with his Dad, having a good time. We were both enjoying being with each other, two naked, hairy bodies—one full of the vigor of youth, the other full of the sensual experience of being with him. It was all over too soon: We were dressed, and I was at the door, given a good-bye kiss, and sent on my way.

I was humming and singing all the way home, so relaxed and yet excited at what had happened. I reviewed it all in my mind—what a wonderful experience. I loved it so much. Had I told him? Had I really told him what a wonderful time I had had, how I loved being with him so much? Perhaps not enough.

I got home, went straight to the computer, and sent him a letter, a love letter, telling him how much I had enjoyed it—loved it, really. Loved sucking him, loved watching him suck me, loved the way he fucked himself with my cock, loved that final cock sucking, his stiff boy cock rigid in my mouth. I was gushing, feeling maybe this was too much; I wanted him again, but would I scare him with all this?

Well, tough shit. I loved it, and I told him so. I sent the letter and then made my supper—it was very late—and gulped it down. Then I sat down at the computer again.

I logged on to IRC. I couldn't wait to tell the other bears what had happened, though he had asked me not to mention his nickname so he wouldn't get a reputation as an easy number and get lots of guys trying to bed him. When I went into the Bearcave channel, he was already there. In fact, he was bragging about the terrific sex he had just enjoyed with a bear dad. I watched the words scroll across the screen and smiled. I messaged him and asked him if he had received my E-mail. He had, and he wanted to let me know how much he had enjoyed it too. And he said, "When can we get together again?"

Sticky Keyboard

By C.J. Murray

Cleaning house has always been a passion of mine. I cannot stand clutter, dust bunnies under the bed, or bits of lint on the carpet. I have an arsenal of supplies under the sink to wage war on the bullies of dirt and disorder. But I am having a hard time (no pun intended) getting the come from between the keys of my computer keyboard. It has dried and is like flaky glue in spots; in other places it is more like wet, white paste. I assume that is where the thicker, whitish lumps and clumps have landed.

I've tried cleaning cloths, electronic equipment spray, sponges, and everything else, but it's still there, wedged in between the keys, and my return key is a bit slow from the sticky film beneath it.

The other passion of mine is young (at least young-looking) men and boys. I am not so stupid as to play with potential jail time for having sex with an underage boy, but I have found that there are a lot of men who look much younger than they are. And despite the obsession of eternal youth in gay society, there are a great many who find us men of middle age attractive. Or at least tolerable and interesting. Besides, Net lovers usually remain unseen. As a writer I spend a lot of time on the computer, and as a gay man always looking for someone I spend a lot of time in chat rooms.

I had listened in on this guy calling himself BarelyLegal for a week. He was always there online, chatting and flirting with other members of my favorite chat room, usually these two guys called

HardMan and WannaLover. A couple of times I entered the chat when they questioned me and commented on my name: EroticRuler.

EroticRuler: How old are you, Barely?
BarelyLegal: Old enough to do you, Ruler, and make your equipment strain its limits.
EroticRuler: Like to try that! How big are you?
HardMan: Barely is really a 12-year-old with big dreams and a big dick.
BarelyLegal: You wish, HardMan!
WannaLover: Sick...all of you.
EroticLover: Answer my question.
BarelyLegal: Eight inches, uncut, and growing.

At that point my own dick, which I had been stroking, was beginning to poke its head out of the slit in my boxers. I glanced down at it and wondered what Barely looked like and tasted like. I wondered if he was clean.

WannaLover: You a ruler? Into S/M?
EroticRuler: Light, mostly young and hot, maybe just bossy.
BarelyLegal: How old are you, Ruler? And how bossy? Looks?
WannaLover: You guys are making me rub it!
HardMan: I still say Barely's 12, and his mommy doesn't know he's online with a bunch of dirty old horny men.
BarelyLegal: I like daddy types. More on your looks?
EroticRuler: 40-ish, tall, hard, nice, and very experienced. This an audition for action?
BarelyLegal: Could be. Wanna go into private chat?
EroticRuler: Great! Meet you there in 10 minutes.
WannaLover: Hey, you guys can't leave us. We want to hear it!
BarelyLegal: You might...later.

I clicked off to check the rooms' members and found BarelyLegal's information profile:

Name: BarelyLegal
Age: Very young but legal...21, but I look 13
Interests: Man-on-man with older guys. Like domination but gentle. No hard S/M. Like light leather.
Occupation: Carpenter

I entered the private chat room he'd set up.

BarelyLegal: So tell me more. What do you like to do and how?
EroticRuler: I want to hold you down and watch you obey me.
BarelyLegal: Are you touching yourself now?
EroticRuler: Sure. Are you?
BarelyLegal: You haven't told me to. I wait.
EroticRuler: Then take it out...describe.
BarelyLegal: About eight, semihard. Stroking the head and leaking a bit.
EroticRuler: I'd have you kneel and take it all, slowly, not touching yourself until I give you permission.

I began to type with only one hand as I pulled on my balls and stroked harder on my swollen dick.

BarelyLegal: And then?
EroticRuler: Then I'd turn you over and lift your legs and enter your tight little O. All the way on the first stroke!
BarelyLegal: O-o-ow!
EroticRuler: Yeah. Then deep and slow, pinching your little nippies in front of you and watching your face.
BarelyLegal: Almost there?
EroticRuler: Oh, yeah. You?
BarelyLegal: When you tell me to. But it's feeling good. Aa-a-ah.
EroticRuler: Come for me, babe. Come for me now!

And I lost all ability to type as my ball sac snapped up, and I came in five heavy spurts that shot up and onto the keyboard and the back of my hand. I could hardly keep my fingers on the slick keyboard as I tried to continue typing.

EroticRuler: Did you come for me?
BarelyLegal: Yes, yes, yes, yes, yes!

After a few more words we clicked off, and I caught my breath and tried to clean the come off my damned computer yet again. So far I have been unsuccessful.

We repeated that encounter several times over the next couple of weeks, and then he suggested that we meet. I was hesitant. I could handle the cybersex, and I could come with the best of them, but to meet him was scary, especially after he had described himself to me. But I agreed to let him come to my apartment the following Saturday.

I had cleaned my apartment until it was spotless except, of course, for the impossible come loads embedded between the keys on my computer.

Promptly at 2 he rang the doorbell, and I opened the door. Todd—I'd learned his real name—was young. He looked about 14 or 15, and for a second I thought he was a neighborhood kid selling something for his school. He was tall, sort of thin, but with a good network of muscles on his lanky body. Black shoulder-length hair hung on the sides of his well-boned face, and his eyes were the color of the sea at noon.

I invited him in, and he sat on the sofa, looking a bit uneasy.

"I enjoyed the chats, and I'm glad to finally meet you," he said. His grin revealed his even, white teeth. He was very tan, and I felt my dick jump in my pants.

"Well, you certainly look young, just as you said. You are of legal age, aren't you?" I asked him.

He whipped out his wallet, dug out his driver's license, and handed it to me. He was like a kid being carded in a convenience store. I glanced at it and handed it back.

I was very aware of his eyes on me.

"I like the way you talked to me online," he said. "I like guys who are a bit older than me."

"Well, I certainly fit the bill," I quipped.

We talked for a while, decided to go out to eat, and talked some more during the meal. He was living with three other guys, his roomies, who were all straight, and he was hooked on cybersex. He worked days as a carpenter and was getting over a two-year relationship that had ended badly. He was a little shy, very natural, and extremely sexy. I found myself very attracted to him.

We were both pretty tight when we returned to my apartment. I shut and locked the door, and as I turned Todd was right there in front of me. He put his hands on my shoulders, leaned into me, and kissed me. It was a soft, shy little kiss. I pulled him to me and shoved my tongue into his sweet-tasting mouth. I pulled his shirt up and rubbed my hands across his back, feeling the muscles that rippled there. Then I brought my hands around front and found his nipples. I pinched as I kissed him and heard the small groan deep in his throat.

I pushed him down to the floor while I stood in front of him, and he opened my jeans, fished out my cock, and then leaned forward and started licking my throbbing dick. I wrapped my fingers in his long hair and rubbed his shoulders. After a while I stopped him, and he stood up. I undressed him then myself and took him to the computer and clicked it on. We found our chat room, and we both watched as HardMan and WannaLover chatted with others.

"Click on and get into the conversation," I told him.

He did, and as he chatted I pulled his legs back a step or two so that he was standing in front of the keyboard with his feet spread and his ass turned to me. I knelt behind him, opened his ass crack, and inserted two fingers at once. Todd moaned and typed. I finger-fucked him awhile, sometimes looking around him to see what he was saying.

Then I pulled my fingers out and stood up directly behind him. I placed my cock head right against his spit-soaked tight hole and then pushed my dick into his softness. I looked at the monitor, and he had printed "xxxxxxx" across the screen. He recovered somewhat, and I began to thrust. I could feel him tremble from the effort it took for him to think about chatting while I fucked him.

"Keep talking. Do not stop," I whispered into his ear, leaning over his back. "Keep talking to them while I fuck you, Todd. Tell them what you are getting."

I reached around him and found his dick. He was hard and dripping. I rubbed the head of it and then pulled on his balls as I fucked his tight little hole. He moaned aloud, and when I checked the screen I could hardly read what he had typed. But I was able to see that he had told the others he was with me and what I was doing to him at that very moment. He began to push his ass back toward me, and I was thrusting harder and harder and stroking his dick faster and faster.

"Don't stop typing!" I hissed into his ear. "If you do, I will punish you!"

> **BarelyLegal:** Oh oh oh oh! EroticRuler fucking me oh oh oh God!

And he came. All over the keyboard and his hands. I filled his ass with my max load a few seconds later. There was no sound except for the hum of the electronic equipment and our ragged breathing for a few minutes. Then I pulled out of him and pushed his head down over the keyboard.

"We've had the fun. Now it's time to clean up," I said, and he began to lick the keyboard clean of his come...and my dried-up loads from the past.

I sat in my desk chair behind him and watched as he cleaned the keys, his beautiful ass still dripping. I felt the beginnings of another hard-on as the blood flowed back into my dick.

He was young, beautiful, and willing to clean.

I decided to keep him around as long as I could. He could always use my computer as long as he cleaned up afterward.

Almost Better Than Sex

By Simon Sheppard

I'd just been stood up by another liar from AOL. Well, maybe "liar" is too strong a word...

I'd just been stood up by another tweaked-out, game-playing asshole shitbag from AOL. It was 1 A.M., and I was horny and itching to go out and pound some butt. So when the guy who said he would phone me after I signed off *didn't* phone me, when the number he'd given me turned out to be a recorded message about transit information, I was pissed off. Pissed off with a hard-on. The first few months I'd been online I'd taken this sort of thing personally—or at least as evidence of the general decline of truth and morality in late capitalist culture. Now I realized it was just the way things were. But it was damned annoying nonetheless.

I signed back on. At 1 A.M. on a weeknight, the online community, such as it is, consists largely of the sexually desperate, the chemically stimulated, and guppies in pajamas who are brushing their teeth in anticipation of another day of designing software—the better to keep their Grand Cherokees purring on down the freeway. It's the time of night when hope springs eternal, only to bang its head against the virtual wall. I'd already opened Netscape and moseyed on over to my favorite porn Web site, anticipating a quick, half-hearted wank into a paper towel to be followed by a deep and dreamless sleep.

I was, though, also still parked in one of the M4M chat rooms, hoping my affair with some porn star's GIFs would be interrupted by the chime of an Instant Message. It was: "Hello, Sir."

My cruising profile instructs boys to call me "Sir." OK, like any minor perversion, it probably seems silly to guys who aren't into it, but I like it. And boys do too.

His screen name was unfamiliar and utterly cryptic. I opened the Get Profile window, typed his name in, and clicked. His profile was nondescript as well.

"Sir?"

"I'm here, boy," I typed. "Age?" I wasn't about to get busted for inadvertently chatting with jailbait.

"18," he returned.

Well, *close* to jailbait.

"And what are you into?"

The answer came up in the little window: "Following orders."

My dick, which had been half deflated from frustration, sprang smartly to attention. "You looking to play now?" I typed out.

"Yes."

"You looking to go out or stay in?"

"I'm in Hoboken."

New Jersey was a mere 3,000 miles away.

"I want you to tell me," he continued, "what to do, and I'll do it and send pictures of it to you while we chat."

I didn't have one of those CUseeMe setups that makes it possible to send blurry, jerky video from one computer to another, so that suited me just fine. "Yes," I typed, somewhat dubious. "OK."

"You've got mail," his next message read.

The E-mail consisted of a photo divided into four smaller pictures. The first two shots were of his dick. In one pic, half hard; in the other, fully erect and tied off with a piece of cord around the base. It was a nice dick. Now I know that just what constitutes a "nice dick" is pretty much indefinable, but let's face it, we all know one when we see one. He'd clipped his body hair really short and shaved around his cock and balls. Not my favorite look, but on him it looked good.

The lower left photo featured a neatly laid-out array of sex toys: three dildos of varying size, two flesh-colored, one bright red;

a cock ring; a bunch of clothespins; several cords; and most suggestive of all, a disposable diaper. The bottom right picture was even more well arranged—nine small numbered panels, each containing a different style of underwear: briefs, boxers, jockstraps, a dance belt. I had to hand it to the kid; he was organized.

"So tell me what you want me to do" was his next message.

I spit in my hand and started stroking. I was more than ready to be a nasty motherfucker, but if there's one thing I've learned about sex, it's that pacing is important. I decided to start slow. "Put on number 6," I commanded.

"Yes, Sir." Then there was a long pause.

You've got mail, my computer notified me.

I opened the message he'd sent and downloaded the file: a nice-looking torso wearing translucent white briefs that just barely hid a prominent erection.

"Nice," I typed. "Now wet them down." I figured the picture with briefs could have been anyone and come from anywhere. But if he sent me a picture on command, he was on the level.

"With piss, Sir?" he asked.

"Yes." While I waited, I spit on my hand again and massaged my hard-on.

You've got mail.

He'd wet his briefs, all right. A damp stain, spreading from his cock head, rendered the cloth transparent. This was getting good. I thought so, and my dick thought so too.

"Take off the briefs and show me your dick, boy."

In a minute a picture of his hard-on, lazing stiffly against his thigh, appeared on my screen. Not a huge dick, which was fine with me. Just handsome and juicy-looking and ready to be shoved around. So my next order was easy: "Take a cord and tie up your dick and balls."

In less than a minute I could see that he had. He'd done a so-so job of dick bondage; I could have done better, made it prettier, but his shaft was bulging now, and his hairless ball sac was nicely stretched out.

"Show me your hole."

You've got mail. A shot from behind, his fingertips spreading his hole wide. It was one of those biology 101 shots, the kind where you can see past the sphincter to the red wetness inside. Way back in my youth, when I first saw split beaver shots in straight porn magazines, I thought they were gross. Now, staring up into a boy's vulnerable insides, I almost came.

"Put a dildo in there."

"Which one, Sir?"

"Start with the small one, the red one."

The pacing of all this was immaculate. A command, a minute of jacking off while I waited to be obeyed, then the results appearing on my screen.

New picture: his ass from behind again. His butt was hairy, but he'd shaved around the crack, and in the middle of the naked flesh he was pressing the dildo into himself. The base was red jelly against his smooth young flesh—like a really perverted Gummi Bear. I had to take my hand off my dick; coming now was unthinkable. Not when I had more to command him to do, limits to push.

The doorbell rang. It was 2 in the morning. *Who the fuck can it be, a neighborhood drunk?* I wondered. Fuck it! Whoever it was would just have to go away. I just hoped it wasn't an emergency. Whatever. I wasn't going to call a halt to this, not even if the house was burning down.

"You still playing with the dildo?" I asked the boy.

"Yes, Sir, is that OK?"

"Take it out and suck it clean. Let me see it in your mouth."

He typed back, "I can't show you my face."

"Just your mouth. Now!"

"Yes, Sir."

A profile from chin to nostrils appeared on my screen. Nice mouth, face just a bit fleshy, apparently. Pretty lips, wrapped around a dirty dildo. I didn't have to touch myself to stay hard. I'd found myself a kinky boy. Or, rather, he'd found me.

"Now show me your pussy again," I told him.

Seconds later the boy's shaved ass reappeared on the screen, a little the worse for wear. His hole was stretched wide open and wasn't altogether clean. *This is incredible,* I thought. *I should write a story about it.*

I gave my dick a tug, squeezed at the tip till I sent myself to the brink of orgasm, then backed off. "Are enjoying this, you sick pig?"

"Yes, Daddy."

"Good boy. Now I want you to..." I typed, and the computer crashed.

Damn, damn, damn! My Mac had frozen, and I had to do a hard restart, wait for the extensions to load, launch AOL, sign on...talk about coitus interruptus!

Finally back online, I brought up an Instant Message window, typed out "Sorry, crashed," and clicked.

A window brought the bad news: "Member is not currently online."

Fuck! He probably figured I'd flaked and gone off to clean up and jack off. Oh, well, at least he wasn't playing online with somebody else. He might be a perverted, exhibitionistic pussy boy, but at least he wasn't a slut.

Then my computer chimed at me. An Instant Message window appeared: "Sorry, Sir, I got bumped." Par for the online course, but now we were back in business. I was in the mood to have him hurt a bit for me.

"Those clothespins?" I asked, fully aware.

"Yes, Daddy."

"I want you to use them."

"Yes, Daddy?"

"Put one on each tit and show me."

His chest was well-built, not quite lean, with close-trimmed hair. Perfect. A clothespin was fastened to each nipple, jutting outward. I was imagining what he was feeling all the way across the country as the wooden clothespins chomped down into his tender flesh, initial discomfort changing to more focused pain, then intense, searing sensation, then something else.

"Now your dick. Put clothespins on your dick. Start with your ball sac."

"Yes, Sir."

There was a longer pause than usual. I guessed he was adjusting the clothespins over the stretched flesh of his sac. Then a message, not a pic: "Daddy?"

"Yes?"

"Where on my dick?"

I told him to put a clothespin where the base of his dick met his sac, then start fastening more up the underside of his cock, stretching out the delicate flesh, clamping the pins down. I loved this; it was delicious.

Eventually the next GIF came: a nice angle, him lying back, shot from below. At the top of the frame the clothespins were still on his tits. Below, closer up, on his dick and balls he had clamped three clothespins on the sac, four more running up the shaft. What a fine lad.

"It hurts, Daddy."

"I know. Have you done this before?"

"No," he said. I almost came.

I looked at the little clock on the upper right of the screen. It was getting late. But I was unwilling to give this up. Somewhere across the continent in frozen moments of time a boy was, somehow, giving himself to me. One of the things I usually like about amateur porn is the giveaway detail: the glimpse of work stacked up on a computer table; an unfortunate choice of carpets or drapes; even in some precious instances, a bookshelf, the exhibitionist's choice of reading matter open to analysis. This boy's photos, though, were tightly cropped. There was no world outside the frame, nothing but the electronic sheen of flesh—and although turned bluish by my monitor, delicious nonetheless. Naked flesh offered up to me.

"Daddy? Sir?" he said, bringing me out of my thoughts.

"Yes?"

"Are you still there?"

"Sorry. Yes."

"What do you want me to do next?"

"Show me your face."

A pause, a hesitation. Then a polite refusal. And I realized he'd made the right choice, even if for the wrong reasons. Maybe all he wanted was the safety of anonymity, but that anonymity was a gift for me. As long as he remained faceless, featureless, he could be damned near anyone, and that meant he could be everyone, everyone I'd ever desired or come on to or fucked. He was in some utterly cyber-erotic fashion the embodiment of desire, only he surely didn't know that, and if I'd told him, he might have laughed at my pretentiousness and offered to stick the dildo back up his ass.

"Stick a dildo back up your ass."

"Which dildo?"

"The big one."

The next picture that appeared on my screen showed his shaved asshole stretched around a larger, flesh-colored toy. His dick, still covered by clothespins, stood straight up.

"Nice," I let him know.

"Now what?"

Now what, indeed. If this were the Real World, we might have come by now. We'd be wiping up, making small talk...about computers probably. If he was like too many young guys, he might be heading out to the back porch for a cigarette. Instead, we each were in ultimate control of our own lusts. There would be no surprise touch of his hand on my dick, a touch that would send me spiraling over the brink of orgasm. There would be no postcoital moment when our eyes accidentally meet. Here in electronic space, despite his apparent surrender of control, despite my losing my head over him—or rather over the pixels that defined his presence—we each had only to flick a button for the whole thing to end. And it was getting very, very late.

I thought about it, then typed out, "I want you to come."

"But, Sir, can't we do this longer?"

"Come."

"Please?"

"Now. And show me."

I planned to make myself spurt the moment I saw the pic of jizz on his belly. I stroked gently, delaying the release. And then the bedroom door opened. My boyfriend, his voice as bleary as his eyes, stuck his head through the living room door. "You still up?" he asked.

"Yeah. I'll come to bed soon."

He glanced down at my hand...my dick. "Slut." He smiled and tottered off to the bathroom for a pee.

When he was safely back in bed, I checked my mailbox, opened the E-mail titled "Last One," clicked DOWNLOAD NOW, grabbed the paper towel I'd left beside the mouse pad, and watched as his picture opened. He'd taken the clothespins off his dick but added two to his balls—a fan of five. His hand was still on his dick, obscuring most of the shaft, leaving the head visible. And just slightly out of focus, come was splashed across his torso, all the way up to one of his clothespinned nipples. I imagined the ocean smell, the way his juice was viscously dripping down over his bare flesh. And I shot off, hard and long, into Bounty, the quicker picker-upper.

"Thanks," I typed out, adding a smile: :-)

"No, thank you, Sir."

"What's your name?"

"Jason," he typed. Maybe it was, and maybe it wasn't.

"I'm Simon. I'll add you to my buddy list."

"And you're on mine," he replied.

"Gotta get to bed," I told him. "Thanks again."

"No problem. My pleasure. Bye."

"Bye." And I signed off, the computer saying *Good-bye* to me as well.

I finished wiping off my dick and used my right hand, the clean one, to click the mouse to shut down.

The base-level directory on my hard disk was still corrupted. I would be short of sleep the next day. Somewhere on the East Coast, a boy was wiping up and cleaning off his toys, and I would never see his face. The hard disk purred to a stop. The computer went silent. The screen went dark. I threw the power switch on the surge protector and headed off to a deep and dreamless sleep.

Dad's Boy

By Jerry Prince

I didn't mean to do it. I just couldn't help myself. There are times I get overcome by my own lust, and I just get carried away.

I was turned on when we finally met; he was my ideal of a "son" to my "dad." Though a little older than what you might conceive of as my son, he was nonetheless my ideal of what I want in a "boy." And add to that the fact that he was in total leather, matching my outfit, it was just a match.

We had chatted online so much about this first meeting. We each knew what turned the other on. He liked my cigars, and I liked his boyish good looks and attitude. And when we met and then kissed, it was that sort of "dream come true" event. That first kiss seemed to last forever. Not only were our tongues exploring each others' mouths, our hands were exploring each others' bodies.

Shortly he had my stiff, dripping cock out of my jeans, and he fell to his knees to give me one of those blow jobs you dream about. I was still smoking my cigar, and the smoke was about to fill the motel room I was smoking so hard while he hit all the hot spots. When he rose up and kissed me again, tasting my cigar spit, and me tasting that great cock-and-precome flavor on his lips, I was just too turned on. I had his belt loose and his jeans around his ankles before he knew what happened. And even though we were lip-locked, I could still get his cock out of his jockstrap and feel the precome on the tip of it. I rubbed the length of his rock-hard shaft and slipped my cock between his legs.

I guess it was the way he opened his legs to let my cock in that so excited me. I could tell he wanted it then, even though he had told me he was HIV-negative and didn't want any raw sex with a poz guy like me. I had my hands up under his shirt working his nips and was kissing and licking his face till he was just a puppy in my paws.

I gently moved him around, kissing his neck and massaging his ass cheeks, until I was behind him and nibbling his earlobes. That was when my stiff meat found his ass crack and set course for his asshole. I was pushing hard against him, trying to get my tongue in his ear, when he sort of fell against the wall and then braced himself against it with both hands, intending to turn back around, but by then I had a nip in each hand, having thrown down my dead cigar, and he was moving in response, enjoying it too much to protest.

My cock head had found his puckered rosebud of an asshole, one of those that seems to have an arrow tattooed above it and a sign saying FUCK HERE. I had him by the arms, holding him tight as I kissed and bit his neck.

"Oh, Daddy!" he kept saying over and over, as if he were trying to persuade himself not to resist. When I pushed and began to feel my cock head penetrate, he stiffened. "Daddy, don't make me do this, please," he pleaded, and he turned his head slightly toward me.

I reached around and kissed him. "It's gonna be OK, Son, just relax," I said, and I made a hip thrust that popped him open. I love that feel on my cock head—when you first pop a boy open like that. There is no feel like it in the world, tight and hot, and then so warm and wet and wonderful. I just couldn't help myself then. I drew him to me, hugging him tight, kissing all over his face and neck, so he didn't notice so much that I was impaling him on my cock. By the time I think he knew what was happening, he was fucked.

I had my cock almost all the way up his ass, and he was loving it. You could tell he was trying to fight the urge—but also wanting it so bad. All the time I was kissing him, I kept telling him it was fine: "You're all right." "This will be great." "Just relax and enjoy it, Son...give yourself to your dad."

Then suddenly he gave a kind of shudder and bucked hard back against me. "Oh, Daddy, take me, take my ass, make me your boy!"

"That's it, Son—enjoy this fuck. Feel your daddy's hard cock up your ass. Love that stiff meat so deep inside you!" He was with me then, meeting every thrust. When I'd hit bottom, he'd grab me hard and tight as much fucking my dick with his ass as I was fucking his hole with my rod.

"Make me your boy, Daddy. Fuck your boy. Show me how much you want me, Daddy!"

I was in the heavy strokes now, fucking his ass hard. My juices were flowing. When I get a hot ass like this, the first fuck is hot and heavy and doesn't take too long. I knew I was getting close. "Where do you want Daddy's load, boy?" I asked as I held him tight and humped him hard.

"Give me your load, Daddy. Make me your boy. Plant that load...*up my ass*!" He was bucking hard, and if I had really wanted to pull out, it would have been difficult, since he was in pace with me so well.

"Oh, God, Son, I can't help it...here it is.Take it, boy! Take Daddy's hot come up your ass."

"Daddy, show me how much you love me. Fuck me...fuck my ass. Give me your juice, Daddy. *Fuck me hard!*"

I lit into him hard then. I could feel the come move from my balls up the length of my shaft and begin to spurt out deep inside him. And I think he must've felt something, even though I know you have to learn to feel it when a guy comes up your ass. There was just something about the way he moved, like he was sucking the come up deep inside himself. We both hit the spot at the same time. "Oh, God!" we were both shouting.

"Here it is, boy...here's Daddy's cream. Take Daddy's load. You're *my boy* now!"

"Hit me hard, Daddy. Show me how much you love me and pound that jizz in my hot hole. Fuck me, Daddy. *Fuck my ass, Daddy!*"

I held him tight and shot my final spurts as deep inside as I could, knowing I was tying him to me in a way no man ever had before. I was converting him to my son in more ways than one. I was making him my boy in a truly positive manner. His ass drew up so tight on my shaft, I thought sure he must be spurting his load. His ass was sucking the come up deep, and he began to flex under me. I could feel his whole body moving as if he were absorbing the sex and distributing it throughout his body.

We held that position a long time. Sweat was dripping down my nose, and he was sweaty as I ran my hands over his chest and caressed his nips. I still had all my clothes on—my fucking cock out of my pants—but otherwise I was still just as I had been when I walked into the room. His pants were around his ankles, but he still had on the jockstrap, shirt, vest, and leather jacket. We both were soaked under all that clothing. But neither moved. We were still in that great Dad-Son connection, feeling the come that bound us together.

Shortly he stopped vibrating, coming back to reality, realizing what had happened. He sort of slumped at that point. I thought he might be crying, so I pulled out and turned him around and kissed him. He was crying. Or at least he had tears in his eyes, so I kissed the tears away, and he began to respond. When I put my hand down to his crotch, I discovered a jock hanging heavy with come. So I pulled off him, bent down, and sucked the come out of his jock, then I pulled his limp, gooey cock out and sucked it clean. He was breathing very heavily now, I think partly because of shock and partly because he was so turned on.

I got up, led him to the bed, and made him sit on it, so I could sit beside him. We kissed again then, another long lovers' kiss, and soon tongues and hands were exploring. Clothes began to fall off, some shucked off by the wearer, some taken off by the other. But our pants were trapped by our boots. We had reached that point again too quickly. The pants just had to stay on—we were at fuck number 2.

I got him into doggy position and stuck my cock back up his ass. It was much easier this time. He merely took a sudden inhalation of breath when I slid my cock home, deep inside him.

We urged each other on again, and soon he had come shot number 2 up his ass. Damn hot boy, he was. He wanted sex as much as I did. We seemed to be a pair, destined to be together. After I added that second load, I just held him close and told him how much I loved him, and he did the same. When my cock went flat and fell out of his ass, he rolled over, and I got on top of him so we could kiss and cuddle again. We took time to get the boots off, finally got our pants off, and we were naked, just kissing and rolling all over the bed, the way lovers do.

We came up for air and took a smoke break. It gave me a chance to really look at him, since I hadn't really seen him naked before, even though I'd planted two loads up his ass. And he did the same with me. I was surprised to see how he blushed when he noticed how I was admiring his boyish body. He had kept himself in great shape, and I had enjoyed it.

The smoke break over, we resumed the kissing, this time being able to be face-to-face for the first time. I didn't intend to fuck him again, but my cock just knew the way to his ass so well by that time that when I got on top and was kissing him, it found the hole and entered easily. He spread wide, put his legs firmly around my hips, and put his heels in my ass. Then he pulled in hard with his heels, making my cock really hit the good spots. Every time I made a stroke that didn't please him, he'd almost kick my cock up his ass.

I couldn't complain. I had my tongue far down his throat. And when I felt the come moving yet a third time, I got his legs up on my shoulders, shoved a pillow under his ass, and began those prying, deep strokes—where you aim for the boy's prostate and fuck him hard.

"Oh, God, Daddy!" he yelled. "I love it when you fuck me like that. Do it again, harder, deeper. Come on, man, put your seal on me—give me the third load and make me your boy forever!"

I got my arms up under his shoulders, pulled him into my fuck strokes, and kissed him hard as I fucked my come into his hot ass—so warm and wet and wild, filled to overflowing with my loads. I wanted to fuck him so hard that the come would flow out his hole and soak the bed. I wanted to fuck him so bad that he could taste my come from the inside out. I wanted to plant my loads so deep that he'd shit my come for a week.

It didn't take long. Spurts of daddy cream joined the prior

loads. My fuck piston planted its third shot, the come pooling around my balls, running down his crack. I pinned him down, legs against his chest, as I pounded the last strokes home, trying to get my come as deep inside him as I could. And he rose up against me on every stroke, making sure he got that jizz as deep inside as possible. When I was drained, I slammed a fuck stroke hard and held it, and he looked up at me with tears in his eyes again, and we kissed.

Then I felt his cock move between us, that steady pulse of a cock as it unloads its seed, a feeling I love. If I don't see or feel a boy come when I fuck him, I'm not fucking him right, and I had fucked this boy right. His cock spurted a heavy load between us, and his come between us and mine up his ass bound us together in many, many ways.

We kissed for a long time. It took us a while to come down off that fuck plateau, where you want to stay as long as you can. When I fell out of his ass, I let his legs down and sucked his limp cock into my mouth and sucked out all the strings of his come that I could get. Then I licked his crotch clean, keeping some of the come in my mouth so we could share it when we kissed. And as I did that, he moved around so he could reach my cock, and he sucked it clean.

When we kissed I could taste his ass, his come, and my come all mixed together—one wonderful taste, a taste every dad wants from his boy.

We fell asleep like that. When we woke the next morning, we were a mess, and the bed was a mess. There was come everywhere, crusted on our cocks and torsos. Time for a piss and a shower. Then we had a smoke and got to examine each other by the light of day. Sometimes that's when it all falls apart, when you come to in the morning and discover that the guy who was so great the night before is not nearly as attractive as you had thought. But there was no change that morning. I still thought he was the best thing I'd ever had, and he told me again that I was his Dad.

We went to breakfast, and it was as if I were meeting him for the first time. We sat there and smoked and drank our coffee and talked about all the things lovers talk about. The waitress finally asked us if we were going to order lunch, and we realized what time it was. We excused ourselves, left a large tip for having had such good service for such a long time, and went back to the motel room.

By the time we'd each had a piss we were on the bed again. The maid's knock interrupted our first fuck of the day. I shouted that we were still in the room, and she went away, and I planted my load. This was a lovers' fuck—that long, slow, gentle fuck of two men deeply in love. There was no hard thrusting, no pounding of a load deep inside guts. He was still moist from the fucks last night, and I wasn't really up to a hot and heavy fuck, but we needed to have sex again...to see if it was still there...and it was.

That wasn't our last fuck, not by a long shot, but those four were the ones that we always remember and talk about. Few men are as fortunate as I have been—to find a guy like this that fits me so well. I can only hope that he continues to feel the same about me.

Lasting Impressions

Having Hot Sex.com

By Trevor J. Callahan Jr.

My senior year of college—which frankly wasn't all that long ago—began on a definite high note. Our football team, on which I was star kicker (if a kicker can ever actually be a star), won homecoming for the first time in five years; my GPA was actually high enough to please my parents; and I started this torrid affair with an offensive linesman named Tommy Grinnell.

Tommy was about 275 pounds of hairy, hard, horny man with florid Italian features; big brown expressive eyes; and one hot, hung cock that, like 7-Eleven, was always open for business. God, for months the two of us sucked and fucked like two horny boy rabbits whenever and wherever we got the chance—in our dorm rooms, in the backseat of his green Pontiac Bonneville, in the third floor bathroom at the library, in the locker room after the game, and even one night underneath the scoreboard at the football field. And believe you me, there was a lot of scoring that night. Tommy liked nothing more than to stick his whopping eight-inch cock up my toned blond butt and plow me for hours, and, frankly, I never saw any reason to object.

I could have gone on like that forever, but unfortunately for me I was dating possibly the only offensive linesman in the history of NCAA football who was not only a great student but eager to go to graduate school. Tommy graduated in December, a semester early, and by January 3 was on the other side of the country at graduate school in Oregon. I knew it wouldn't be long before he found another hot ass to plug, but I still found myself sitting in my dorm room—or underneath the goalposts—pining away for the lost "love of my life."

I know what you're thinking: When you're young, these things seem much more serious than they really are. And you're right. But to me, losing Tommy was awful. Not only did I think I'd never fall in love again, but I wasn't even all that interested in cock anymore. January and February melted into March, and there I was, still pining away for Tommy, having gone two and a half months without even sucking on another guy's dick. And, frankly, it was starting to get to me. By the time midterms rolled around, I was as horny as hell, and I wasn't gonna take it anymore.

Of course, midterm exams and papers should have been more on my mind than cock, but nothing doing. I spent two weeks chasing after every hot guy I saw on campus. I didn't care if he was gay or straight or what—I just wanted to suck some dick! I took condoms and lube with me everywhere "just in case." But I kept striking out, and after repeated failures, reality hit me: I had two important papers due that very next day.

Normally, I would have been screwed. But lucky for me, my little college had a computer lab that stayed open 24 hours a day. I got to the lab right after dinner and hunkered down, knowing that only a serious all-nighter would pull me out of my jam.

I finished the first paper sometime after 1 in the morning. It was pretty good, and as I printed it out, I noticed that the lab was totally empty. *Figures,* I thought, as I headed quickly out to take a fast piss. I passed into the outer room, where the computer lab workers sit along with a whole other set of computers. The only person left in the lab was the night assistant, some redheaded kid who looked like he was sound asleep on his desk. I took my whiz, got a drink of water, and headed back, refreshed and prepared to finish my second paper.

Swinging past the lab assistant again, though, I noticed how cute he was. He was a short guy—and compact with nice strong arms and a broad chest. I recognized him vaguely; his name was Ryan, and he played rugby. I'd met him once at a party, and I remembered him being mostly shy and mumbly. His sleepy green eyes told me he'd rather be home in bed, but, hey, that's work study, right? I headed back to my paper.

Walking past Ryan, though, had stirred up the Mr. Happy in my pants. I felt my cock getting stiff in my jeans. *Fuck,* I thought, knowing I'd never be able to finish my paper while horny. I decided to give myself a minute to let it go away. I cranked up the Internet connection and checked my E-mail. After reading and responding to a few letters, I closed up my mail and found myself still pretty horny.

I sat in front of my computer and thought to myself, *Well, why the fuck not?* I glanced furtively side to side, and then I cranked up this hot porn site I know. Almost instantly cocks paraded before my eyes. God bless the Internet! I felt my own cock get stiffer in my jeans and slowly began rubbing it. God, the pressure of my hand on my cock felt so good, and there—out in the open where Ryan or security or anyone could catch me—damn, that made it feel even better. It got me pretty horny pretty fucking fast, and I found myself seriously contemplating whether I should just whip my dick out and jerk it off right there in the computer lab.

You gotta be crazy, Callahan, I thought. I knew that if I got caught I would be in deep shit, and besides, I still had that paper to write. Sighing, I was getting ready to exit Netscape when I noticed something I had never seen before. This Internet site had a chat function. I'd always heard lurid tales of Net sex, but I'd never actually done it. Curious, I clicked on the icon and was asked for my handle. Well, I was totally blanking, so I put in the name derived from our college mascot: RocketBoy. (We were, quite naturally, the Rockin' Rockets.)

Right after I clicked on the log-in feature a dozen or so names popped up before my eyes. I scanned them for any names really interesting: BigDickGuy, ReallyBigDickGuy, and HugeAssM*FingDick were a few I remember. One, however, really got my attention: HornyNY. Well, I was in New York, so what the hell? I sent HornyNY a message, and sure enough he responded almost instantaneously. We went into a private room and began to chat.

HornyNY: Hey, man, what's up?

RocketBoy: Not much, buddy, what's up with you?

HornyNY: My eight-inch boner. How about you?

RocketBoy: I'm pretty horny myself tonight.

HornyNY: Yeah? What do you look like?

RocketBoy: I'm 21, 6 foot 1, 175, blond hair, blue eyes, in great shape. I work out every day. What do you look like?

HornyNY: Dark hair, dark eyes, toned bod, ripped and cut, 26. Throbbing eight-incher. How big is yours?

RocketBoy: Seven, fully hard.

HornyNY: Nice. What do you like to do with that cock of yours?

RocketBoy: Whatever...I'm versatile. Suck, get sucked, fuck, get fucked—I can do it all.

HornyNY: I love to fuck hot ass. You got a hot ass?

RocketBoy: Yeah. It's a muscular, round bubble butt.

HornyNY: Nice and tight?

RocketBoy: Yeah.

HornyNY: Awesome. You want to get it fucked right now?

RocketBoy: Yeah. How?

HornyNY: What do you mean, "How?" Haven't you ever done this before?

RocketBoy: No, not really. Sorry.

HornyNY: Hey, that's OK, dude. It's kinda cool, actually—I got me a Net virgin. :-)

RocketBoy: Thanks. So what do we do?

HornyNY: We just type about what we'd want to do to each other. You know, like, *I want to suck your cock so bad,* and stuff like that. And while we type, we jerk. Got it?

RocketBoy: I can't jerk right now. I'm in a computer lab at school.

HornyNY: At 1 A.M.?

RocketBoy: I have a paper to write.

HornyNY: Anyone else around?

RocketBoy: Not really.

HornyNY: Then jerk it. Come on, it gets me real hard to think about you stroking it in some computer lab.

RocketBoy: Well, OK.
HornyNY: Good. Take it out.
RocketBoy: It's out.
HornyNY: Cool. I'm totally naked right now, hard and ready.
RocketBoy: Awesome. You sound totally hot.
HornyNY: So do you, bud. Ready?
RocketBoy: I guess so. Wait a sec. What's your name? Your real name, I mean?
HornyNY: Rico.
RocketBoy: I'm Trevor.
HornyNY: Nice to meet ya, Trevor. Now get on your knees and suck my dick, Trevor.
RocketBoy: OK, Rico.
HornyNY: Yeah, suck it, boy. Suck my hot, eight-inch Mexican dick. Yeah, how's that taste, Trevor?
RocketBoy: Awesome, Rico. You have such a hot cock.
HornyNY: Yeah, suck it good, man, and get it nice and wet, yeah. Why don't I just fuck your face a bit?
RocketBoy: Go for it, Rico.
HornyNY: Yeah, watch me pound this thick piece of cock meat in your mouth, buddy. Yeah, I can feel my balls slapping against your chin, man.
RocketBoy: God, that's hot.
HornyNY: Yeah, play with my balls, man...tug on 'em good.
RocketBoy: Yeah. Oh, fuck, Rico, you have the hottest cock I have ever tasted.
HornyNY: Don't I know it, man. They all say that. Hey, you wanna eat my ass out?
RocketBoy: Sure.
HornyNY: OK, then eat that ass out, Trevor. Shove your tongue up my crack and suck on that hole, man.
RocketBoy: Mmm. You have a hot ass too, Rico.
HornyNY: Yeah, lick it, man...suck my ass. You still stroking it, dude?
RocketBoy: Sure am. Totally hot to be jerking in the open like this. I am oozing precome like fuck already.
HornyNY: Me too, man, me too. Keep eating that ass out.

Yeah, fuck! Lick it, man! That feels good. You ready to get worked over now?
RocketBoy: You bet!
HornyNY: Turn around then, Trevor, and let me lick that hot ass of yours. Oh, man, what a nice piece of boy pussy you got.
RocketBoy: Ah, fuck, Rico, your tongue feels so good, man.
HornyNY: Your pussy tastes good, boy, let me tell you. Mmm, I could eat you all night.
RocketBoy: Go for it, man!
HornyNY: I don't think so, stud pup. I got something else planned for your hole, Trevor.
RocketBoy: You wanna fuck me, Rico?
HornyNY: You know it, boy. Bend over and prepare for Rico's rocket, buddy.
RocketBoy: Yeah, Rico, fill my ass with that huge cock, you stud.
HornyNY: Here it comes, man. I'm gonna shove it in fast and hard. Ye-e-eah!
RocketBoy: Fuck! Shit, man, your cock is so fucking huge!
HornyNY: Yeah, take it, buddy. Fuck, your ass is so tight! Yeah!
RocketBoy: Fuck me, Rico. Fuck me hard, man! Shit, I need to get fucked, man. Do it!
HornyNY: Yeah, you're taking my cock like a pro, stud. God, your pussy is hot. I'm loving it, man!
RocketBoy: Me too, stud!
HornyNY: How are ya doing, Trevor?
RocketBoy: I'm real close, Rico.
HornyNY: Do it, man—jerk that cock. I'm right with ya, buddy.
RocketBoy: Oh, fuck, Rico…man, I'm gonna shoot. Man, I'm gonna shoot!
HornyNY: Me too, buddy, me too. Do it…come on!
RocketBoy: I'm coming! Fu-u-uck!
HornyNY: Yeah, shit! Fuck, yeah! Ye-e-eah!

My cock was pumping a steady load of sticky, hot come. Jeez, what a fucking mess! I tried to catch most of it in my hand, but a couple of globs got away; one shot even hit the computer screen.

Sweaty and wiped, I took a couple of deep breaths and wondered what I should do now. God, that shit had been hot. But, man, I had a fucking mess to clean up, and I had better clean it now! I looked back at the computer screen and saw that HornyNY was long gone. Oh, well, I guess Rico was having the same problem I was.

I took out a Kleenex from my bag and wiped the computer screen clear. I shoved my cock back into my pants and somehow managed to zip them back up. But that huge load of come in my hand—what was I going to do with that? I could already feel it seeping through my fingers. I could always just lick it down, but that shit only sounds hot when you're still horny. I had to go to the bathroom and clean it off, but a trip to the bathroom meant having to walk past the lab assistant. And, gee, he'd probably think it odd that I had a huge wad of come in my hand.

Still, there was no other choice, so I carefully got out of my chair and walked toward the bathroom again. The lab assistant seemed preoccupied by something else, so I pretty much slipped past him unnoticed and managed to make it to the bathroom. I washed my hand good and cleaned the rest of my self up too and in record time. After all, it was almost 2 A.M., and I still had a paper to write. I ran back to the lab, feeling slightly less horny, ready to churn out another student masterpiece of complete and utter bullshit.

Walking through the outer lab, I could still strongly smell come. *That's odd,* I thought. *I shouldn't be able to smell come in this part of the lab. I was in a whole other room when I shot.* I sniffed my hand—smelled only like soap. That's when I noticed Ryan. He looked like he was busy wiping stuff up with some paper towels—the countertop, his hands.

Wait a minute. Wait just a minute! A smile crossed my mind as I realized what Ryan probably was doing. Looks like I wasn't the only one who got horny here late, I thought, heading back to my computer. Funny, though, what were the odds that we were both gonna be jerking off at the same time?

I stopped with a start when I realized just how small those odds were. I walked back over toward Ryan. He looked pretty red and flustered; I could see beads of sweat on his forehead, and there was a bulge in his jeans that still looked pretty solid. He looked up at me and, boy, did he look nervous.

"Can I help you with something?" he asked.

I stared at him for a full five seconds before I finally spoke: "Rico?"

His face completely and utterly turned white, and for a second I thought he was gonna lose it. But then a small smile came over his face. "Trevor," he said with understanding.

Boy, talk about awkward! You think you're gonna jerk off with some guy and that's it—only, it turns out that he's in the next room. And Ryan looked worse than I did.

"Big Mexican dick?" I finally said, and we both laughed.

Ryan shrugged. "Sorry," he said. "It's just that, you know, online you can be anyone."

I waved off his explanation. "I don't see what's so wrong with being just you," I said. And I didn't. He was really damned cute—with dimples and deep green eyes—and I tell you, the more I looked at his body, the more muscles I saw. The guy may have only been about 5 foot 6, but he was built, that's for sure.

Ryan turned even more red. "Thanks," he said. "At least you didn't have to lie. You look hot just the way you are. In fact," he said, his voice going really low, "I've kind of had this crush on you for a while. I just think you're totally hot."

"Really?" I said, surprised. It was one of the sweetest things I had ever heard anyone say. It's funny. I always drool over all kinds of guys, but I never stop and think that anyone might be drooling over me. Sure, maybe I hadn't noticed Ryan much in the past, but I was certainly starting to notice him now.

"I know it's kind of...well...dorky," he said. "Sorry."

I shook my head. "I think it's awesome," I told him. I laughed. "After what we just did back there, hell, I'm getting a crush on you."

Ryan lit up. "Yeah?" he said.

I nodded. "Sure. But let me ask you something. I know you don't look like Rico. But, well, do you fuck like him? I mean, is that how you like things to be, you know, in bed?"

Ryan nodded eagerly. "Hell, yeah," he said, grinning. "Why? Did you like it?"

I smiled. "A lot."

Ryan eyed me cockily. "Maybe we can make it come true sometime," he said.

I looked around the lab. "No time like the present."

That surprised him. "Are you kidding?" he asked.

I nodded my head. "Absolutely not. Come on, this place is deserted, and I'm ready to go again." And I was. I could feel my prick getting stiffer by the second.

Ryan seemed to be mulling it over in his head.

"Come on," I prodded. "I've got some rubbers in my bag. I'll let you fuck my tight ass." I turned around to make sure he got a good view of what he was considering turning down.

He didn't have to think much more. "Sure," he said, returning my grin.

I leaned over the counter, and we started to kiss. God, what great lips he had! Thick and wet. And he was a good kisser too—the right amount of torque and tongue. It took me about 10 seconds to realize I was in the hands of an expert. I relaxed, sat back, and got ready to enjoy the ride.

Ryan sat me in his chair, went to the other lab, and returned with my bag. After taking one more glance around the empty lab, he grinned, stood directly in front of me, grabbed the back of my head, and began to grind my face into his crotch. God, it felt so good to have another guy touch me after almost three months! I could smell both Ryan's sweat and his last load as he shoved my face into his bulge, rubbing my mouth over his denim-covered dick. It didn't take long for me to pull those pants down, and I knew by the telltale mesh fabric covering his cock and balls that he was wearing a jockstrap instead of underwear.

Ryan shrugged. "Ran out of underwear," he explained. "Now lick it." Eagerly I obeyed, lapping my tongue over the salty mesh until his dick got as stiff as a board.

Ryan's pants were around his ankles, and he quickly stepped out of them. I was intensely rubbing his incredibly firm ass with my hands, wondering just how big his tool was gonna get, when he gently backed my head off of his cock. He turned around, and there was his sweet, muscular ass right in front of me.

"Suck that hole, Trevor," I heard him say.

"Sure thing, Rico," I replied, and before he could he say another word, I plunged my nose right between his cheeks.

Damn, did he smell good! Sweaty and hot, just like a man should. His ass was sweet-tasting to me, and I licked that crack up and down fast, shoving my tongue in as far as it would go. I surely hoped he'd soon return in kind, but instead Ryan reached behind and grabbed the back of my head again. Holding it firmly in his hand, he began to rub his ass crack over my whole face. I just stuck out my tongue and let him move that sweet, hot butt over my eager tongue and face.

"Damn, Trevor, you slut," he said, "you sure do have a hot mouth." He released my head and whipped around again. With one finger he casually pulled down his jock and out popped his dick. "Let's see just how hot it is."

If there was one thing Ryan had been telling the truth about, it was his cock. It was a whopper: about 7½ inches long, thick, and fat, surrounded by a wild tangle of fire-red bush, and already dripping with precome.

"How does a little guy like you get a cock that big?" I asked.

Ryan grinned and said, "Just suck it." And I did, popping that hot redhead's hot head into my mouth.

I tasted sweat, grime, and precome as well as come from Ryan's previous load. "Mmm," I said as I slowly moved down his thick shaft.

"Suck me, Trevor," Ryan was saying. "Suck that big cock...come on, yeah."

I was about three inches from his pubes—planning to go no farther—when Ryan grabbed my head with both hands. "I'm gonna flick your face, boy," he announced, and then he shoved the rest of that shaft right down my throat. I gagged, but I recovered. And damn, it felt good to have my throat stretch with cock once more. "Yeah, fucking your face, man. Feel my balls slap against that chin. Damn, that feels nice. Suck me, buddy. Come on, suck that cock."

"Damn, Ryan," I said, coming up for air, "your cock is so

fucking hot!" I slid his dick right back down my throat and watched him as he pounded my face senseless. His balls were slamming against my chin, and he seemed to like that so I tugged on them and squeezed them some too.

"Yeah," Ryan said, "play with those nuts while I fuck your face."

I could tell by the way Ryan's legs were twitching that he was getting kind of close. When he sensed the come churning up from his balls, he yanked his cock out of my mouth abruptly. "Maybe you deserve some of the same, huh?" he said.

"Oh, yeah," I answered as Ryan slid to his knees in front of me. I took his shirt off so I could rub his muscular back while he worked my cock out of my jeans. God, it felt so good when it came out! Seven inches of taut, hard dick. Ryan slurped it into his mouth right away, and, damn, did he give good head.

He started by circling the top of my dick with his tongue, getting it nice and slick before trying to shove that tongue of his right up my piss slit. "Damn," I moaned, "that feels fucking fantastic." And it only got better as Ryan lowered himself onto my throbbing cock. By the time he got to my pubes with his lips, my toes were tingling, and I watched in ecstasy as his red head just bobbed up and down on my lap.

Ryan sucked me for a good 10 minutes, sometimes getting me kind of close before slowing down and backing off. I ran my hand through his hair and over his back, encouraging him the whole time: "Suck me, buddy. Suck that cock. Yeah, faster, man...take it. Suck that precome out. Fuck, yeah!"

"Take those clothes all off," Ryan said, surprising me. But I did, standing up and tossing my clothes into a corner. "Turn around," he ordered, "and put your leg up on the chair." I did just as he said, and as he leaned in to my puckered, sweet asshole, I could feel myself tingling with excitement all over. The instant his tongue hit my crack, I jumped in ecstasy.

"Ah, fuck, man! That's so fucking good!" I said as Ryan's tongue probed, licked, sucked, and flicked my hot, willing ass. He grabbed my hips and shoved his face as far as it would go into my crack. "Fuckin' A!" I yelped, loving every second his tongue was in my hole.

Finally, Ryan stood up behind me. I heard the condom come out of the wrapper and knew what was about to come. He shoved a lubed finger up my ass and whispered hot in my ear, "You want my cock, boy?"

I could only nod eagerly, gasping with pleasure as his finger worked wonders up my butt.

"Then beg for it," he barked.

"Please, man...come on, Ryan. Fuck my tight ass, please. I want it bad...please."

I could practically hear Ryan grinning behind me. His finger slid out of my butt, and he steadied himself behind me. I could feel the head of his whopper dick right at my hole.

"Brace yourself," he said, and then without another word, he shoved at least four inches of his dick right into my hole.

"Fuck!" I screamed in ecstasy, loving the feeling of this guy filling my ass with his huge cock. Another brutal shove, and Ryan's balls banged against my ass.

"You ready, slut?" he hissed, and I could only nod as Ryan began to plow my eager, willing hole with his huge throbbing cock.

Standing there in the computer lab with this redhead's enormous prick forcing itself up my ass, I began to suddenly feel very exposed. I mean, shit, anyone could literally walk in at any moment. And, damn, here I was getting fucked by this stud in the middle of the fucking room! But it only heightened my excitement to think of shit like that, and so when Ryan reached around me to grab my hard-as-rock cock, I knew it wouldn't take me long to come again.

"Oh, man, your ass is so tight and hot, buddy. Fu-u-uck, yeah. I can't *believe* how good it feels!" Ryan was ripping me apart, but I was loving every second of it, and so was he. And as sweat dripped from his forehead onto my back, I could tell we were both pretty close to blowing our wads.

Our moans and pants filled the still lab, and Ryan's hand began to jerk my dick faster and faster. "Fuck, man," I said, "I'm gonna shoot!"

"Do it!" he ordered. "Shoot your load for me all over the fucking floor!"

"Ah, fuck, yeah, Ryan. Here it fucking comes. I...shit!...I'm coming, man! I'm coming! Aah!" Glob after glob of sticky juice shot out of my cock and all over the fucking place. Ryan jerked me even faster to make sure he got every drop pumped out of me, and my cock tingled every time he rubbed his raw hand over the head in search of that last drop of jizz.

My orgasm caused my knees to buckle and my ass to spasm, and that was enough to put Ryan over the edge. "I'm coming, buddy! Here it comes," he shouted, "right up your ass!"

I squeezed my cheeks as hard as I fucking could. "Do it, man! Shoot up my butt!"

Ryan was panting hard now. "Fuck! Shit, yeah. Yeah, oh, fuck ye-e-eah. Ye-e-e-ss!" I could feel his cock jerking around as he tossed his load up my sweet hole.

We stayed like that for only another moment, savoring the feeling of just having lost our loads. Quickly, though, we realized we were naked in the middle of the lab, so Ryan took his cock out of my ass, and we started to clean up.

"That was hot, so fucking hot," he said as he wrapped the rubber in some paper towels and put it in the trash can.

"Sure was, Rico," I joked, ruffling his red hair and sorting out our clothes.

Ryan grabbed my tighty whiteys before I had a chance to put them on. "A memento," he said with a cocky grin.

I reached over and grabbed his jock. "Then I get one," I said. Ryan took the jock and wrapped it around my neck. I could smell his cock and come all over it.

"Until I come for it," he said.

I laughed. "*Come* for it, you mean," I said.

Ryan laughed for a second, then looked serious. "Uh, Trevor, do you think maybe, I mean, do you think you might want to do it again sometime?"

I smiled. I couldn't believe that the same guy who just a few minutes ago was plugging my ass in a public place and telling me to "eat his hole" was suddenly shy again. I reached over and snuggled my fingers into the red hair at the back of his head. "What time do you get off?" I asked.

Ryan shrugged. "Six," he answered.

I smiled. "Good. I'll be done with this paper by then. We can go back to my place."

Ryan looked somewhat skeptical. "I'll be real tired by then," he said with a hint of sadness, "and I've got class at 11." And he turned around to step into his jeans and zip them up.

I wrapped my arms around his waist from behind so that my crotch was against his butt and my mouth right up to his ear. "I think I'll need some sleep too," I told him. "I thought maybe we could sleep together, wrapped in each other's arms."

"Yeah?" Ryan asked, clearly perking up at the idea. "I've never done that before, not really."

"Well," I answered, "maybe you should get used to it."

Ryan wriggled out of my grasp, turned to face me, and wrapped his arms around my waist this time. "Maybe I should," he said. "Maybe I should at that."

Submission to the Editor... and Then Some

By Jay Starre

I am a writer. A writer of gay "erotica." In other words, I'm a gay porn writer. I was directed toward an editor who took submissions through E-mail, and so I decided to get online for the first time. Well-versed in the use of computers through my daily grind of writing, pumping out hot stories about men pumping other men, I still somehow had not made the time to get hooked into the Internet. This was the perfect excuse to get on the information superhighway.

I was guided by Greg, the editor I mentioned, through the E-mail world, submitting "attached files" and "rich text files," wending the highway of the Internet. There is one thing about editors: They are busy and tend to accept or reject without much feedback. But suddenly I was getting E-mails (a new experience in itself) with more than just a simple rejection or a contract.

E-mail from Greg: "Pretty hot, this one. But a little heavy on the adjectives—'His long, hard, throbbing prick dripped leaky, musky precome.' I think you could cut a word or two there. I liked the part about him licking butt hole. That was definitely exciting, but we can't use that in this safer-sex version, so it will have to go. And you should replace with a good finger fuck or something like that. Rewrite and return, and I'll take it."

I am accustomed to such explicit language; I write it all the time. But it seemed so personal in his comments, and E-mail is instantaneous. Like the phone, except you can say these kinds of things without actually speaking them. It was weird, but, I admit, from that first E-mail it was downright sexy. I was intrigued—this faceless guy, what did he look like? I was sending him such raunchy, intimate stuff. He was definitely getting a look into my psyche. But he was an enigma to me, except for his E-mails and his comments.

From Greg: "I was a bit put off by this one. 'His fat butt was up in the air, spread wide. I plunged my greased whanger between the big cheeks and reveled in the sensual feel of those giant mounds in my hands as I pounded in and out.' I don't like references to 'fat butt' or 'big' or 'chunky.' It makes me think the guy is fat and out of shape, a definite turnoff."

I wondered at that. I like all kinds of bodies; that was one reason I could write this porn stuff. Men are sexy to me, all kinds of men. And I did have a penchant for a nice, padded butt or a guy a little on the chunky side. But that was fine. I knew that editors had their preferences, and you just had to go along with them. I did wonder if perhaps Greg was fat and I had insulted him. My curiosity was further piqued.

So I sent him a story about a coach, actually using a close description of myself, and a hefty football player he fucks. As usual I submitted a couple of stories together, but I wondered if he would get the hint and comment on that particular story. He did.

From Greg: "Good story, although I don't like coach stories normally. I tend to find coaches dull and witless with nothing going for them except their physiques. Sorry, I know you are a trainer in a gym, and you aren't brain-dead. 'Tall with long limbs, short sandy hair, and a blond mustache, Trent's entire body was muscular, from neck to calves, but not grossly so. He kept in shape, but was not a fanatic. His cock was not a giant sausage either, although it suited his body in its substantial length. His butt was full but hard too. And he did have stupendous balls, swollen with seed where they hung down between his thick thighs. He smiled when he stroked his cock to erection, comfortable with his body, his sexuality. He looked like he knew how to fuck, not just how to play games.' I think of this guy as not a doughbrain and sexy as hell. The story was great sex; he spreads the football tackle's ass on a locker room bench, fucks him all over the floor and shower and in every position imaginable. It is exciting. But there isn't much else to it—perhaps a bit of a story, a conflict? Could they have an argument that is settled through the means of the fuck scene? Something like that. Rewrite and resubmit."

He liked the coach, which was a fair description of myself! All the better. I was still curious as hell about him but didn't want to ask outright if he'd describe himself. Why? Basically I am shy, and strangely enough I cannot talk aloud about sex without being uncomfortable. Perhaps that is why I write porn—as an outlet where I can let myself go completely. Anyway, enough of the self-analysis.

So I banged out a story about a guy, Jeff, who looked a lot like the coach character, except I darkened his hair and gave him a bit of hair on his chest; otherwise, he was myself again. This time I had him fuck the hell out of a character, a cop, who I imagined to be like Greg:

"Jeff lifted the hunky highway patrolman's large thighs and buried his face in his crotch. The tall bodybuilder sank his mustached lips over the hefty cop's swollen pole. Jeff reached up and took hold of each of the man's huge tits, squeezing the hairy pecs between his fingers, reveling in the thickness of the chest muscles. He loved having the huge guy sprawled out and moaning as he sucked both the jizz and the will right out of him."

Every word was a fantasy of sex with Greg. So off I sent it.

E-mail from Greg that very night: "Again a hot story. When Jeff finally sank his dick up the patrolman's asshole, I was practically begging for it myself. Nice climax building. Another thing, as I've mentioned before, the use of 'big,' 'fat,' 'chunky' puts me off somewhat. I am 6 foot 2 and well over 220 pounds, not all muscle by any means and with a paunch I hate, so I am a little touchy about references to 'fat.' I know you are a trainer and probably in perfect shape, but not everyone is. And once more, perhaps a bit of a story would help. I'm sending you one of mine from an anthology I did last year. Perhaps you can see what I mean from reading it."

Well, he had inferred I was a real hunk, and he was describing himself as less than perfect. But I liked guys with some fat on them, even big too. He sounded great to me. Then I read his story, "Bear Goes for a Ride." (Porn titles are not usually too creative.)

Excerpts from E-mail attachment with Greg's story: "Ted was a large man, hairy and powerful. His ass was a work of silken art, and when he raised it up above his seated lover, Lance eagerly ran his fingers through the dark curls of hair and squeezed the hard mounds as he pointed his twitching rod up into the warmth of the parted crevice. They both sighed when that pole slid into the hair-ringed pit of heated flesh."

Whatever the hell the story was didn't concern me, just that pole sliding up that hairy butt and imagining Ted was really Greg. I will admit that I read the E-mail about 11 at night in my home office with the lights out and the computer casting its soft glow. I was naked, my cock was hard, and I was stroking it while I read. When the characters climaxed, so did I, shooting jizz on my thighs, careful to keep the gooey stuff away from the computer keyboard. I'd just had my first online sex session!

E-mail to Greg: "The story was fantastic. I wanted to fuck that hot bear myself. I haven't really written about bears as such before. You have definitely given me ideas. Thanks."

E-mail from Greg: "There is a site on the Internet you can go to." Then he quoted the location address for me.

I had rarely used the Internet for other than E-mail since going online. I was just too busy. I spent eight hours or more a day at the computer yet found myself unwilling to expend the effort it required to surf that confusing universe. But I definitely wanted to see where Greg was directing me. I had the hots for him—in all ways.

So I found Bearmania on the Internet. Wow! Pictures galore of every manner of bear type. There were definitely the fat ones, many of them not exactly fit, but there were also hairy guys, chunky guys, big, muscular, dark-haired brutes too, with mustaches, beards, goatees, really just about every kind of masculine hunk. There was a chat line, lists of guys to meet, and links that I spent the next two hours following. I was amazed at all the gay porn sites, and I had just discovered the tip of the iceberg.

But it was back to Bearmania for me at midnight, exhausted

from a barrage of bright images and kinky Internet sites. I clicked through the gallery, wondering if any of the men looked like my fantasy E-mail partner. Before I went to bed I E-mailed Greg:

"Cool site. Lots of hot guys. Not everyone has to be muscle-bound to be attractive. At least that's what I think. Sexy is as sexy does! Thanks for the direction. You are always helpful, and I appreciate it."

I wanted to say "What do you look like? Can we meet? Can we fuck? I am mad for you!" But there was no way I would be that bold. For one thing, we had a professional relationship—he was an editor and I was a writer who needed him to accept my work. And one thing about E-mail: Distance does not matter. In the real world it does. He was on the East Coast in Boston; I was on the West Coast in Vancouver.

But things have a strange way of working out. He wanted some stories by the end of the month, and I E-mailed him this: "I am going to San Francisco the last week of the month. Can I send them to you when I get back?"

From Greg: "I have to go to San Francisco that weekend. Perhaps we could get together."

I stared at the computer. I was so excited, I was shaking. Then doubts assailed me. I had described myself as hot, and maybe he wouldn't like my looks after all. He had not indicated he liked my type; in fact, he didn't like coaches. He had not said anything about wanting sex.

Yet cowardice does not get you anywhere. I was going to meet him.

To Greg: "Can we meet in the Castro on Saturday afternoon? I don't know the names of any of the restaurants, but how about the corner of Castro and Market? It would be great to meet you in the flesh!"

I realized I had typed *flesh* only after I had sent the message. I fretted over the innuendo. After all the raunchy sex I had sent him, I worried about that one innocuous word.

From Greg: "Fine. See you there."

It was hot for the end of September in San Francisco. I was in shorts and a tank top; of course I wanted to reveal my shoulders and my tanned legs. I leaned against a storefront and watched men pass by—so many men, gay, hot or not, but men, men, men. I stared at them all. They must have thought I was very horny, which I was. I saw a few guys I imagined could be Greg—tall, handsome, dark-haired, and bearish. A couple of them grinned and winked, but they were not my editor friend.

Then I saw him. I just knew it was him immediately. He was walking down Mission about two blocks away. He was looking for someone—I could tell from the way he checked out the passersby—but I was across the street on the opposite corner, and he did not see me.

He was blond, which I had not expected at all, with a thick golden goatee that shone in the brilliant afternoon sun. He was tall. I'm six feet tall exactly, but he was that extra two inches that make a guy stand out, and he did, well above the crowd. How did I know it was Greg? I think it was his walk and the casual way he looked around. He did not hurry, and there was no swagger; he was an economy of motion for such a big guy. He wrote sparingly, and he walked sparingly. And he seemed nice, unaffected. It had to be Greg.

I crossed the street and walked up to him. He turned and saw me. He grinned at once. "I thought I'd recognize you," he said. "You're the spitting image of Trent from your coach story." His voice was soft and deep. His eyes were green. His broad face was sunburned pink above the blond goatee. His eyebrows were blond. He was the man of my dreams.

He shook my hand, his grip gentle but firm. "I didn't know what to expect," I said. "You never described yourself except to say you were tall." I laughed, staring into his eyes and mesmerized by his face.

"Are you disappointed?" He hadn't let go of my hand.

"Not by a long shot. How about you?"

He just laughed, genuinely, before letting go of my hand. "Do you want to go for lunch?"

We ate while I stared at him unashamedly. He was huge. His arms were giant with a furry swirl of blond over the forearms. His chest looked mammoth under the green T-shirt he wore. There was a spray of blond hair erupting from the collar. He exuded quiet power.

I was a blabbermouth of excitement. I wanted to get him in bed, and after a good hour of conversation I was on the verge of just blurting it out.

"Let's go for a walk down by the ocean," he said, forestalling me. It was a beautiful day. He had a car, and we drove down to the water. We walked for hours. He said that walking was his main exercise. He didn't really like running but walked everywhere.

The sun was setting and was brilliant on the edge of the ocean. He turned to me, his green eyes twinkling. He was grinning when he spoke: "Do you want to come to my apartment and have sex?"

"Whatever gave you that idea?" I burst out laughing.

We sat on the couch in his room, making out. He was big, bigger than me, which was a turn-on in itself. He kissed tenderly but not tentatively. He leaned into me and slid his tongue far into my mouth, filling me with slowly massaging flesh. I imagined his dick was like his tongue, then I searched for it with my hands. It was fat beneath his jeans, fat and swelling, not quite rock-hard but thick and meaty and getting harder as I squeezed it harshly. He moaned in my mouth, his chest rumbling against mine.

His hands were large too, and they clasped my back, down low, sliding lower, and then they were beneath my tank top and into the waist of my shorts. I had to unbutton my fly to let him in, and I did it willingly, gurgling around the steady tonguing he was giving me. His fingers slid down over my butt. He moaned appreciatively and clutched at my ass, then lifted me slightly and stuck his fingers deep into my crack, finding my pulsing asshole. He teased it, playing with the rim as he pulled apart my ass cheeks and lifted my hips up into his lap.

My hands were busy too. I fished out his dick, eager to feel it without anything between its heat and my fingers. It was fat, throbbing, and still not quite hard, which was exciting too. I imagined it growing even larger, and it did as I stroked it up and down.

Then we got into a wrestling match. We struggled on the couch, pulling each other's clothing off as he kept grabbing at my ass and I tried to get hold of his. Our mouths disengaged as we rolled around on the sofa, tangled in clothing, our dicks out in the air, mine as hard as a fence pole and his fat and bobbing at his belly. I got hold of his ass before I saw it, and it was big and plump and hairy—exactly how I loved them to be. I ran my eager fingers through the silky down that covered the cheeks, seeking the crevice between, but he rolled me on top of him while he pulled my pants and underwear down over my feet.

"Who is going to fuck who?" He grinned up at me, his breathing rapid. He wasn't so cool and calm now.

"I gotta have your big fat ass!" I smirked, gazing into his green eyes.

"For that insult you're gonna get a big fat dick instead!" His smile was crooked, but I could see he didn't really mind the teasing. Then he was on top of me, and I was on my belly. He was bigger than me, although I was the one with the years of weight training.

I didn't mind that either. I am ambidextrous and ambifuckable too. I can dish it out, and I can take it too, in other words. When he lay on top of me, all his considerable bulk burying me in furry flesh, I thrust my thighs wide and opened up for him. He buried that mammoth pole between my butt cheeks, poking and prodding all along the crack as he laughed above me.

I trusted him, even though I had only met him in the flesh a few hours earlier. I really did. I knew he wouldn't hurt me, and I knew he wouldn't fuck me without protection. So I wasn't surprised when he rose up and stood beside the couch. I remained on my belly and wiggled my naked ass as I turned my head and stared up at him.

"What a fucking hot butt! OK, muscleman, stay on your belly with your hard ass squirming like that until I get the condoms and lube. Then my love muscle goes up your tempting anal cave!" We both laughed at that, appreciating the joke. As porn writers, we were always searching for those exotic synonyms for *butt hole* and *cock*.

I watched him walk away. Man, oh, man, he was a big guy, and he was not fat; he was just large. His legs were big, like the legs of all men who have to carry around 220-plus pounds. They were trunks, covered by the swirl of light blond hair that also graced his hefty butt mounds. As he walked, those big cheeks pumped up and down enticingly. I actually groaned out loud and reached down beneath my belly to stroke my dick. I wanted to bury my face in those sexy ass cheeks!

He came back with condoms in hand and a bottle of exotic German lube. My eyes focused on his belly, which did protrude from his body a bit. But it was as sexy as his ass, a trail of hair snaking down from his furred chest to his crotch, where it joined the mass of blond curls surrounding his bouncing cock. That belly was lush, and I wanted to bury my face in it too.

He stood beside me with his dick right above my face while he rolled a condom over the plum head. It grew completely rigid as he stroked it and grinned down at me. "Can you take a fatso like this up your chute?" he teased. He rubbed it along my neck and laughed.

"Plow my aching love furnace with that battering ram!" I laughed back. But I was shaking. I was so hot to have his dick inside me. He continued grinning as he squirted that clear German love lube over the swollen head of his dick. It glistened in his hands, slick and huge.

He straddled me on the couch, shoving my thighs farther apart and placing his body between them. His hands grasped my ass, squeezing and pulling the cheeks apart. "You got a muscular butt, coachie. Let's see how good you are at exercising it. I want to see you squirm when I get my cock up your butt hole!"

He was spreading me apart and squirting more of the slick lube in my crack, his fingers digging into it and tickling my hole. He didn't put them inside, preferring to stretch the hole open by the rim and tease me.

It was too much, his joking and baiting. I guess he was getting me back for saying he had a big fat ass. "Fuck me, you idiot!" I shouted, half laughing and half gasping as I thrust up with my hips and attempted to get his wriggling fingers into my eager fuck hole.

At that moment I felt the blunt head of his cock poke directly into my lubed entrance. He had managed to heat me up to the point where I was ready for it. We both shoved, and half his cock plugged me in one plunge.

It was heaven. I felt stuffed. And then he lay over me, and I was engulfed by hot, hairy flesh. He used his hips to work his cock deeper, then deeper yet. I was helpless beneath him, except for the one fact that I could will my asshole to open up for the invasion. I did just that.

I took him all the way. He felt my surrender. "Good man, you take a fat cock like a champ!"

We began to giggle, the both of us, even while he rammed into me with less than tender enthusiasm. I gasped and laughed and shouted for him to "plow my sweet cavern," and he slobbered in my ear while telling me how he was going to "shove his enormous love bat all the way to my tonsils" between snorts of laughter.

It all dissolved in moans and grunts as he lost his wits and really fucked me. I could barely breathe as he did shove his enormous love bat almost to my tonsils. I managed to worm my hands down beneath my stomach and grip my stiff cock while he rode me to orgasm.

"Oh, yeah, fuck the man cream out of me!" I gurgled hysterically as I began to shoot.

He did. He kept up his assault right to the end while I shuddered and spewed uncontrollably. He slowed down then as my body's convulsions lessened. Then he sat up, his huge cock still in my battered asshole. While I lay there totally fucked out, he worked his cock in and out slowly for about five minutes. He grasped a cheek of my butt in each big hand at the end, squeezed, and then buried his cock to the balls as he unloaded.

"Yeah, coach, you can suck the juice right out of a guy with this liquid love hole!" he managed to say through his gritted teeth. I had to giggle helplessly at his words.

We didn't even bother cleaning up until round 2. We both had more stamina after having unloaded once. I got his legs in the air and got to bury my face in his delicious belly while I finger-fucked his butt hole. I got three fingers up there with the aid of that miraculously slippery German lube before shoving my rubber-wrapped cock to the hilt. His guts were warm and slick. I had him that way for a while, then had him on his hands and knees on the carpet while I took my time watching my glistening shaft disappearing and reappearing from his distended hair-ringed butt hole. His ample butt cheeks quivered with every shove, absolutely beautiful to my lust-filled eyes. That's how I came—with my cock buried between his ass cheeks. He spurted on the rug.

We had the night to experiment. He fucked me more times than I fucked him; it was a battle of wills I had to lose. After all, I was the writer and he was the editor.

Two weeks later, an E-mail from Greg: "Re: 'Big Guy Learns a Lesson.' Great story, but I think it would work better if the protagonist, the bearish stud, Dirk, ends up with his cock up the bodybuilder's asshole rather than the other way around. Don't you? Rewrite and resubmit."

What can you do? Besides, I can take a little criticism of my work, and as long as the editor accepts the story, I don't mind a rewrite. Especially when I may get a little rematch out of it as well. I'm planning another trip to San Francisco in the spring, and Greg says he can meet me there. We'll see who ends up on top then.

The Reunion

By William Holden

The night started out like most of my nights: get home from work, let the dog out, and continue my love affair with the computer. It's not that I'm unattractive or shy. I certainly keep a pretty active social life with my cyberfriends. But I just happen to live in a small, Midwestern town where the hottest place for gay men to meet is a patch of woods behind the baseball diamond in the local park. There are no gay bars where I live, and the closest city with anything like a "community" is three hours away. But I shouldn't complain. I have a lot of great friends, and I spend almost every night with them. What else could a man ask for?

That particular night I was online only a couple of minutes when the Instant Messages started bombarding my computer screen. It's amazing how you can actually keep six different conversations going at the same time.

"Hey, Kyle. How are you?"

"Not bad for a Thursday night." Ken was one of my best friends. We could chat well into the early-morning hours. I guess you could say that we have spent many nights together. "Have you found any prospective husbands?" Ken asked.

"You know me," I replied. "I can't seem to ever get one to call me. It's online chat or nothing for me."

"Well, you know those people on the East Coast," he replied. "They're pretty fickle."

"Yeah, yeah," I said jokingly to him. "I'm one of those East Coast men, and don't you forget it."

"I'm sure you would rather be chatting with a possible fuck for tonight instead of me, so I'll let you go. See you later."

"OK, wish me luck!"

As I sat there waiting for my friends to respond, I heard that old familiar voice: *You've got mail.* I opened my mailbox to read the message: "Hi, stranger. I bet you'll never guess who this is? It's been about six months, but I'll never forget what you look like. Those gorgeous blue eyes and blond hair that always hangs down to your shoulders. The way your smooth, hairless body shimmered on the beach in the warm California sun. I'm in a private room called Love Me, waiting for you."

My pulse perked up. Could it be Andrew? I couldn't believe that he would be looking for me after all this time. I quickly said goodbye to the friends I was chatting with and went to the private room.

"Hello?" I said with a bit of caution.

"Hi there, hot thing. Do you know who this is?"

"Not exactly." I told the truth.

"I can't believe you don't remember me! Let me give you a hint. The dance floor, you flat on your back, your legs in the air. LOL."

"LMAO. I can't believe it! Where the hell have you been?" It was Andrew, the man who opened my eyes to the gay world. I was with him for only six days, but those days hold some of the most memorable moments of my life.

"I'm sorry I haven't been in touch," Andrew said. "I was transferred to Germany for four months to open our new plant. I just got back to California two weeks ago. And you?"

"My life's been dull compared to yours."

"I have a way to spice it up," he said. "Like to have a visitor for a few days? My company is giving me extra time off. Can't think of anyone that I would rather spend it with than you. Besides, I want to see the hell hole of a city you say you live in."

"Great!" I couldn't believe my eyes. "When do you want to come?"

"Well, there's a flight that leaves tomorrow afternoon. If I can get a seat, I will arrive at the airport at 6:30 P.M. Can you take some time off of work next week?"

"If I have to," I said, "I can just call in sick for a few days."

"Great! I can't wait to see you again. I need to sign off and make my reservations. If there's a problem, I'll let you know. Otherwise, I will see you tomorrow night."

"OK. Have a good night."

After making my phone call to work, I decided to turn in for the night. I undressed and crawled into bed. As I lay there, my mind raced with thoughts of Andrew. In less then 24 hours he would be lying next to me. My cock twitched with the thought. I lowered my hand and began caressing the soft skin just below the head. My cock was fully erect within seconds. I gripped it at its base and began slow up-and-down movements as I thought of the night we met.

I had been online and in one of the all-male chat rooms. I wasn't chatting with anyone in particular, just following the conversations of the other people and putting in my two cents every now and again. The conversations were just heating up when I received an Instant Message: "Nice profile! What are you up to tonight?"

"Not much," I responded. "Just hanging around and checking out the rooms." I immediately went to view his profile. I never like chatting with someone without knowing their vital statistics. He was 28, three years older than me. He listed himself as 6 foot 2, clean-shaven, with black hair and brown eyes, a strong, muscular build, a hairy chest, 34-inch waist, and a very nice seven-inch cock—or so he said.

"Yeah, it's pretty quiet here tonight too," was his next comment. "Where are you? Your profile doesn't say."

"Indiana."

"Damn, that's a little too far to drive for a meeting. I'm in California. Do you at least have a picture for trade?"

"Sure. I'll send one." I waited for a few minutes to receive his mail and to also get his reaction to the picture of myself I had sent.

"You're cute!" he said. "By the way, my name is Andrew."

"I'm Kyle—and thanks. You're not bad yourself." Actually, he was gorgeous. He appeared to be sitting on a brick wall. His legs, which were crossed in front of him, were dark and well-toned. His smile seemed to be genuine.

"I wish you were here with me right now," Andrew said. "My cock is needing some attention tonight."

"I know what you mean," I told him. "The bulge in my pants is getting really uncomfortable."

"Well, why don't you do something about that?" he urged me. "If you're there alone, you can always take your clothes off. Then you can describe your body to me in more detail."

"Right now I'm sitting here in a white pair of briefs and nothing else," I let him know. "My cock is fully erect at seven inches, and there is a small wet spot on my crotch from the precome that's already oozing out."

"Oh, man!" he exclaimed. "That sounds so hot! Imagine my mouth on those shorts of yours, sucking that juice out of the fabric. Then I pull them off and lick that cock dry."

"Let me take my cock and rub that precome all over your face, teasing your hungry mouth with its tip," I replied, keeping up with his storyline. "Feel the heat from my rod against your forehead, moving slowly down to your cheek." I tore off my underwear and began jerking my cock. The precome was dripping down my left hand and making that soft, wonderful noise as it was squeezed through my fingers. My nuts ached. I couldn't believe how hot he was making me.

"Oh, shit, Kyle, you have gotten me so horny. All I can think about is that cock of yours in my face. I don't know how much longer I can keep this up."

"My hairy balls are begging for your mouth on them," I egged him on. "Come on, man; let me feel your tongue lick my balls. Oh, yeah! Swallow them whole." This was getting too hot. One hand was trying to type my fantasies to Andrew while the other was busy with my own meat. "Oh, Andrew," I typed to him. "I'm gonna shoot!"

"Oh, yeah, give it to me. Shoot that hot load."

"Oh, man!" That's all I could manage to type before my cock exploded. The first release of hot come hit the monitor and began sliding down the screen. The second and third landed on my keyboard. I squeezed my shrinking dick one final time to get the last drop of come out of my shaft. I had nothing to clean myself up with, so I began to lick the come off my hand. The taste of my own hot juice made my cock come back to life.

Completely unaware of what was happening on Andrew's end, I looked up at my monitor and saw his final words. They were blurred as I read them through my drying come: "I'm going to shoot!"

"Hey, Andrew." I got back to my keyboard. "Are you there?"

"Yeah, I'm here. I'm not going anywhere now," he said. "Damn, that was so hot! I can't imagine what it would be like if we ever got together."

"I would really like to meet you too," I told him. "It figures that I finally meet someone I like on this damn computer, and he's thousands of miles away."

"I know that we have just met, but how would you feel about flying out here for a few days?" he asked. "You can stay with me to cut down on the expense. That would give us some time to spend together. Who knows what might happen?"

"I would like to meet you," I told him truthfully, adding, "but I don't think flying out there is a good idea."

"Oh, come on," he said. "I'm not going to kidnap you. You can come out early in the morning; if you don't feel comfortable, you can stay at a hotel in town and leave the next day. What do you have to lose?"

The movement of my hand increased, and I began thrusting my hips to the rhythm I was pumping away at. Beads of sweat formed on my forehead as I continued my thoughts of Andrew.

My hand played with my damp pubic hair as I reached for my balls. I gripped them tightly, forcing myself to hold back. The blood in my cock had turned a deep purple as I jacked myself to within seconds of an orgasm. I pulled my legs up over my chest and opened my mouth, awaiting my release. My muscles tightened, and I felt the first wave of my hot juice hit my upper lip and drip onto my tongue. I continued jerking my cock and shot another four spurts directly into my mouth.

Releasing my cock, I scooped up every drop of come and licked it off my fingers and hand. My sheets were damp with sweat. Relaxed and contented, I put my arms up over my head; my thoughts remained on Andrew.

Andrew had been right back then. What did I have to lose? Within a few weeks I was on a nonstop flight to San José. As I entered the airport terminal, I looked around and didn't see anyone who resembled the picture he had sent to me. I stood there, not quite sure what to do next. I walked over to the wall opposite the gate and waited. As the minutes passed, my fear of being stood up grew. I had been on the ground for 40 minutes and still no sign of Andrew. I couldn't believe how stupid I had been to fly out to California to meet someone I had only known for a few weeks—and on the Internet. I guess that's what makes situations like mine so ridiculous. It's the risk involved that makes us continue to do these things.

"Kyle?" I heard someone say. I turned toward the strange voice and saw Andrew standing next to me. A nervous smile stretched across his face. His voice was deeper than I had expected. That same familiar smile I noticed in the picture made his face glow.

"Hi," I said after my eyes finished taking him in. "I was beginning to think you stood me up." I put my arms around him and gave him a hug. He returned the gesture.

"I'm sorry to keep you waiting," he said. "I was given the wrong gate information. Do you have any more luggage?" He reached down and picked up both of my bags.

"No, this is it," I told him.

"Great," he said. "Then let's get to my place, and we can decide what to do from there."

As we made our way through the crowded terminal, he placed his arm around my waist. It was strange for me to be so free and open in public. I was never one to hide the fact that I was gay, but walking arm in arm with another man is something that just doesn't happen in the Midwest—I mean, outside of Boystown in Chicago. We arrived at his house and put my luggage in his room.

"If you are comfortable with it," he began, "you can sleep in my room with me. If not, I have two roommates, and both of them are out of town for a couple of days, so you can stay in one of their rooms."

"No, I'm OK," I said, trying to sound confident. "Your bedroom is fine with me."

His room was open and spacious. A king-size bed was against the wall nearest the door. On the wall opposite the bed, there was a large stone fireplace. Sliding glass doors, which led to a small garden patio, made up another wall, . Hanging from the ceiling were dozens of large silver Christmas ornaments.

"I have to ask," I said, staring upward. "Why do you have these ornaments hanging on fishing line from your ceiling?"

"It's my own little invention to detect earthquakes," he said. "The ornaments are so light that the smallest movement in the earth starts them swaying. They've worked for me every time." He walked over to me, turned me toward him, and wrapped his arms around me.

"You feel so good in my arms," he said as he held me. "I'm glad you agreed to fly out here."

Since he was six inches taller than I was, my face fit nicely against his solid chest. It's funny that you don't think of that when you're reviewing numbers in profiles. He felt warm, and the smell of him filled my nose. His finger moved under my chin and brought my face to his. He leaned forward and kissed me gently. His lips were firm and moist. We looked at each other for what seemed like minutes. I was lost in the deep color of his eyes. I inched closer to him and lightly pecked at his lips; he kissed back. I could feel his heart beating against my body. He kissed me again; this time I felt his tongue begging to be let in. I opened my mouth, and our tongues met.

I had never been kissed so deeply before. His tongue moved over my teeth, my gums, caressing every inch.

"You're a great kisser, Kyle," he told me. "But maybe we should hold off for a while. How about we go out to dinner and then hit some of the dance clubs?"

It sounded good to me: "I am curious to see what the clubs are like in California. I can't even begin to imagine."

"Given what you're used to in Indiana," he replied, "I would say that you have quite an experience ahead of you tonight. I'm really glad that I'm the one you're sharing this with."

We ate dinner in a quiet Italian restaurant. Our conversation was smooth and easy. I couldn't get over how well we were getting along. We had many of the same interests. He loved to dance and told me a little about the clubs he was planning on taking me to. We discussed what we both wanted in life and what kind of men interested us. Before we knew it, it was well after 10 P.M. We left the restaurant and headed south to our first stop.

We arrived about 20 minutes later at an almost-full parking lot. The outside of the club was decorated like an beach resort. Wooden planks suspended on ropes led the guests from the parking lot to the screened porch. Even outside, the music was loud and inviting, the bass beating against my chest. We walked through the front door and entered a world like nothing I had ever imagined.

The bar was sexually charged. Men from all walks of life mingled and toyed with each other. The club broke off into three separate areas. To the left, we walked through a large open room. A bar stretched almost 30 feet. The other walls were lined with soft, plush couches. I glanced around, watching the other men. There was a three-way just finishing up in the corner and what looked to be several others in the beginning stages. My heart was racing with excitement. Andrew stood there watching my expressions. He put his arm around my waist and guided me over to the bar.

"What would you like on your first night in town?"

"Rum and Coke will do, thanks," I told him. I didn't want to stare at what was going on around me, but I couldn't keep my eyes off the local activities.

The drinks came, and Andrew motioned for me to get up, saying, "I want to show you the dance floor."

I followed him through a small door. The next room was full of hot, sexy men too. Their sweat-covered, shirtless bodies glistened as the lights flashed to the intense music playing from all sides. I stood there, my head filled with alcohol, music, lights, and smoke. It seemed to consume every ounce of my being. I felt as if the music was coming from within me. The feeling was overwhelming.

So overwhelming that I began to say, "Andrew, I'm not feeling real well. Can we..."

The next thing I remembered was waking up flat on my back in the middle of the dance floor. There was some strange man standing between my legs, holding my feet up in the air. There seemed to be 50 other men standing around, looking at me. My shirt was soaked with sweat. My body was hot, but I couldn't tell if it was from the heat of the room or from my own embarrassment.

"Are you OK?" Andrew asked with concern. He sat down next to me. "What happened?"

"I...oh...I'm fine," I muttered. "I can't believe I just passed out like that. It must be jet lag. It just hit me so quickly." I could hear voices of concern all around me. The bartender brought over a glass of orange juice and handed it to Andrew.

"You need to drink some of this," Andrew said. "Then we need to get you home. Do you think you can make it to the car?"

"I'm feeling fine now," I lied. I just wanted to get out of there. I finished my orange juice and slowly stood up. Andrew was right there, holding on to me. We walked slowly from the bar, down the wooden planks, and out to his car. The drive home was quiet. I sat, staring out the window into this strange city. Andrew kept his right hand on my lap.

I was feeling pretty embarrassed. "I can't believe what happened back there," I said. "I'm sorry to wreck the evening."

"Kyle, don't worry about it," Andrew said, trying to soothe me. "I just want to get you home. We have five more days together. There will be plenty of time for us to go out."

As we pulled into the driveway, Andrew insisted that I wait in the car until he could get around to help me out. I loved how caring he was being with me, and at that moment I believe that I actually could have fallen in love with him. He reached in the car and picked me up. He used his hip to close the door.

"Andrew! I am feeling fine," I said, amused. "Carrying me into the house is not necessary."

"I know, but your fainting makes for a good excuse. Besides," he said, "when am I ever going to have another chance to carry someone I met online into my house?"

"Gee," I replied, "that depends on how much cybering you actually do." I smiled as if I were joking, but I was curious how often he met people from the Internet.

He put me down at the front door. "Now that we're home," he said, fumbling for his keys, "I want you to get straight into bed."

Inside, we sat down on the edge of his bed, his hand in mine. "Let me help you out of your clothes." His words came gently. He knelt down in front of me and unlaced my boots. As he pulled my foot out of the first boot, the smell of damp leather filled the room. He pulled off my sock and rubbed my foot. His hands were so strong. The pressure felt good on my tired foot. His fingers worked the tip of each toe and then worked their way down my arch and over my heel.

I leaned back on my elbows and enjoyed his touch. He unlaced the other boot, sliding it off along with my sock. I thought he would start massaging that foot like the other, but instead he kissed each toe. His tongue caressed the soft skin under each joint. At that moment I noticed the first sign of life coming into my cock. I watched as the bulge in my pants grew.

"Andrew," I whispered to him, "that feels so good."

"Just lie back and enjoy it," he urged me, letting my foot fall from his face as he climbed up my body. When his face was next to mine, he looked into my eyes and said, "I can't help myself tonight. I want to be with you." Then he kissed me full on the lips.

He kicked his shoes off and rolled to the left of me. I began to unbutton his shirt and noticed for the first time the thick, dark hair that blanketed his chest. I wondered how I could have missed that in the photograph. I fumbled around for the remaining button and threw open his shirt. His nipples were dark and inviting. I brushed my tongue across one and then the other. Andrew's body shivered at my touch.

I pulled his shirt off. My hands held his arms over his head. My tongue massaged the soft tender skin of his armpits. The smell of his hairy pits brought my cock to full attention. I washed his sweaty pits with my tongue, licking and cleaning every inch. He pretended to struggle under my hold, but I could tell he loved the sensation. I raised myself up, sat on his stomach, and pulled my shirt off. His hands were on me instantly. The strength of his hands left red prints on my chest as he squeezed and caressed me. I leaned over and kissed him, slowly bringing my mouth down his neck. I could feel the stubble of his beard against my lips. I continued my downward movement, ignoring his nipples and heading straight down his stomach to stop and caress his belly button. I moved lower and grabbed hold of the center of the waistband of his pants with my teeth; the button snapped easily. I ran my tongue over the zipper, feeling his swollen rod, which lay just beneath the fabric of his clothes. Seizing the tab with my teeth, I slowly started to unzip his pants.

The front of his underwear was damp with precome. I could see his cock head pushing at the material, struggling to be let out. I slid off the bed and stood between his outstretched legs. I pulled down on his jeans, bringing his underwear down right along with them. His body was nearly perfect, much better than what he advertised in his profile. Every muscle was well-toned and covered by a thin layer of hair.

I stripped down to my underwear. The head of my cock poked out of the waistband. The tip was covered in a thick, shiny layer of precome.

I crawled up between his legs, running my tongue up one thigh and into the dark crevice of his crotch. Andrew arched his back as I made my way down below his low-hanging balls, circling the area just below his ass with my tongue. I pushed his legs up to his head. His ass was in perfect view. His tight, puckered hole was pink at the innermost point but was soon hidden in the dark patch of hair that covered his crack. I lowered my face to his ass and ran my hot, wet tongue down his slit. His body convulsed as my tongue hit his fuck hole. I stopped and toyed with him a little longer—gently tonguing his hole, then blowing my warm breath against it.

"Oh, man, Kyle, that feels so good," he said and sucked in his breath. "Keep it up. I don't want you to stop."

Ignoring his wishes, I continued past his hole and back toward his balls. I placed both of his hairy nuts in my mouth and began to massage them with my tongue. I could feel the hair of his balls getting tangled together with my saliva. I released them slowly, one at a time, enjoying the texture and shape as they slid out of my mouth. I returned my attention to his ass. He was flexing his ass muscles: getting tighter, releasing, tighter, releasing. What would it feel like to have that talented ass of his working its magic on my cock?

"Do you want that ass, Kyle?" he said, basically reading my thoughts. "I see you watching it."

"Yeah, I do," I told him firmly. "I want to shove my cock deep inside and fuck you."

He reached over to the nightstand and brought out a box of condoms and some lube. I opened up one of the packages and slowly unrolled the condom down over the damp, swollen head of my cock. I could tell Andrew was getting really turned on by this act. The condom seemed to intensify the look and size of the bulging veins that covered my thick shaft. I turned the lube upside down, high above his ass, and let it slowly drip down into his hole. His ass muscles tightened as the cold wetness of the lube touched his hot puckered skin. I rubbed the lube all over his ass and then applied some to my cock. He held his legs firmly in the air, giving me a perfect view of his ass.

I watched as the head of my cock first touched his butt. His hole responded to the first sensations of being invaded. I placed a little pressure on him and could feel my cock head slowly entering his dark cavern.

"Kyle, you're so big!" Andrew blurted, seeming a little taken aback.

That's another thing you don't quite allow for when you're online. It's one thing to read the numbers and another to have them inside you. He licked his lips, anticipating my next forward thrust. I leaned into him and felt his ass give way to the entire length of my rod. The warmth of his ass was incredible. I slowly moved around inside of him, brought my cock up and down against the walls of his hole.

Then Andrew's readiness was apparent. His muscles began to grip my rod with enormous strength. It felt as if my cock were going to be squeezed in half. And he half yelled, "Come on, man, fuck me!"

I raised myself up and brought my cock almost completely out of his ass, then shoved it back in. I continued my in-and-out movements, each time increasing the force of the downward thrust. Every time I pulled out, his muscles contracted, applying the most incredible force along my shaft. Then he released his muscles as I pushed in. Our rhythm was magical, his muscles expanding and contracting with each and every thrust of my hips. Sweat began sliding down my body onto him. It glistened in his hair from the small light on the nightstand.

But I couldn't keep the pace up, not with that intense feeling, and I shouted, "Oh, Andrew, I'm going to come!"

"Yeah, man!" he screamed. "Pull it out, and shoot that hot load all over my cock."

I pulled my throbbing shaft out of his hot ass. It came out with a wet smack. I pulled off the condom, grabbed my pulsing cock, and began jerking it violently. Within seconds I felt total release building from deep within me—deeper than ever. The first stream of come landed on his chin. I watched it drip down his neck. I aimed my rod downward, forcing the final four or five shots to cover his cock and balls.

"Your hot come feels so good on my cock," he cooed, foretelling how close he was to climaxing.

I continued stroking my cock as he smeared my come over his own, using it as a nice lubricant. He held his cock at the base and began thrusting his hips up and down. The head of his dick was a deep purple—the pressure was about to release. He pulled his cock backward, then thrust his hips through his clenched hands, showering me with his hot juices. I rubbed his warm come all over my sweat-dampened chest and stomach. I lay down next to him and fell asleep in his arms.

I looked at the clock; it read 3:15 A.M. I had not slept at all. My mind would not settle down long enough for sleep to take hold. My thoughts were on Andrew, of course. That trip had been one of the most exciting times of my life. I won't have the bars or gay nightlife to show Andrew when he arrives tomorrow, but I don't think that's going to be a problem. We both know what it was like that first five days together, and now after six months of separation, I can only imagine what the next few days will bring.

Home Is Where the Heart Is

RumpRider

By Joel Valley

December 4, 1998. That was the day I bought my computer. I had used a PC at work for years, but I wanted my own at home in order to pursue an interest in creative writing. At work I used word processing, spreadsheet, and database software; however, E-mail and the Internet were unknown to me. For home use I required a basic model for word processing and little else. I was thinking cheap but upgradable. I tried to keep that in mind when I entered the computer store in Liverpool, the city where I live. What I actually ordered was the most expensive, top-of-the-range model in the store. What can I say? The salesman was cute! It was delivered the following Saturday. Within a few hours of its arrival, I was on the Internet and in my first gay chat room.

Of course I'd heard of cybersex, or E-sex, and chat rooms, but I never really took much notice until then. I had a vague understanding that the Internet had been originally created by the U.S. military but was now being used by some people to circulate pornography and by others to chat and interact with each other. I'm not a technophobe, but I had no comprehension about how it was done.

Friends talked about guys they'd met on the Internet, and if I'm honest, I thought myself above them. I maintained a kind of prudish snobbery. Meeting people on the Net was impersonal, remote, and unsexy, wasn't it? I'd much rather meet a guy at the baths, in a park, or in a bar. Meeting people in real life lets you at least see what they really look like: You can weigh them up, get to know them a little. This Internet really wasn't for me, right? Wrong! The minute I tripped into that first chat room, I was intrigued. I immediately adopted my nickname, RumpRider.

What I had never considered was the fact that the Internet lets you be direct—blatant even—about sex and what you want. I'm a top (well, 90% of the time anyway), and in real-life situations, as Joel, I was never really able to be as up-front as I would like to have been; call it my English reserve if you like, but as RumpRider, I was totally to the point. I liked fucking ass and said so.

After some experimenting, searching, and lots of chatting, I discovered that I preferred chat rooms that allowed for a profile as well as a nickname. While a nick can make a guy's proclivities obvious (FukMe, Sucker, TopGuy, Scatman), a profile adds further detail and ensures less time is wasted in finding the guys you are really looking for. It makes things so much easier. I like fit, 30-something guys. All I had to do was check out the list of nicks in the chat room and single-click on any that sounded interesting (HotBtm35, FukMe37, etc.) to check their profiles. If the profile seemed worthy of interest I would double-click their nick to chat privately. Similarly, any guys could do the same to me if they liked my nick and profile (36, 30w, 39c, 5'8", 150 lbs, 7 uc, gymed body, hairy ass/legs, brn hair/eyes, iso btm guys, pref 30s). If the chat was horny or I just wanted to know what they looked like, I would swap pictures with them. I got a digital camera with the computer, so I took a series of G- and R-rated photos for that specific purpose.

I would sometimes get off just by chatting and viewing their pictures—what I see as cybersex. Otherwise, I would exchange phone numbers and have phone sex. After a little while, however, both became increasingly boring. I mean, having to type with one hand and try not to come on the keyboard was a real pain in the ass! Cybersex and phone sex, while having their merits, can't replace skin on skin.

At this point I need to mention that I was (and still am) in a long-term relationship. At that time we'd been together for eight years and, as now, the relationship was supposedly monogamous.

Cybersex meant that I never felt like I was cheating, but it did nevertheless whet my appetite. However, since I was in a relationship, I made sure that I chatted with guys outside my hometown. I didn't want to be found out, after all, and, as I said, I knew a lot of our friends regularly used the Net.

Sometimes I chatted with guys in other parts of Britain, and on occasion in other countries and on other continents. Over time I came to predominantly chat with guys in the northwest of England. This was because the northwest (mainly the Manchester area) was far enough away for guys to be interested in me without being too close for comfort. Generally, interest in chatting declines in direct proportion to the distance separating those concerned. While I could lie about where I lived, I found that it was more exciting not to. There was always the possibility that we could meet and fuck.

I eventually got to the point where I arranged meets with a whole list of guys. I never showed up, though (sorry about that, GoodFuk, Gee, FukULike, TiteHole, and anyone else I stood up). I was full of enthusiasm when online, but as soon as I logged off, my hard-on sagged under a wave of guilt. This continued into early summer—when things changed.

I was chatting to a bottom guy in the Manchester chat room one evening. He suddenly invited me to a sex party in London. He told me that the party was organized by two of his friends and E-mailed me a collage of pictures, maybe 30 in all, showing the guys who would be attending together with the E-mail address of the organizers. The collage and the thought of an orgy was such a turn-on that it is hard to describe. For two weeks I used that collage as jack-off ammunition. I became obsessed with the thought of it. All those men, all that ass, all that action. I was interested in the majority of guys in the pictures—they were all seemingly fit 30-somethings—but particularly two hunky guys that appeared together in one picture. They were obviously a couple.

Eventually I could stand it no longer, so I E-mailed the organizers with my photo. By that time the party had come and gone, but I received an E-mail stating that they liked my photo and that I should get in touch if I wanted to meet them. I E-mailed back that I was interested, and they sent several hot pictures.

Guess what? That's right. They were the two guys I fancied. In addition to the pictures, they supplied their phone number.

I remember sitting in front of the screen, literally in shock. These things rarely ever happen to me. Here were these two hot, hung, and hunky guys, Gerry and Harry, who wanted me to fuck them both. I literally came in my pants as I read the E-mail. They gave their stats: Gerry, 41, 5 foot 10, 200 pounds, eight uncut inches, brown hair and eyes; and Harry, 36, 6 foot 1, 190 pounds, nine cut inches, and brown hair and eyes. I phoned them then and there.

Gerry answered the phone, and I stuttered my way through an introduction.

"Hi. Th-th-this is Joel. I j-j-just got your E-m-m-mail."

Gerry soon put me at ease. He had a low, sexy voice. I was honest about my partner's existence, and he was thoughtful enough to warn me about how I might feel about any infidelity. I explained that we had an "If I don't know about what you get up to behind my back, I won't get hurt" type of relationship. I chatted about what I liked—fucking, sucking, jacking off, rimming, poppers. "I'm Mr. Vanilla," I explained.

He asked, and I told him about my favorite positions: doggy-style; having a guy sit on me; fucking over the corner of a bed. He explained that he and Harry were versatile and that I could fuck both of them, one after the other, all night long if I cared to pay them a visit sometime. I said I liked the idea of a daisy chain, and he said that was fine too. Hell, he could even get a few other guys to come along if I wanted! I threw a boner. The thought of other guys was a turn-on, but I decided that, initially at least, it was better to meet just the two of them. I presumed that the more bodies around, the more nervous I would feel. I'd never had a threesome before, never mind any other multiples. We arranged to meet the following Saturday.

I'm a rarity—a 30-something who doesn't drive—so I bought my train ticket the next day. I told my partner I had to go away on business for a few days. He didn't doubt a word. On a warm Saturday afternoon in May I arrived in London. I phoned Gerry and Harry to announce my arrival, and they duly met me at the station.

My first impression was that they were big, buffed guys, bigger than I imagined. I initially felt that despite the exchange of pictures and the phone conversation, they wouldn't want me. That wasn't, however, conveyed in their greeting, which was warm and sincere. After the initial recognition—I'd informed them that I was wearing black 501s and a khaki jacket—we shook hands, hugged, and introduced ourselves. My delight was so great that I would have kissed them, but it was an unknown place, the street was busy, and I felt nervous already. Having a homophobe confront us was the last thing that I wanted. After a few brief questions ("What was the journey like?" "How are you feeling?" and "Are you ready to go?") we headed for their vehicle. As we walked along we smiled at each other, and I realized that they were as nervous as I was, which was reassuring. I also got a proper look at each of them.

Gerry, the hunkier and older of the two, had short dark hair, slightly longer than in his picture and graying at the temples. He had broad shoulders and big biceps. Harry was the younger and sexier of the two. He was taller than Gerry, had short fair hair, and was leaner. They both had light but noticeable tans.

Since it was a warm day, they wore T-shirts and khaki shorts. They both had muscly, well-shaped legs. Harry in particular had a firm, round ass, which I stole glances at as we walked. I recalled that although both of them were versatile, Harry was more often the bottom when they fucked together. It was difficult concealing the boner in my jeans. After a few minutes' walk we arrived at their Jeep. I hopped in after them. They sat in the front; I sat in the back. We didn't say much on the journey to their place. Harry drove, and Gerry occasionally criticized his driving, which I found amusing.

Several minutes later we arrived at the town house where they lived. Gerry jumped out of the Jeep and disappeared into the kitchen while Harry showed me to the bedroom. He helped me find a home for the small bag of clothes and toiletries I had brought with me. He explained that there was a spare room "in case things got too much" or I wanted to sleep alone, which was considerate of them.

I sat on their huge double bed, and Harry sat down beside me. I had a raging hard-on, and he started to stroke and caress me through my jeans. I trembled with desire but felt awkward because I felt that Gerry should have been there.

"What about Gerry?" I asked as Harry unbuttoned my fly and put his hand into my 501s.

"He'll be here shortly," he said and leaned over to kiss me.

Still trembling, I lay back on the bed. Harry undid my trousers, pulled my dick out of my Calvin Kleins and put his mouth around the head of it. I heard Gerry's footsteps on the stairs. I closed my eyes. As Harry worked on my cock, I suddenly felt Gerry's warmth next to me. He kissed me on the side of the face and began unbuttoning my shirt. He ran his big hands across my chest, gently rubbing my nipples with his thumb. I turned to face him and opened my eyes. We kissed, exchanging hot breath and sweet-tasting saliva. Harry began to work his mouth up and down the shaft of my cock a little vigorously. My body tensed. I sat up slightly and gave an involuntary sigh. I leaned forward and lightly pushed Harry's head away from my groin.

"Not so fast—I'll come," I said.

"OK," he said. "Shall we strip?"

Both stood up and stripped naked. They had great bodies, as I knew already from their pictures. Gerry was moderately hairy, a feathery, dark-colored fur covering his arms, chest, and legs. As he bent down and removed his white briefs, he revealed a firm, pale, hairy ass. Harry on the other hand was smooth. His tan was less pronounced, but he, like Gerry, had a visible tan line above and below his cute, well-formed ass.

"You both work out," I said, removing my CKs.

"No," Gerry said, "we just fuck a lot."

My seven-inch dick was small compared with theirs. Gerry's erection was particularly impressive, his thick, uncut dick having a large, almost mushroomlike, purple head. "Nine cut inches" was no exaggeration. His balls were huge too. Although Harry was taller, his dick was shorter and thinner, in fact, not much bigger than mine.

We stood nervously looking at each other a moment before we fell back onto the bed. They immediately began kissing me all over—face, mouth, neck, back, nipples, abdomen, ass, legs, sides, balls. They eventually settled on my dick, each in turn taking it in his mouth. Hands caressed my chest, stroked my nipples, traced my sides, and kneaded my ass. I closed my eyes, and one of them took control of my cock, sucking and slurping at it.

I heard a drawer being opened and something being removed. The mouth left my cock, and after a moment I felt breath at the side of my face. I opened my eyes to see Gerry wink at me before kissing my lips and nibbling the side of my face and neck. I felt cool lube applied to my cock by a firm, warm hand that caressed the glans, making me squirm and sigh. Harry withdrew his hand a moment, then expertly sheathed my cock in a condom. I looked back at Gerry, who leaned over and started to tease one of my nipples with his tongue. I then felt Harry straddle my waist and my cock enter the warm pit of his ass. I lifted my head to see him sitting astride me.

"Like that, do ya?" he said.

"Yeah, too right I do," was all I could think to say.

Harry began to slowly ride up and down on my rigid cock. I placed my hands on each hip and pushed my cock farther into him. He smiled down at me. Gerry got to his knees and kissed Harry. They embraced and exchanged wet, sloppy kisses for a little while as Harry slowly rode my dick. They unlocked, and Gerry leaned down to place his lips on mine. I sighed as Harry's rocking quickened. As he rode my dick, I thrust my hips up, driving the head of my cock deeper within.

Harry said, "Ah, I like that."

"Go on," Gerry said, "fuck him."

I didn't answer, just smiled back and carried on fucking Harry's accommodating hole. He started to buck faster, and the force of my cock ramming into him increased. Harry was soon literally jumping up and down on my hard rod. I grabbed his hips and thrust up as he brought his ass down against me. The pace got faster, then frantic.

"I'm gonna come," I was barely able to say.

"OK," he said. I took control, grabbing the cheeks of his arse, pulling them apart, and ramming my cock deeper still within him. I thrust as hard and fast as I could and seconds later erupted inside him. As my body crumpled under him, Harry began to jack off, quickly coming in a gush of milky, warm juice.

Meanwhile, Gerry was on his knees, stroking his prick vigorously. He moved toward me, and I joined Harry in licking his huge balls as he stroked himself to fruition, coming over my face and chest.

Harry climbed off me. Using several tissues from a box on the bedside cabinet, he cleaned the sperm off me.

"Thought you were gonna fuck me too," Gerry said.

"Sorry," I replied.

"There's always later," Harry pointed out. "Let's shower, eh?"

Harry and Gerry kissed me, then each other. Hand in hand they disappeared into the bathroom together. I lay on the bed and drifted into sleep. I awoke hours later to Harry's voice.

"Wake up," he said. "Dinner's ready."

We ate steak, salad, and potatoes and chatted for a little while before watching TV for several hours. It was 1 A.M. when we eventually went to bed. I was totally beat despite my earlier sleep. Gerry intimated that he wanted to be fucked. Both Harry and I took part in kissing, caressing, and fondling him, but Gerry soon sensed that he was the only one who wanted sex. He seemed disappointed but acquiesced. I fell asleep between them.

When I woke there was only Harry in bed beside me. I could hear Gerry downstairs in the kitchen. Harry was also awake. He snuggled up to me and then reached down to grab my cock. We kissed and in a matter of seconds had embarked upon another fucking session. I fucked him face down on the bed. I was conscious of Gerry's presence downstairs; he whistled while he cooked breakfast. The sex was hurried but exciting. I feared that Gerry might return and catch us. Our fucking seemed wrong without the participation of Gerry. I don't know if Harry felt the same; I never asked. I came in what seemed hardly any time at all. Harry got up and showered. When he vacated the bathroom I entered, then dressed.

We ate breakfast in silence. I wasn't sure if Gerry was annoyed.

"Is everything OK?" I asked. Gerry looked completely baffled. "It's just so quiet," I explained.

"Everything's fine," Gerry replied. "We're not big talkers in the morning." That seemed to be the truth.

After breakfast I traveled to the local garden center with them where I helped to pick some garden furniture—a bench, a table, and several large terra-cotta pots. It was a typical suburban Sunday with lots of hetero couples picking through the shrubs and plants of the garden center. As I watched them, I felt like some kind of revolutionary. I suppose gay men are sexual revolutionaries. I wondered what those respectable heterosexual families would think about our fucking the previous night. How would they react if they knew that each day thousands of gay guys met and fucked as a consequence of the Internet? As we wandered around, no one gave us a second glance, which took the drama away from my thoughts.

I helped carry the items of furniture to the Jeep and then we drove to the train station. We said our farewells in the Jeep. I kissed and hugged Gerry, then Harry. I felt unexpectedly sad. Three and a half hours later I was home. I phoned to say thanks and inform them that I had arrived safely, as Gerry had insisted I do.

We still keep in contact, exchanging the odd E-mail and phone call, but we have not met again. I definitely intend to visit them in the fall, and although we have talked about it, we have not set a date. They have had several sex parties since May, but I haven't had the nerve to attend any. One day, maybe.

My relationship with my boyfriend seems to have perked up in the meantime. We have better sex and get on better generally; the boredom is less evident. I'm not saying that the sex with Gerry and Harry is the only reason for this. Ours, like any relationship, has its ups and downs, but I do feel that it has nonetheless contributed something.

Since May I have not, as I thought probable, met any other guys through the Internet. In fact, I have not been frequenting the chat rooms very often at all. This is largely because I have been busy writing—this piece among many others. The computer is unexpectedly serving its intended purpose after all.

Roger, the Trucker, and Me

By Donny Buckman

My boyfriend, Roger, is a workaholic. He's an architect, and if he gets home before 10 o'clock, it's only with a box of work under his arm.

We've been together six years and have lived together three, so at some point you'd think I'd get used to this routine. But I don't. That's partly because even though he works too much and doesn't get to the gym as often as he should, Roger is hotter than Alabama in August. At least that's how I see him. He's 6 foot 2 with curly brown hair that he keeps cut close to his scalp, sparkling blue eyes, a cleft chin, and a slyly sexy smile. He still makes my heart pound after all these years.

And when he's naked, I can barely maintain myself. His thick chest and flat belly are covered with curly hair, and his dick is a work of art. Clipped and shapely, it hangs a good five inches soft, snuggled against fat, hairy balls that hang low against strong thighs.

I love to suck it until it gets hard, swelling and stretching in my mouth until it reaches its full nine inches, my tongue tickling the popping veins that writhe along the shaft.

And he fucks me like a dream, slow at first and then faster and harder until I'm pure crazy and half crying, it's so good.

Sometimes he lets me fuck him, and his ass is like warm velvet on my cock.

Which explains why it drives me crazy that he works so much. He's always so tired that I usually only get my loving on weekends.

But I would never cheat on him. For one, I love him too much, and two, we've been monogamous ever since we got serious. And now since we've both been tested every year since we've been together, we decided it was OK to fuck without condoms. And let me tell you, nothing is going to make me trade the feeling of Roger shooting inside me for anything.

But I decided it's OK if I go into some of the computer chat rooms while Roger is at work. It's pretty harmless, and it makes me less bitchy when he gets home all tired and in need of sleep.

At first it was kind of hard because I didn't really know what to do, but after a while I realized it was just like phone sex, only typing. Ever since, I've been kind of the slut of cyberspace, sucking dick and fucking and getting fucked out there among the stars or satellites or whatever. I've been a little blond twinkie, a straight schoolteacher, a slave, a leather daddy, and I've even been a woman a couple of times in the straight rooms.

And if I feel a bit guilty afterward, well, I guess it's better than letting the frustration of having a hot husband who's never around get the better of me.

But one night it all came together.

Roger was working in the den that he calls his office, and I was in the bedroom on the computer, supposedly booking our vacation to Maui, when I decided to check out my favorite chat room. I knew Roger would be busy for another couple of hours, and then he would want to watch the news in bed—or, more accurately, fall asleep during the first commercial—and I would be too horny to get a good night's sleep.

So I went into a private room with some guy who said he was a logging truck driver in Spokane, Washington. Who knows, he might have been.

I was really nervous, since this was the first time I'd done this with Roger in the house, and at every noise I jumped. But after a while I settled down and started stroking my cock while this guy described eating my ass out and sucking my dick.

I had my pants down around my ankles, had tossed my T-shirt across the room, and was telling him how I was sucking his log, running my tongue up and down and flicking it in and out of his piss slit when something poked me in the back of the head.

I jumped like a cat set on by a pack of wild dogs and whirled around, coming face-to-face with Roger's gorgeous hard-on.

I didn't know whether to blush or burst into the "Hallelujah Chorus." I looked up, and he was grinning at me fit to split his face in two. I smiled back, and he grabbed the back of my head and slammed his dick between my lips, and I went to work like a starving man. I was moaning and slobbering so hard, bouncing my forehead into his hard abs and sucking his fat balls, that I didn't hear him start typing.

I had pulled off for a minute and had started stroking him from base to head, hard and slow like he likes, when I noticed he'd taken over online with my truck driver.

"Hey, buddy," he had typed. "I'm Roger, and your fuck buddy is sucking my cock right now, so he can't type anymore."

The trucker typed right back, "Oh, man, I bet that's hot."

Roger was chuckling while I stroked him and typed, "Oh, yeah, his mouth is better than your best wet dream."

I started sucking him again then, so I don't know what the trucker typed back. I was just so happy to have Roger's hot come stick in my mouth, I couldn't have cared less. I opened my throat and let him pop the head past my tonsils a couple of times while I worked my tongue on the rock-hard underside of his shaft.

"He wants you to eat my ass," Roger said to me.

I got behind him and pulled his muscular cheeks apart, burying my face in the hairy crack. I ran my tongue along the ridge of flesh between his balls and ass and felt him shudder, but I could still hear him typing. I reached my hand around his waist and grabbed his iron rod while my tongue found the hard pucker of his ass ring. My tongue went crazy at his sweetly sour taste, and I pumped his cock while my tongue dove into his slick chute.

He bucked his hips into my face, fucking himself on my tongue and driving his cock in and out of my fist.

"Now he wants me to fuck you," Roger laughed.

While Roger got behind me and rimmed my hole into readiness, I took over the typing duties.

"He's getting me all slicked up for his monster dick," I typed.

"You like a big cock, huh?" the trucker typed back.

Roger's tongue on my manhole sent waves of pleasure rocketing through my body, but I managed to type, "The bigger, the better."

I felt Roger spit into my fuck chute. Then he stood behind me, and I heard him spit onto his dick. Then the sweet cushion of his mushroom head pressed against my back door and popped through. He stopped and worked the head in and out, driving me crazy like he knew he would, and then pushed all the way in until his furry pubes scratched against my ass.

He leaned over me, his hairy chest tickling my back, and put his hands over mine on the keyboard.

I moved my hands out of the way, one reaching down between my legs to pull on his swaying bag as it banged into me and the other going to work on my own throbbing pole.

"God, his ass is so tight and hot," Roger typed.

I got my fingers back to the keyboard. "He's fucking me nice and slow," I added.

"You guys are too fucking much!" the trucker said.

We fucked and groaned and sweated and typed and laughed until Roger started jackrabbiting my ass, which was a sign that he was close.

I put my hand back on my cock and started stroking because he liked to feel me come while he was still inside me. With my other hand, I reached back for his balls again. They were pulled up tight and hard, ready to blow.

"I'm gonna come," Roger typed.

"Me too," the trucker responded.

"Me three," I said aloud.

Roger put his hand on my back, pressing me down over the desk, and pounded my ass while I fucked my fist until the tickle in my balls turned into a spasm, my cock pulsed, and thick gobs of cream shot through my fingers.

Roger grunted and buried himself inside me, holding me tight as his cock exploded, and I felt four thick, hot jism blasts paint my insides. Then he pulled out and shot the rest over my sweaty back.

We slumped to the floor and held each other, kissing passionately until we remembered our pal in Spokane.

On the screen were three words: “Thanks, guys. Bye.”

We laughed and, kissing me, Roger said, “So this is how you spend your time when I'm not around?”

“How did you sneak up on me like that?” I had to know.

“I was walking to the bathroom. You left the door open a crack, and when I saw you sitting there with a hard-on, it was too good to pass up.”

“Well,” I said, “now I'll have to do it when you are around!”

“I guess I'll have to be around more then,” he said with that smile that makes me fall in love with him all over again.

About the Contributors

Donny Buckman runs a catering service and dabbles with floral design. He lives in Kentucky.

Trevor J. Callahan Jr. has written fiction for numerous anthologies and magazines. He lives in southern New England.

Michael Edwards is a journalist who lives in Los Angeles and spends countless hours in front of his computer every night exploring the vast realms of cyberspace—and the men who dwell there. Eventually he did find Mr. Right—and he found him online.

Larry Fuller is a financial analyst and self-described fitness fanatic who lives in Bronxville, N.Y.

William Holden is a native of Detroit but currently lives in the heart of Atlanta within walking distance of Piedmont Park. During the day he acts as an accountant, but he spends the evenings and weekends in the park, writing and watching for future stories. He also enjoys dancing at some of the darkest clubs in the city. This is Holden's second published short story, with two others forthcoming.

Cameron King has spent all of his 30 years in the same small, pleasant town. He first knew for sure he was gay when he spent all junior high gym class trying to look up the cute guys' shorts. Not much has changed really. Always one for a cheap thrill, King also enjoys fantasizing about men he'll never have (although he's sure Brad Pitt will one day give in) and cruising town, checking out college boys.

Conrad Max MacDonald has written tales for various publications globally. He holds a college diploma and university degree and considers his husband, Suneel, to be a muse. MacDonald's mission is to create erotic tales with ethnic and racial diversity. Though no one author fuels his style of writing, MacDonald takes his inspirations from the works of Truman Capote, James Baldwin, Jacqueline Susann, and Gordon Merrick. He lives in Toronto, Canada.

Phillip Mackenzie Jr. is a freelance writer and entertainment consultant who lives in Los Angeles.

C.J. Murray lives in the Mississippi/New Orleans area. He is the author of *The Legend of Cazaunoux, The Magic of Isha Swift,* and *Different Dancer.* He has short erotica published in several anthologies, including "The Water Boy" in Alyson Books' *Men for All Seasons: Stories of Sports and Sex.* Murray is working on a novel, *Zu: The Diary of a Vampire,* and *Sun Perch and Summer Tomatoes,* a collection of gay erotica. He lives with daughter Halley.

Jerry Prince lives in the Maryland suburbs of Washington, D.C. He has had stories published in *Bear* magazine as well as on the Net. He is active in Hot Ash, the club for cigar-smoking gay men. He also operates the Cigar Picture Trading Club, which can reached at cigarpics@egroups.com, on the Net. He may be reached by E-mail at CigarDadDC@aol.com.

Raymond, the author of "The One," was born October 29, 1970, in Atlanta. Childhood experiences answered the questions of his existence in this lifestyle: His fondness for men, stares from guys in the locker room, and midnight rendezvous. "The One" is just one example of his world that's tucked away in a closet.

slave mike, a recent graduate of the University of Chicago, grew up in the Midwest, where he lives with his current Master. "23 Hours" is his first published story. He plans to pursue freelance writing while dealing with more of life's questions.

Simon Sheppard is the coeditor, with M. Christian, of *Rough Stuff: Tales of Gay Men, Sex, and Power* and the author of the forthcoming *Hotter Than Hell and Other Stories,* both from Alyson Books. His work has appeared in dozens of quality smut anthologies, including *Best American Erotica, Best Gay Erotica,* and Alyson's *Friction: Best Gay Erotic Fiction* series. When he's not jacking off at the keyboard, he can be found writing the column "Sex Talk," which is published on Web sites and in (very) hard copy throughout the world.

Jay Starre lives in Vancouver, Canada, where he has been writing for the past 10 years. He has written gay erotic fiction for the past three years. His stories have been published in magazines such as *Honcho, Blueboy, Torso,* and *In Touch* and in the anthologies *Rent Boys* and *Skin Flicks #2.*

Jm Tella is the author of numerous short stories and lives in Boston, Mass., where he's employed as a copywriter. He holds a bachelor's degree in English from Boston College and a master of arts in writing from the University of San Francisco.

Joel Valley is 30-something and lives in Liverpool, England. "RumpRider" is his first published writing. Valley dreams of emigrating to Canada and writing full-time. In the meantime, he works for a small community group. Although no longer a regular in the Internet chat rooms, he still occasionally makes an appearance and uses the nickname RumpRider. Try looking for him in Gay.com's Liverpool chat room. Alternatively, E-mail him at joelvalley@yahoo.com.